Viking Slave

Viking Slave

Book 1 in the Dragon Heart Series

By

Griff Hosker

Viking Slave

Published by Sword Books Ltd 2013
Copyright © Griff Hosker First Edition

The author has asserted their moral right under the Copyright, Designs and Patents Act, 1988, to be identified as the author of this work.

All Rights reserved. No part of this publication may be reproduced, copied, stored in a retrieval system, or transmitted, in any form or by any means, without the prior written consent of the copyright holder, nor be otherwise circulated in any form of binding or cover other than that in which it is published and without a similar condition being imposed on the subsequent purchaser.

A CIP catalogue record for this title is available from the British Library.

Cover by Design for Writers

Contents

Viking Slave i
Chapter 1 1
Chapter 2 10
Chapter 3 23
Chapter 4 35
Chapter 5 47
Chapter 6 59
Chapter 7 72
Chapter 8 85
Chapter 9 96
Chapter 10 108
Chapter 11 120
Chapter 12 132
Chapter 13 146
Chapter 14 156
Chapter 15 168
Chapter 16 180
Chapter 17 193
The End 200
Glossary 201
Historical note 202
Other books by Griff Hosker 203

Viking Slave

Chapter 1

It was a misty and damp spring morning when the Vikings first came. I was with the other boys by the river, hauling in the nets filled with the salmon caught overnight. It was hard to see anything with the low mist which we called a sea fret hanging over the river. The cold chilled you to your very bones. I had taken off my hare fur boots before I entered the water as I did not want them to be wet and soggy all day. It was better to have cold feet. I waded to the furthest point from the shore.

The other children did not like me. The boys called me Crow. The name was meant as an insult for I was the only dark-haired boy in the whole village. It marked me out as different and that was a bad thing. I was also thin and frail. I think I inherited those qualities from my mother. I looked a lot like her. She had been taken in a slave raid by my father who had been a warrior of some renown.

She had lived on the west coast and, it was said, that she was of the old people of Britain. My father treated her well and she was better off than most of the slaves but I did not fare well. My father also resented my dark hair and, as he called it, my weedy appearance. All the other boys looked like true Saxons with their broad chests and blond hair. I was the freak that they could all gang up on. Of course, I learned to run really quickly to avoid their beatings. Tadgh, Saelac and Rald were my worst tormentors.

That morning, as we worked in the water before the Vikings came, I was safe. Work time was not the time for bullying. It was not the time to hold my head under the water until I nearly drowned or to burn my feet with a brand from the fire. Work was my safe time and I volunteered for work as often as possible.

I say the Vikings came but we did not call them Vikings then. We just called them the men from the north or wolves from the sea. That was what they appeared like. They just arrived without any warning. They were something new. Their ships sailed from somewhere over the edge of the world in the east and they came silently. We had heard of raids further north but, until that cold, spring day they had never ventured to our river. It was called The River because no river was as big and it was ours in that we ruled the small part on the northern shore where we could trap salmon and steal heron's eggs. We might have been a handful of

Viking Slave

families but we had a palisade and ditch around our homes and we feared no one.

And so on that cold morning, the eight boys from the village trudged down to the river. I took with me, as I always did, an offering for Icaunus, the river god. That was another reason for my misery at the hands of the others. My mother and I followed the old ways and the old religion but the rest of the village followed the White Christ. I did as my mother did and, before I stepped into the water, I said a prayer and dropped the piece of wood I had carved the night before. I intoned the words quietly so that the others would not hear; if they did it would result in a beating later on. "I come as a supplicant, Great Icaunus. I exchange this gift for your bounty." I dropped the wood into the icy dark waters and then waded out into the icy current.

I was up to my chest in the water, holding on to the net when I first saw the dragon boat. All that I saw was the red-painted dragon prow of the ship heading silently for the bank. It came from nowhere as though some wizard had summoned it. Even had I wanted to I could not have evaded capture. I was too far into the river. Aelle, who was closest to the bank tried to run and to shout a warning but an axe flew through the air and split his skull in two. I had seen that happen before but only to the pigs and sheep when we slaughtered them. The raiders leapt from the boat and while two of them secured it to a tree four warriors began to grab and bind the other six boys. I was the furthest out and I began to wade in. I could not swim. As I struggled against the water I reflected that my offering had not been enough and the village was being punished because they worshipped the White Christ and not Icaunus. A toothless old man waited for me. He smelled of sweat and pig grease. He turned me around and bound my hands behind me. He was accomplished and skilled and I was tied to the other boys in a heartbeat.

The warriors began to leap onto the river bank. The mist still lay like a blanket over the bank and they quickly made their way to the village. Our chief, Rald, was proud of the fact that the village was on a high piece of land, well away from the unpredictable water. It was at least four hundred man paces from the water and I watched as the fierce warriors trotted off. Most had a helmet and two had long coats of mail but all had a sword or an axe and a round shield. My heart sank. Most of the men in the village were naked in comparison. There were just two helmets in the village and only three swords. The old toothless one began to lift us one by one into the boat. I was the last one to be hauled unceremoniously on

Viking Slave

board and I watched as the others were lifted up. Raldson, the son of the chief began to struggle as they lifted him. He was the eldest of the boys and had seen eleven summers, he was almost a man. The old man took out an axe handle and stuck him so hard on the back of the head that blood poured from the wound and he fell unconscious onto the deck. No one else fought. When my turn came I obeyed meekly. I was no Raldson.

The six of us stood on the thwarts of the ship and found that we could see to the village. None of us had the courage to voice a warning and I fear we would have been silenced like Raldson had we shouted. We could only watch as the warriors entered the open gates of the settlement unhindered. The guards both lay dead. We had not seen them killed but I knew the two men; they had probably been asleep. We heard the screams and the clamour of metal on metal. Our men were putting up a fight but I had seen the warriors, the fourteen men of the village would not be able to do much against the thirty hardened pirates who carved a path of death through my home. When the noise stopped we saw the first of the captives being led down towards the boat. The mist was beginning to be burned off and we were able to watch them as they trudged down the well-worn path to the river. It was the women and the children who were driven down to their ship. There were no men. I saw my mother walking in the middle of the first group. I would not be alone.

The warrior who led them wore a helmet that had a face mask. He looked terrifying. You could see nothing, not even his eyes and it made him seem inhuman. He wore a fine mail shirt and carried a shield with a dragon's head painted upon it. He carried a long sword. There was blood on the blade. His men formed two lines on either side of the captives and, at the rear, four of his men drove the few animals we possessed: a handful of sheep and goats, two pigs and a milk cow. The sow was heavy with young.

Suddenly we were yanked from behind and we were pulled away from the side. The old man said something. Parts of it sounded familiar but none of us understood a word. We were pushed and dragged towards the dragon's head prow of the ship and I noticed there was a piece of cloth rigged to cover it. Raldson was slumped there, his head still bleeding. None of the others paid him any attention. All of us were looking for our mothers and sisters as they were pushed towards us. My mother was not popular with the other women and they rushed to their own children, pushing mother out of the way. I was used to being patient and I waited.

Viking Slave

She threw her arms around me; there were no tears and there was no fuss. She had been taken as a slave once before and she had survived. She would survive this. "You are safe?"

"I am safe." I looked up. "Father?"

"He was the last to die and he died well. You are now the man, Gareth." A further reason they all despised me was my name. It was not a Saxon name and a further reminder that I was not one of them; I was one of the old tribes.

How they managed to haul the cow on board I shall never know but we had turned east and headed back to the sea almost before we knew. I looked to the small settlement on the slight rise and wondered what would become of the deserted village filled with the dead. The village was now packed into the prow of the boat and heading towards the land of the raiders. The only memory of the old place would be in our hearts and heads. I would not miss it for I had never been happy there.

When we reached the sea I expected them to continue east but they turned south. South of the river was a different land with people we did not know. My mother held me tighter. I did not want the other boys to hear me and so I whispered, "Why are we going south, mother?"

"I know not." I felt her fingers squeeze into my scrawny back. "They may be going to sell us to others I do not know." She looked down at me and, for the first time, I saw fear in her eyes. "If we are separated then do all that your new masters ask. It will make life easier. There is no point in fighting it only results in beatings or worse."

I nodded and lowered my head into the comfort of her body. "You were taken once."

"Aye, and my father was killed. I found a life with your father who was a kind master and I was given the gift of you my son. We never know what *wyrd* has in store for us." She surreptitiously slid the necklace she wore from around her neck and gave it to me. "Hide this and keep this. It has protected me and it will protect you." I knew what it was without even looking. It was a piece of stone carved into a wolf's head and in the eye was a tiny piece of blue glass. Mother said it was a precious stone from the lands far to the west. I was about to refuse when she tightened her hand about mine. "Take it! My mother gave it to me and I pass it on to you. We have had this in our family for generations. So long as it survives then the family will also survive."

The raiders had left just two young men with spears to watch us. They looked as though they would happily spear any of us who moved. The

Viking Slave

rest of the crew rowed steadily along the coast. The leader had removed his helmet and was standing at the stern holding on to the tiller. I could see his face now. His hair was a frightening white blond. His beard showed that he was not an old man. He had a scar running down the right-hand side of his face and crossed his eye. It gave him an angry look. Later we found that his name was Harald One Eye and that this was his first expedition as a leader. Perhaps that was why he had not returned to his home across the sea.

I wondered how far we would travel when suddenly the ship began to turn. We had just passed an estuary and there was a cliff with buildings at the top. The dragon boat ground up onto the sand at the foot of the rocks. The leader shouted orders and the warriors leapt from their oars and followed him up the cliff. I could hear a bell tolling. There were four men left to guard us. I heeded my mother's words but Scald, one of the boys who followed Raldson, suddenly tried to leap overboard. It was almost impossible as his hands were still tied; I suspect he thought he was close to shore and might be able to survive the surf. I do not know if the guards had been expecting something but as he stood on the ship's side he was speared through the back. His lifeless body dropped into the foaming sea. Scald's mother began to wail and the toothless old man walked up to her and punched her in the side of the head. She whimpered instead. The old man then examined Raldson who had not moved since he had been deposited. He lifted an arm and dropped it. Raldson was dead. They threw his body over the side too.

The splashes of the two bodies in the water seemed ominous. I knew that we would be slaves and that we had value but I now knew that we were disposable and my mother's words rang loudly in my ears. I would do all that I could to survive. The truth was that my life in the village had not been the best. I was lonely and I was beaten. As I peered around at the boys I saw that none of them was my friend nor would I wish them to be. The life in this new land could be no worse than the old life in the Saxon village.

The boat seemed to be on the beach longer than I would have expected. The men they left as guards had to push her into the water once to avoid her being stranded on the tide. Eventually, we saw a straggly line descending from the building at the top. "What is that building?" I whispered.

"It is an abbey and a church of the White Christ."

Viking Slave

I had heard of these churches and abbeys. When tales were told around the fire they spoke of great riches and gold within. I could see that the raiders were heavily laden as they descended. This time, however, there were just two slaves. They were young women. Both looked tearful and afraid. They were being carried by two of the bigger warriors. I had not counted the raiders as they had left the ship but I did not think that they were fewer in number. However, as they began to board the ship I saw some small boats put out from the estuary we had just passed and other armed men running down the cliff path. I began to wonder if we would be rescued.

The warrior who led the raiders barked out his orders. The two women were dumped with the other prisoners and the warriors took to their oars. These were strong men and they began to pull away from the shore. I was right at the prow of the ship and I peered over the wooden edge. The ships which were coming out to meet us were small boats, mainly fishing skiffs. It looked like the warriors from Streonshal were trying to rescue the two prisoners. They began to close with us and I was surprised that the crew did not seem more worried. Three of them leisurely strode forwards and stood just behind us. They each had a bow and they began to loose arrows at the nearest boat. It only took them six or seven arrows to make a hit. The boat slowed and I heard one of the men say something to a companion who laughed. They kept loosing at the first boat and had two more hits. The crews stopped following. We were now picking up speed as we headed eastwards. The archers walked along the centre walkway and positioned themselves at the side where they kept up a flurry of arrows until the boats gave up their pursuit.

It was then that we learned of the leader's name for, as they rowed, the men all chanted, "Harald, Harald!"

It was almost noon; we could work that out from the position of the sun and we were all now, effectively slaves. There would be no pursuit and these raiders would take us to their home. When the coastline was no longer in sight the leader took off his helmet and strode towards us with another, older man. The older man had many scars on his arms and he had necklaces and bracelets on his neck and arms. Even I knew they marked him as a great warrior. Rald had had but two and I saw that Harald wore both of them now; he had killed our leader

The older man spoke Saxon, "You are now the thralls of Harald One Eye and we are going to his home, Ulfberg. There you will be given to warriors who have pleased the chief. Some of you will become his slaves. The two boys who died were brave but you are now his property and he wants no more bravery. Any further attempts to escape will result in blinding."

He turned to leave and one of the two females taken from the abbey suddenly shouted. "I am Aethelfrith, the daughter of King Aethelred of Northumbria. I demand you take me to my father's castle!"

The older warrior smiled as he translated for Harald who burst out laughing. "Jarl Harald cares not what Saxon princesses want. If your father wishes to buy you then he will set a fair price."

They returned to the stern and we all looked with new interest at the two women who had survived from the abbey. We knew that we had a king but none had ever seen him. The only contact we had was when the fyrd was called to war and the men went off. We had had years of peace and I had never heard of the king summoning his farmers to fight. Looking at these raiders it was a good thing for I could not see them standing for long against such muscular and well-armed men.

As we hit the open water the motion of the boat became more severe and, added to the smell from the animals, some of the villagers began to empty the contents of their stomachs over the side. I stared ahead, watching for the new land where I would soon live. I could hear them vomiting behind me but I just peered towards the horizon. When it became dark I became hungry and thirsty. I turned to mother. "Will we be fed do you think?"

She smiled, "Probably, my little man. They do not want us dying but I think it is just you and I who will be eating."

Eventually, the older man who had spoken to us came down accompanied by the toothless warrior. They had some bread and some water. "I am Butar Ragnarson. This old one is Olaf the Toothless. Would anyone like some food and water?"

Mother was the only one of the women who had not been sea sick. "My son and I will eat and drink." She flashed a look of superiority at the other pale women who would normally have claimed any food going first. They only wanted the water. Olaf gave us a loaf to share and poured some water into two wooden beakers.

Butar stayed with us while Olaf saw to the other women and gave them water. "You two look different from the rest."

"I am from Cymri. I was taken as a slave by the Saxons."

"And now you and your son have been taken again. You seem calm about this."

Viking Slave

"It is the first time that is hard. I survived then and I will survive now. I do not know if you are to be good or bad masters. That may change my opinion but for now my son and I eat, we drink and you have not beaten us."

I could see this man called Butar, appraising my mother. I did not know her age; I could never judge a person's age. She must have had me when she was quite young for she looked younger than most of the other women and seemed to be about the same age as the Saxon princess. I know she laughed a great deal and played more with me than the other mothers did with their children. He smiled, "What is your name?"

"Myfanwy and this is Gareth, my son."

"Well, Myfanwy, you might just have the right attitude to help you to survive. I will watch you."

She caught me staring at him. She tore the bread in two. "Eat while we have food. When the others become hungry, they will regret not eating any of this food. I fear we will not be offered more."

I did as I was told. "When will we reach their land?"

She shook her head, "I know not. It depends on the weather and how far they sailed. When the Saxons came they only travelled a little way across the German Sea but these sometimes travel from the land of the ice."

"How do you know so much, mother?"

"I listen and I learn. You will do well if you can do the same. Now get some sleep while we can. If a storm blows up we will get precious little rest."

Surprisingly I did get some sleep despite the fact that I thought that we would sail off the end of the world. I was in my mother's arms and I was safe. Nothing could hurt me there. When I awoke the next day my mouth felt salty and I was incredibly thirsty. Olaf brought the water around. The other mothers and children tried to clamour for the water first but Olaf beat them back and served first my mother and then me with the precious liquid. I saw the hate in the eyes of the others and I did not care. I devoured the stale, rock hard bread and then peered over the prow again. The horizon was still empty. We had not reached our new home.

After another two days of tortuous sailing, a thin smudge appeared in the distance. It was land again. I would be happy to reach the shore. The main reason was my fellow slaves. They wailed and they complained. They were sick. Three small children, all girls, had died and their bodies

Viking Slave

thrown to the fishes. Their mothers were now looking drawn and haggard. My mother and I had continued to be treated courteously, compared with the others. I did not know why. I had expected the Saxon princess to have been afforded such treatment. I suspect their haughty attitude did not endear them to our captors. My mother and I grew closer and we were able to speak on that long voyage. We had rarely had that luxury. She told me of the land she had lived in before she had been taken. It was Cymri, the land the Saxons called Wales. Her father had been a warrior and a leader of his people. I wondered if that made her a princess. She had been taken when her father had been visiting the borderlands and she had been the only survivor of the savage ambush.

She had shaken her head and become quite tearful at that point. That was not my mother who was strong. "I think my father died because I was with him. I was precocious and wanted to be a son for my father. I had begged him to take me on that journey and when we were attacked he protected me instead of fighting the enemy. He was a mighty warrior but he died and so did his oathsworn." She shook her head and closed her eyes. When she opened them she said, "Now promise me that if you get the chance to escape you will do so. I do not want someone else to suffer because of me."

I was about to say no when she became angry and gripped my shoulders, "Promise me!"

I was a little afraid of her and I blurted out, "I promise." Deep inside, I thought that it would be unlikely that I would ever escape. How would I cross the mighty sea we had just traversed? I agreed to her request but I never thought that I would have to keep that promise.

When the crew began to clean themselves up I knew that we were close to their home. That meant that I was closer to my new life as a slave and a parting from my mother.

Chapter 2

When we reached Harald's home I saw my first fiord. It was much later that I learned the name but it was something I had never seen before. It was something I could never have dreamed up. We sailed through a rocky inlet that was as wide as our river. The rocks just rose straight from the water and it was hard to see how anyone could live here. Even the sea birds would have struggled to find a nest on those sheer walls. Suddenly we turned a bend in the fiord and saw a beach and there, perched on a rocky ledge, was the village that would be my new home. There were a few people waiting to greet us; mainly women and children with a few old men and they stood, expectantly at the wooden quay. The ship was made secure and then the important passengers, the animals were taken off. The crew followed carrying their oars, weapons and treasure and then Butar, Olaf and Harald came to us with four men. The women were led off by the four men. Butar put his hands on his hips and looked at the six of us who were left grinning broadly. He pulled out a wicked-looking knife and sliced our bonds. I noticed that Harald One Eye also had a sly smile on his face.

"Now then, Saxons, you are here in your new home. Before you are assigned to new masters you have a task to perform." The lower part of the boat was empty. He pointed at the bottom. "Your animals did not have the luxury, as you had, of sticking an arse over the side. We want all that valuable fertiliser collecting and putting in these sacks. Olaf will oversee the work. When he is happy then you get to go ashore."

Tadgh said, "Do we get shovels."

Butar translated for Olaf. Bearing in mind Olaf's previous reaction to any kind of dissent I thought that this was brave but the old gnarled warrior suddenly cracked his face into a toothless chortle. Butar smiled, "Use your hands!"

The others hesitated but I heeded my mother's words and took a sack and descended into the bottom. I saw a nod of approval from Butar. I began to grab handfuls which I dropped into the sack. The smell was bad but I had smelled worse. Some of it had dried into hard lumps which made collecting easy but some of it was liquid slurry and that was harder to harvest. The others behind me hesitated and then I heard a crack and suddenly the other five each had a bag and had joined me. They glanced belligerently at me as though I was the cause of their work. I just kept working. When I had filled my sack I looked at Olaf who pointed up the gangplank. I swung the steaming pile onto my back and tried to climb up the short ladder. The dung was heavy and as, as I reached the top I began to overbalance. In a heartbeat, I was pitched forward by Olaf's hand and found myself balancing precariously on the narrow plank. Thankfully I regained my balance and I struggled to the quayside.

Butar was there supervising the division of the spoils. He turned when he saw me, "Take that up the hill. You will see the dunghill before you. Then return here with the sack."

By the time I returned the other boys had filled their sacks and were heading up the hill. Butar restrained me as I tried to get back aboard the ship. "No, it is done, little one. You did well. Go to the river and wash." I began to take off my short tunic." He shook his head. "That will need washing too. Jump in and wash everything."

The river might have been icy cold but it felt good as I jumped in. The smell soon went and the icy water woke me up. I washed as quickly as I could. The main reason was I did not want to be in there when the others jumped in. They would pay me back for their own punishment. I managed to reach Butar by the time the others trudged slowly down the hill. My little run from the river had warmed me up but as I stood there I began to shiver. Butar took off his fur cloak and draped it around my shoulders. I wondered why but I was too grateful to ask and I just wrapped it tightly around my shoulders. The warmth gradually came back into my bones.

The other boys were almost blue with the cold when they emerged. Butar did not spare them a glance he just strode up the hill to the palisaded settlement. Olaf trudged behind with the flat of his palm ready. I could see that everyone was waiting for us and we ran to our mothers when we saw them. I hesitated and went to return the cloak to Butar. He smiled and shook his head. I also noticed that my mother seemed happier than the others.

Butar stood next to Harald One Eye as he translated his words. It was obvious that Butar's role was to assign the slaves to the warriors. The princess and her companion were led to Harald's sharp-eyed, thin-faced wife. They did not look like they would have a happy time. Then the other women were each given to a different warrior. My mother was not and she stood, calmly, with us six boys and the gaggle of girls. Tadgh was given to Olaf who had an evil grin on his face. The younger girls were all given to their mothers but the boys were apportioned randomly. Some to the same owner as the mothers but others were not. Finally, there was just my mother and me. Harald One Eye said nothing but smiled and everyone left.

Butar turned to us two; the last ones left. "You are to be my slaves. Your mother already knows this. You," he struggled to say Gareth and it came out Garth, "young Garth, will look after my aged father." Despite my best efforts and those of my mother, I became Garth. My mother fared even worse. No-one could get their tongues around Myfanwy and so she became, 'my love' to Butar who took her to his bed and 'Butar's woman' to the rest of the village. Those who had come with us from Northumbria called her Butar's Whore but only when they thought my mother and Butar were out of earshot.

I was fitted with my wooden collar, the mark of the thrall, as were the other women and slaves. The exception was my mother. At the time I did not understand but as the months passed by it became clearer. The collar felt uncomfortable and I wondered how I would bear it. I discovered that the human being is an adaptable animal and within a few weeks I barely noticed it. Old Ragnar was the half-blind father of Butar and he had just one arm. He was scrawny and he was cantankerous. After one week with him, I was not sure that I would be able to cope but, as with the collar, I adapted.

Ragnar Haraldsson lived almost like a hermit outside the palisade. He had his own hut tucked into the rock face. It was a good walk from the village. Butar led me up the slope. He had given me a clean tunic to wear. I idly wondered where he had got it but I discovered that later.

"My father is the oldest man in the village and he is very independent. The trouble is that he cannot see well enough to look after himself and his one arm prevents him from doing simple tasks. Your job is to be his arm, his eyes and his guard. You will leave him, at night, when he is abed and you will return in the morning before he wakes." He looked at me as though he expected a complaint. I nodded. "You are a strange one Garth. I saw that on the boat. You seemed calm when they were angry and you were willing when they were not. I can see that you and your mother are different. It is why I asked Jarl Harald for the two of you."

It may sound strange but I felt proud that I had been selected. I might only be a slave but I was a chosen slave. It is important to find good in life; it makes it easier to bear the disasters when they come. He paused before the door. "Always announce yourself. He has sharp ears and

Viking Slave

knows where the door is. I would hate for you to get an axe in your head. He was a fearsome warrior in his time and could take a maiden's pigtail with an axe." I wondered why anyone would want to do that. "I will tell him who you are. You will need to learn our language quickly." He rapped on the old wooden door. "Father, it is Butar."

The door was held to the wall by a piece of leather and Butar had to lift it slightly in order to open it. "Who is that with you?"

"I told you he has good ears." He changed to his own language. "It is a thrall from across the sea." He told me what he said. The old man shouted loudly and I did not understand one word. Butar shook his head. "He says he needs no foreigners. We will return to the village and I will get some food for him. You can bring it back. He may be in a better mood later." Butar spoke, for a time, to his father who seemed to argue with his son. I peered around the room. I could see that it had been cut into the rock and the sleeping part was in a cave. I wondered how warm that would be. The furniture was basic, there was a table and the old man was seated on a log which had been carved into a chair. His missing arm was his right one. I could see how that would have been a problem for a warrior. He was thin but I could see that, in his prime, he would have been a powerful warrior. He kept turning his head when Butar spoke and he reminded me of a bird. Butar sighed and, shaking his head, we left.

As we walked down I asked, "Lord, how will I avoid having an axe in my head."

He laughed, "Firstly, I am not lord. You just call me master and secondly, you are clever. I will teach you the words to say." By the time we reached the village I could say. "It is your thrall, Garth the Saxon!"

I was still not confident but I was determined to earn this warrior's respect. My mother was busy working in Butar's hut. It was the second-largest in the village and only Harald One Eye had one which was bigger. There was even a separate sleeping section with an actual bed. It just convinced me that no matter what Butar said, he really was a lord. Mother just smiled and continued preparing the food. She never shirked work.

"That will be where you sleep." He pointed to a pile of straw by the fire in the middle of the room. It was better than the bed I had had before. He then spent the time until the food was ready teaching me words. I may not have been strong but I had a good mind and could learn quickly. As long as the old man didn't speak too quickly I would be able to speak a little with him.

Viking Slave

I took the metal pot with the stew, the black bread and the jug of beer up the hill. Both were heavy and the hill was steep. When I reached the door I was out of breath. I laid Ragnar's food on the ground and rapped on the door. "It is your thrall, Garth the Saxon."

I heard no reply but I steeled myself and lifting the door slightly, opened it. Thankfully no axe came my way and I hefted the pot and the jug into the room. He was seated still on the carved wooden chair next to a fading fire and he was asleep. I placed the pot of food next to the fire and then fed the fire. I could see that he would need more wood and I was about to get some more when he stirred. His eyes opened and then widened when he saw me. His hand went to his axe. "No sir, I am your thrall. Garth the Saxon! I bring food. Butar!" My phrases were exhausted and I waited for the blow which, thankfully never came. I took the lid from the pot and held it to him. He sniffed. My mother is a good cook and I could see he liked the smell. I gave him the bread, which he snatched from me and he began to eat.

I went outside and looked for the log pile. There were a few logs but not many. I put them in my arms and went inside. I put some on the fire and then placed the rest next to it. He looked up at me. I pointed to his axe and mimed cutting wood. He shook his head. I pointed to the small pile of wood and spread my arms. He said something which I didn't catch. When I didn't do anything he pointed to the wall where there was another, smaller axe. I took it down and then realised that the small axe he had was a fine weapon, it was a throwing axe. The other was a more functional axe. I was learning the old man's ways.

As I went outside I tested the edge and found that the axe was dull. I sharpened it on the stone outside the door and then began to chop the wood. It was harder than it looked and I did not seem to be making headway. I was suddenly aware of the old man behind me. When he laughed I turned around, "No, no" was all that I caught. The rest was indecipherable. He put his good arm on my right and moved it the way he wanted me to then he did the same with my left. Finally, he took his own axe and swung it one handed to show me the action. This time, when I swung the axe a chip of wood flew off. The old man showed me the direction of the next cut and soon the chips were littering the ground. I laughed. I was cutting logs! He tapped me on the shoulder and mimed for me to bring them in. I did so and then he took me back outside and made me pick up all the chips which I also carried in. I saw that he had a wooden pail next to the fire. This was obviously his kindling.

I noticed that it was getting dark and wondered when he would sleep. He shouted something at me which I didn't understand. He waved his arm at me. I repeated the word he had said and he nodded, "Go!" I had learned another word.

I felt afraid as I raced through the woods and down the hill. I had no idea what kind of monsters lived up here. There were all sorts of trolls, aelfes and fairies who could bring harm upon you. I would need to make a sacrifice to the gods of these woods when I found out who they were. We had no forests such as these at home on the river. I gripped the wolf head charm my mother had given me on the ship and I felt happier. There was a guard at the gate. He looked at me suspiciously until I said, "Garth, Butar, thrall!"

He laughed and waved me through. I almost burst through the door and my mother's face became cross. "Gareth, I thought I had taught you better. This is not your home. This is the master's house. Next time, knock."

"Sorry."

Butar said something in his language and I repeated it. He laughed. "Well done. You have now learned the word for sorry. Let us hope you do not have to say it too often." He came over to examine my head and my mother frowned. "I am just checking that my father did not throw an axe at him."

I smiled, "He had his food and he showed me how to cut logs. I took in the logs and the kindling and he told me to go."

Butar ruffled my hair. "Well done, Garth, then you have earned your food. Sit and eat."

I wolfed the food down for I was starving, having only eaten bread and water the past days. Butar and my mother seemed oblivious and they talked incessantly. When I had finished my food I drank the small beer they had poured for me. I was tired but I was curious. I waited for the conversation to die and Butar took a drink and I asked, "What made you come to our village?"

"Garth!" My mother was outraged at my rudeness.

Butar held up his hand and smiled, "Let him ask his questions. It is a reasonable one and it shows he has an inquiring mind." He stood and poked the fire to make it burn brighter and hotter.

Viking Slave

"We are, as you can see, a small village. I know that you have only seen a little of it but there are many empty huts. Last year a terrible disease laid waste to us. I lost my wife, my son and my three daughters. My mother died. Everyone in the village lost someone from their family. Most of our slaves died. Harald One Eye had gone a-Viking before and knew that your land was peaceful and unprotected. He decided to lead his own raid for the first time. That way we could find women to replace those who died and get slaves who would work for us." He smiled at me and emptied his beaker. "Does that answer your questions?"

I thought about it, "Almost. How many warriors do you have?"

"Gareth!"

"It is all right. There are but twenty-eight warriors left. We had many more and could have filled every bank of oars last year but the disease killed many." I opened my mouth to speak and he laughed, "A last answer. We do need more warriors for others could raid us but we will have to wait until the young men are old enough to go to sea." He held up his hand. "And now it is time for our bed, if not yours. Your mother will wake you with father's food. Sleep well tonight you will need it."

He was correct of course but sleep took some time to come for I could hear my mother and Butar coupling in the sleeping room. I had heard it before with my father and her but this time it seemed noisier. Normally it had just been my father I had heard. Tonight my mother was making as much noise as Butar. Eventually, I fell asleep.

I seemed to be asleep for no more than a moment before I was woken. I was given a bowl of porridge and then the old man's food. It was pitch black dark when I left. The guard grumbled as I approached but Butar must have spoken with him and I was allowed through. The forest seemed even more terrifying than the night before. When I finally reached the door I wondered if I should just go in for the old man would probably be asleep. I had to put down the pot of food anyway and so I knocked and shouted my greeting. I was surprised to hear a shout from inside and I entered.

The old man was awake and beckoned me over. He handed me the empty pot from the night before. He said something and rubbed his stomach with his good arm. I took the word to mean good and I repeated it. He nodded, seemingly satisfied. I took the lid off the pot and he sniffed appreciatively. He said another word; I repeated it and he grunted. So the day passed. I learned words by his pointing, speaking and me repeating. It tended to be objects but soon I was picking up the sound of the word. He worked me hard. I was given a brush and told to clean. I was sent to climb into the upper part of the cave and take away the nests and spider's webs I found there. I chopped more wood. He took me into the forests and he showed me which berries we could pick to eat. He had to bend down and peer at them closely but he could find his way around the paths quite easily. We went to his hives and he showed me where they were. I was thankful I was not asked to get any honey combs. I looked at the sky and saw that it was late afternoon. It was time for his meal. I had learned the word for food and he waved me away with a, "Go!" As I turned and ran I think I saw a ghost of a smile but I could not be sure.

This became the pattern of my day for the next weeks. I only ever saw four other people, Butar, my mother, the guard on the gate and Ragnar. There was a change in me. I learned the language very quickly. I seemed to have an ear for it. I began to fill out. We ate better here than we had at home. Back across the sea I was given whatever my father hadn't eaten and he could eat a lot. Here, even for a slave, there was plenty. These people liked their meat and they ate huge quantities. The fish and shellfish were plentiful too. The constant climbing of the hill with heavy weights and the cutting of the logs all seemed to make me more muscular. I was no longer the scrawny crow who would blow over in a strong wind. Soon the hill and the wooden collar meant nothing to me.

There was a change in the old man too. He seemed to be less frail and slept less than he had when I had first arrived. He still rarely smiled but he did not scowl as much as he used to. One summer's morning he was waiting for me. He had a bow and a quiver of arrows. He had learned to use the words I knew and then he would teach me the new words I needed.

"Today, when we have eaten we will hunt. Now go and chop wood."

He came out and I was still chopping. He handed me a bow and a quiver. "Have you hunted before?"

"No."

He sighed, "If I want to eat well then I must teach you."

He began to teach me how to draw and release an arrow without an arrow and then with an arrow. He did not seem bothered if I could hit anything, just as long as I could draw a bow. Then he led me through the woods. He pointed to the ground and taught me to track animals. He would ask me to describe the tracks I saw. He told me what the animal was. He was in the mood for some game and he wanted hare. I wished

Viking Slave

that he had picked something bigger. He must have been a good hunter when he was younger for he brought us to the edge of the forest and a patch of bare hillside. He seemed to know how to get there almost by touch. We would walk with his good arm on my shoulder. When we reached the bare ground we could see the hares but they seemed too far away to hit. He led us around the hillside until they could not smell us. We managed to approach to within fifty paces of our prey, sheltered by the trees, and he handed me an arrow. He pointed at eight hares which were close together. He mimed aiming at them. I took an arrow and pulled back. Looking back now I can see that he could not have given me an easier target. I loosed and, to my delight, a hare was pinned to the ground. As we hurried over he explained to me how I could have done it better. He criticised everything I had done. I did not mind. I had succeeded. I retrieved the arrow; to the old man they were precious and put the game in my bag. He then taught me how to make a trap which we laid outside the burrow.

"Tomorrow you can come back and find another hare."

I did and so another pattern began to emerge; chopping wood, cleaning and hunting. I learned that his one arm was very strong having had to do the work of two and he could see things but they tended to be shapes rather than detailed images. His hearing and his sense of smell were uncanny. He could smell me approaching when I was not making the slightest sound. Under the old man's tutoring I became quite adept. When I killed my first deer the old man insisted on coming to the village so that my mother could skin it and cook it under his supervision.

Ragnar and my mother approved of each other as soon as they met. While they talked Butar took me outside. "Thrall I am pleased with you. Come with me." He took me to the blacksmith's, Bagsecg. "Take off his collar." The blacksmith was surprised but Butar was an important man and the smith did as ordered. "You are still my slave but I do not think you will run."

As we passed through the village I saw some of the boys from the village and they all had their collars on. I might not have seen them for months but their looks were still murderous. I suppose they now had another reason to hate me. I was given special treatment and they were not. When the skin was cured my mother made it into my first jerkin. As we killed more deer during the summer it meant that all four of us had fine footwear and jackets. I was growing so much that mine had to be renewed quite frequently. My Norse was now fluent. There were few words that I did not use. Ragnar and I would come down to see his son once a week. My mother told me that this was a good thing for the old man had lived alone too long since his wife had died.

One summer's evening, when the day was so long that the night lasted less time than it takes to fell a tree, I asked Butar why he had chosen my mother and me. My mother, of course, shook her head at my questions but Butar smiled. "I liked your spirit. You did not take the capture as the end of your life and, besides, the others followed the White Christ. I do not like that. You two follow the old ways and we like that. Besides, I think the Norns had much to do with it."

"The Norns?"

"They are three sisters who weave webs which entangle men. They decide on what we will do and how we will do it."

Mother nodded and said to me, "*Wyrd.*"

"Ah. Now I understand. You had lost your family and the Norns gave you another one." I pointed to my mother. "So you will soon have more children."

My mother blushed and Butar's face darkened. "We have been trying but the Norns have decided otherwise."

The next few months seemed to fly by and I found, for the first time in my life, that I was happy. I had no contact at all with my past as I was rarely in the village and I was learning to do things I had never done before. Once I had mastered the bow I was taught how to use a javelin and I looked forward to the time when I would hunt wild pig. Ragnar was, really, a wise old man and a wonderful teacher despite his grumpy ways. Everything he taught me seemed to be an effort for him and yet he taught me well. The amazing thing was he seemed to grow younger as the year went on. He was old but he began to sleep less and eat more. I think it was my mother's food and we both grew well on it.

It was at the turn of the year when leaves began to fall and the nights became longer than the days when he took me to the back of the cave. He made me climb up to a rocky ledge and bring down the object wrapped in sheepskin. I handed it to him and he took it into the light. When he unwrapped it, I saw that it was a sword. Even though it had been wrapped up it had been well cared for. The light from the fire made the shiny blade seem to sparkle and I could see that there were runes all over the two sides. He carefully explained what they meant. The sword was called Odin's Fang and belonged to Ragnar. He was proud of the blade and what he had achieved. He had told me, after much questioning, how

Viking Slave

he had lost his arm and it been when wielding the sword and protecting his Jarl, Harald's grandfather and his father. His voice became so gentle I thought that he was crying as he told me of the times he had used it.

"I have not held it since I lost my right arm. No one has." He looked at me, "Hold it."

I gripped the sword and suddenly I felt as though I had grown a head taller. It felt light and seemed to sing to me. Without realising it I began to swing the blade gently. If I had tried this when I had first come it would have fallen from my feeble arm but it felt comfortable. Ragnar smiled. "When the days become longer I will teach you how to use a sword."

My eyes widened in excitement. "This one?"

His face became irritated and angry, "No, you stupid boy! This is the sword of a warrior and not a thrall. We will make a wooden sword for you. That will be your task this winter and it will take all winter believe me. Then in the days of flowers and the days of new birth we will practise and I will teach you, thrall, how to fight like a warrior."

I loved that hard cold winter. I struggled up the hill each day through the snow and the cold but it was worth it as Ragnar told me how to cut the wood to make the shape of the sword and then how to make the blade and the handle. I became quite excited when it was finished and I showed him my handiwork. He laughed at me, his toothless face breaking into a cackle, "This is a lump of wood. We need to make it live and make it a sword."

I spent the months when the sun rose for a brief moment, carving intricate runes and messages onto the wooden blade and making the hilt look as though it was embedded with rubies. When I had finished I had to agree that it was worth it. It was beautiful and I could not wait to use it. It was only a wooden sword but it was mine and I had made it.

Ragnar seemed to take malicious pleasure in taking me out during the short cold, snow filled days to practise with my wooden sword. He also insisted that I take the bow and quiver in case we discovered any game. He was wrapped in his bearskin whilst I just had my deer hide jerkin. It was better than my tunic had been but little good at keeping out the cold. He had me hacking and slicing at a particularly thick blackberry bush. He chortled as he saw the thorns ripping into my bare arms. "When you can direct where the blade goes then you will avoid the thorns."

He was right of course and I did improve. Just as I had that first day when I had struggled to cut logs for the old man with the axe. He had told me that when I had the speed of the swing and the angle correct then I would be able to chop the bushes. He was right. Of course it had the added benefit not only of strengthening my arms but clearing the blackberries for a better crop the following spring. He was a wise old warrior.

After a week I was feeling stronger and more skilled. Never one to let me rest on my success, he took me deeper into the forest. He made me climb the lower branches of the huge fir trees and, whilst I hung from my left arm, I had to hack away the dead wood from the lower part of the tree. I had not used my left arm as much and it burned so much that I thought I would drop.

"What use is this? When will I have to hang from a tree and wield a sword?"

"If you ever have to then this is a good lesson but heed my words thrall, you may have to hold a shield in your left arm and that is harder than hanging from a tree." As I came to discover, he was right.

It was the next day when we came close to death. We both made a small sacrifice to Joro the goddess of the earth as we always did and set forth. We had not been out for two days due to the severe storm. I had slept in Ragnar's home where it was warm and we had the food I had managed to hunt. Squirrel stew is neither the most nourishing nor the tastiest but when the alternative is to fight your way through a blizzard to the village, it will do. After we had sacrificed I cleared the snow from the door. It warmed me up considerably. Ragnar took his staff and we headed into the woods.

There was an eerie silence in the woods. The snow was without any prints. Not a bird had ventured down to the white blanket covering their food. There were no signs of deer or hare. Ragnar found an empty piece of land and decided to have me dodging snowballs and smacking them with my wooden sword. I had to make the pile which I then had to make into a pyramid before him. He then began to pelt me with them. I was just a blurred shape to him but he was effective enough. Although I was warm from my exertions, the icy balls of wet snow soon chilled me and I began to hit more than I missed. It was a good exercise and speeded up my reflexes.

"Move your body too!"

I heeded his words and none of the last four snowballs struck me. He then made me make him some more. This time I was only struck once and that was due to the cunning of my mentor. He feinted and then, with

Viking Slave

the speed of a snake striking, he hit me full on the face. It was funny enough for me to laugh and the old man to smile. Then our smiles left us as we heard the howls of the wolf pack.

Ragnar's face fell. "Come this is no place for an old man and a boy. The blizzard has driven the wolves from the high places." We struggled through the snow. Ragnar led us along our own steps in the snow. "Notch an arrow!"

I did as I was bid. Suddenly he stopped. There were other tracks in the snow that were not ours nor were they deer or hares. They were wolves and they were ahead of us. Ragnar held up his hand and we stopped. He sniffed the air. I remembered our first hunt. Were we upwind or downwind of the wolves? The path we trod was wider than most but it narrowed close to the house. I hoped that the smell of man would make the wolf fearful but it had been a harsh few days and who knew how desperate they would be?

We hurried through the woods both listening and watching for danger. I am ashamed to say that it was the rheumy, fading eyes and ears of Old Ragnar who sensed the wolves. I had no idea they were there. When I did see them I saw that there were three of them. Ragnar held up his hand. "Which is the largest one, thrall?"

"The one in the middle."

"Then he is the leader. You must put an arrow into him but one will not kill him or even slow him. You will need a second. When you have loosed your second then you will have to use your wooden sword as a weapon."

I was going to die on this remote path in the forest and our bones would only be discovered when the snow melted. My wooden sword could not kill a wolf.

The old man chuckled as he sensed my fear, "This is a test sent by Ullr."

I had not heard of the god but I assumed he could help us. I aimed the arrow and held a second in my teeth. As soon as I loosed it the mighty beast leapt at me. I notched a second and loosed that too. Both struck him but he kept coming at me. I dropped my bow and grabbed my wooden sword in both hands. His mouth seemed to be a cave filled with huge teeth and it was coming directly for me. I managed to get the wooden sword out and in front of me. It was none too soon for its foaming mouth was almost at my throat. I was knocked to the ground and all went black.

Chapter 3

I awoke and thought I was still aboard the ship. I seemed to be moving up and down. I opened my eyes and saw above me the trees. I shouted, "Ho!"

The motion stopped and Ragnar's face loomed above me. His half blind eyes came almost to my face and his ancient foul breath oozed over me as he chuckled. "You are not dead then. The gods must look kindly upon you. As you are awake then you can stand. We are almost at my home."

When I stood, I felt a little woozy and faint but I could see the smoke rising from Ragnar's chimney and, leaning on the old man I struggled into the safety and security of the hut. The old man plunged a brand into the fire and said, "Take off your jerkin. I want to see if there are wounds."

I wondered how he would see with half blind eyes but I complied. When he found the necklace he had put his milky eyes close to it and then felt it. He laughed. "Had I known you had this then I would not have worried. This is a wolf charm. Who gave it to you?"

"My mother."

"Then she is both wise and caring; as well as being the best cook in the village. You can put your jerkin on and we will go back."

Terror coursed through my veins. "Go back! There are three wolves there."

He laughed. "There are two and they have slunk away. You killed the leader. Your bow, quiver and wooden sword are there and wolf makes good eating. This time we will take a real sword. Take the weapon down and carry that."

I lifted the precious sword down and handed it to Ragnar. "You may be brave but I wonder about your intelligence. I have one arm and can barely see. How would I use it? Strap it on."

I put the sword belt around my waist and coiled the rope Ragnar gave to me around my body. I followed our footsteps through the snow. It was coming on to night and we both hurried. Ragnar, surprisingly, kept up with me. When we neared the body we could hear the foxes. Ragnar screamed and they fled yelping. I found my bow and quiver and secured them about my body. Then I looked at the dead wolf which seemed as big, if not bigger than me. I wondered how we would get it back.

"Find your wooden sword and then tie this rope around his forelegs and head. We will drag him back." He suddenly whirled around with his stick and two foxes which were sneaking towards their spoiled meal ran off. I found my wooden sword. It was buried in the wolf's neck and had entered his skull. I had not had the strength to do that, it had been the force and the power of the beast which had done that or perhaps I had been aided by the gods.

We dragged the carcass back to the house. It was easier than it might have been as it was all downhill. When we reached the house night had fallen and I was chilled to the bone. Once inside Ragnar said, "Put the cauldron of stew on the fire we need warming; especially you." I hurried to do his bidding, grateful for the warmth of the fire which began to thaw me out although I noticed that my fingers were a strange shade of blue. By the time I returned Ragnar had slit the animal open down the middle. "Take out the stomach and throw it outside. The foxes will eat that. If we leave it in here it will stink and attract rats."

I had gutted enough animals to know where the stomach and the bowels were. We always discarded them. I ripped them from the warm body, my blue fingers grateful for the body warmth of the dead wolf. The stink almost made me gag. I opened the door and threw them as far as I could. Almost before I had closed the door, I could hear the foxes racing for the offal. "You watch the stew. I can do this by touch."

Even with just one hand he was skilled. It helped having a knife as sharp as his.

I tasted the stew. It was hot enough. "It is ready."

We ate the stew and afterwards I helped Ragnar to skin the wolf and prepare the meat for cooking. Both of us were so tired that we fell asleep almost as soon as we had placed the raw meat on to the table.

I was awoken by a banging on the door. It was Butar's voice. "Ragnar, it is me Butar."

Ragnar stirred but did not wake. I yelled, "Come in, Lord Butar, it is safe."

"Who is it?" Ragnar had woken from his sleep.

"It is your son, master."

The door opened and Butar, my mother and two of the men from the village were there. Butar looked relieved. "When we had not heard from you for a few days we worried."

Ragnar spat phlegm into the embers of the fire. "You need not worry about us." He pointed to the table. "My thrall killed a wolf last night; with a wooden sword."

The two men with Butar exchanged a smirk and my mother grabbed me and hugged me. "Is this true?"

"Yes, mother, we were hunting when three wolves attacked us."

One of the men, Olef said, "How did you kill it then, thrall?" His tone implied I had not done so.

Ragnar growled, "Did you not hear? With a wooden sword."

I saw the disbelief on their faces. "I first put two arrows in him but he did to stop and then he fell on my sword."

Ragnar struggled to his feet and went to the wolf skin; he threw it at the two men. "There is the wolf, Olef the Doubter. See the wounds and look at the size of the beast."

They opened it out and gasped. "I am sorry, old one. You are right." He looked at me. "He looks like a strong wind would blow him over and yet he has the heart of a dragon."

That is how I came by my name for Butar clasped me to his chest and roared. "You are Dragon Heart and that shall be your name from now on. Now come, both of you. We will hold a feast to celebrate the kill; unless the two of you wish to eat the whole beast yourselves?"

Ragnar sniffed, "No, we will join you but the heart belongs to the boy. He will take the strength of the wolf." My mother was close and the old white eyes could just make her out; he probably smelled her. "Your son was saved by your gift and I will come to your home, not for the food but to get to know you. I would like to know about the wolf charm and, of course, enjoy your cooking. Your son's does not compare."

Mother cuddled me and smiled. I did not mind. I was not a cook. I was a killer of wolves and I felt like a giant as we wound our way through the trees to the village. The warriors with Butar carried the animal. When we reached the hall mother set too, preparing the food, and Ragnar and I were taken to the hall where Harald One Eye held court. All of the warriors were there. In the long winter nights the warriors drank much and told sagas and tales of bravery and heroism. The two warriors who had carried the meat and the skin down had already begun to tell the tale of the thrall and the wolf. Harald One Eye shouted at them to be silent as we entered. "Would you deprive us of a good story? Be silent fools, or you shall be the guards tonight when we celebrate this kill.

Come, Butar and revered Ragnar. Bring this thrall who still looks like a leaf but appears to have the strength of an oak."

Harald himself helped Ragnar to a seat. Butar stood behind his father and next to the Jarl. He spoke, "This is the son of my woman and his courage saved my father. He has earned the name Dragon Heart."

The warriors who were all seated at long tables began banging the tables with their fists and cheering. They were already a little drunk but I felt flattered to have the warriors cheering me.

Ragnar told, quite simply, what had happened without embellishment or fine words. Someone else would make it into a saga. We were cheered, again, as we left. We returned to Butar's home and he put an arm around me. "You have saved my father's life and given him purpose again. I thank you thrall. The Norns must have directed us to your village that day."

"Master, why did you choose our village?"

"I spied the boys in the river and knew there must be a settlement close by. We were headed up river to the bend where there is a choice of villages."

Once again *wyrd* had intervened in my life. Ragnar was seated by the hearth in Butar's hall and I could hear him and my mother chattering away. Butar had three other thralls. All were young girls from my village. They all had the sullen look of the others. I sighed. If they accepted that this was their destiny they would find the burden much easier to bear. My life was better than it had been. Apart from the odd clout around the ears for carelessness I had not been beaten and I had certainly never been bullied. With the thrall collar gone I could live as normally as any. I could not flee but where would I go? I would either starve to death or be eaten by wild animals. I was suddenly aware that all three of the adults were looking at me. Ragnar's white eyes were fixed on my shape framed in the doorway.

Butar chuckled, "Dragon Heart is dreaming while awake my love."

"Come in, my son, and close the door. You are letting out all the warmth."

"Speaking of warmth," Butar went into his sleeping quarters and returned with a fur, "Your mother has spent the long nights sewing together the hare and squirrel fur from the animals you hunted. You have a cloak. My father told me you nearly froze to death. I cannot have my father's thrall dying on the job." He handed me the cloak. The fur was soft and downy. There was a leather tie to secure it. I put it around my shoulders. It was fine.

"Thank you, mother; thank you, master." My mother nodded her approval as she prepared the food.

Ragnar stayed in his son's house and ate his food there. "I do not need to see Harald One Eye and the others making fools of themselves. I know that already and I do not wish to hear them butcher the saga of Dragon Heart the Thrall. I will sit by the warm fire and speak with the mother of the Dragon Heart."

I would have loved to stay there with them but Butar insisted that I attend because the feast was in honour of my deed and they wanted to compete with the telling of the tale. "Master, how can they tell the tale? They were not there. Even I do not know all that happened and your father's eyes would not bear true testament."

"The detail matters not. They all know that a youth of twelve summers or so went out and defeated a wolf pack with a wooden sword and two arrows. They will enjoy competing to give the most stirring saga."

When we entered the hall they all cheered. A place for Butar was cleared next to Harald and a wooden log placed behind Butar for me. I was still a thrall. Butar and Ragnar did not treat me as such but here, in the hall of the Jarl, the proprieties had to be observed. This was the first time I had seen all of the warriors since the raid. There were more of them. Old Olaf was there and he was still scowling. They were all busy drinking and eating and I was able to sit and watch them. I also saw the other thralls, most of them taken from my village, as they served the jugs of ale and brought in the hunks of steaming meat. They all had their wooden collars on and they all gave me hateful glances. I sighed. I was still the outsider. Even here where we were all strangers I was still not accepted. I think that was the night I decided that I did not need them. I had done nothing to offend them and yet they treated me badly. So far, I liked these people amongst whom I had been planted. I would grow to be like them and I listened and I watched just as my mother had urged.

When the food was finished Harald stood up. "We have a new tale to tell today, the saga of Dragon Heart the Thrall. Who will begin?"

Many of the warriors fancied themselves a poet and they all vied to be the first. Harald was the arbitrator of all disputes over seniority. Butar told me later that it should have been my role to tell the tale but I was still a boy and I was a thrall. I did not mind. Eventually, six of the men

Viking Slave

told the tale. One of the things I discovered was that they loved to have sagas repeated and each one was told and retold until the final version was reached, delivered by Harald One Eye. This one, of course, was greeted by the loudest cheer and was the one which would be retold each winter.

The Saga

The winter snow lay on the ground
The cold ate like the wolves
Old Ragnar left to find the food
And hunt with just his boy a thrall
Ullr watched down with hard cold eyes
To see what they would do
With deepening step they struggled on
The eyes of wolves glowing red around them
The pack had gathered to feast on men
In the forest land of Harald the Brave
With dripping jaws and savage teeth
They stalked the one armed warrior
And child with wooden sword
The cunning wolf surrounded them
And they readied to feast on flesh
One armed Ragnar had no sight
But his heart was true and strong
With his thrall close by
They faced their foes
Joined together by bonds and oaths
The arrows flew swift and true
But still the wolves came on
To feast on man flesh and gorge on blood
Until with sword made of wood
The thrall bravely stood his ground
With snarling teeth and eyes of fire
The wolf opened his mouth to feast
Dragon Heart stood fast and strong
Like a rock against the flood
The wolf fell dead and the others fled

Viking Slave

Ragnar had prevailed
And the wolf died there
While the pack all fled
Beaten by Dragon Heart the thrall
And Ragnar the mighty

After the saga Harald stood, a little unsteadily and addressed his warriors. "Men of Ulfberg, we have had a fine year and we are now richer than before the disease came which took so many." They all nodded and Harald swept an encompassing hand around the table. "I see before me another ten warriors who have travelled here to join my band!" This was greeted by the banging of hands on the table. "When the ice and the snow melt we will return across the water and we will take more from that honey pot that is the land of the Angles. We will build a second ship to join my ship '*Sif*' so that we can take even more plunder and make this hall even better and finer. And make the name of Ulfberg feared across all the northern seas."

The evening then became a drunken orgy of drinking contests, arm wrestling and fist fights. I only saw this briefly for Butar, who had drunk less than most, took me back to his hall. "Thank you for taking me, master."

He looked at me strangely, "It was in your honour. You had to be there."

I shook my head, "I was the saga but I am a slave; I was not needed there so I thank you."

He shook his head, "You are wise beyond your years. Come, my warm hall calls."

My mother awaited us and she held her finger to her lips. She pointed at Ragnar curled up by the fire with furs about him. She kissed me on the head and led me to the other side of the fire where she had laid furs for me. Butar wrapped one of his huge arms around her and led her to the sleeping room. I could hear them trying to make me a brother and then I fell asleep.

We spent the months of the lengthening days continuing my training. The main difference to my life was that we visited the settlement more. Ragnar enjoyed the company of my mother who fussed over the old man. I was now afforded a higher status and, whilst still a thrall, I was seen as a human being rather than an object. My fellows from the village across the sea were less than friendly. I still used the wooden sword to practise but now the warriors often asked to see it. The wolf blood still stained the wood and they would look at me and shake their heads at either the bravery or stupidity of taking on a wolf with a wooden sword. Opinions were divided.

The preparations for the raid to the land of the Angles occupied everyone. Weapons were prepared; arrows and spears gathered. Blades were sharpened and those who could afford it had their helmets and shields improved. I noticed that only three warriors wore mail shirts; Harald, Butar and Knut. The rest all had leather byrnies. The one thing they all had in common was a shield. They all had a design painted upon them and each warrior took the time to painstakingly repair any flaws. Some of the wealthier warriors studded their shields with iron but all of them spent the majority of time with their swords or their axes. The late winter saw them practising all the time with their weapons and the winter fat became muscle once more.

Ragnar fell ill just before they were due to leave. It was probably just the normal colds we all suffered but Butar insisted that we return to his hall. "Father, you need care. Dragon Heart is faithful but he is no nurse. My woman will care for you both."

Ragnar relented although he was so ill that he had little option. I helped Butar carry the old man down to the hall where a bed was built close to the fire and my mother took charge of him. She became quite bossy but I think Ragnar enjoyed it. His wife had died when the disease had ravaged Ulfberg and my mother reminded him of her. I had mixed feelings about the return. I liked being close to my mother again but I enjoyed my status as Ragnar's thrall. The village had too many of my enemies within its wooden walls for me to be happy.

The snow had gone from the village although it still remained in the hills when *'Sif'* set sail. There were ten old men and young boys left to guard the village. Olaf the Toothless was, to his chagrin, left in command. He was not happy about his role and took his displeasure out on the thralls. The ship slipped silently down the fiord. After it had gone both the anchorage and the village seemed empty somehow. It should not have been so for there were well over a hundred people left in the settlement but it seemed desolate and lacking life. I saw that my mother was unhappy that Butar had gone. They seemed very close; much closer than she had been to my father. I suddenly realised that I could barely remember my birth father's face. I had forgotten my own father.

Ragnar was becoming better and he sent me, one day, to return to the house and bring his sword. He had been too ill to make a fuss but now he wanted it close by. I did not know why for he could not use it but I was glad to be away from the hateful stares and the depressing atmosphere. I took my bow; Ragnar had gifted it to me after the wolf attack. I was more aware of the danger I might be in. I was almost at the house when I was suddenly aware of being followed. There was someone behind me. I think the time I had spent hunting with Ragnar had honed my senses. I would not turn around for that would mean they would know that I knew they were there. I continued up to the house. The skull of the wolf peered at me from its wooden perch outside the front door. It marked our home and warned the wolves of our intent. I carried on beyond the house. I knew the land as far as the mountain top better than any other and I knew how to set a trap. Whoever was following me would follow my prints in the snow which lay beyond the house. The path wound around the rock and I would be able to ambush my pursuers.

Once I turned the corner of the large rock I hurried. I needed to gain a lead. The path entered the forest and turned back to head down the slope. I began to move through the trees and I found a spot from which to watch the path. I saw Tadgh and Saelac, two of the boys from my village. They both had cudgel like sticks in their hands which confirmed that they wished me harm. I slipped my bow around my body. I would use my wooden sword.

I heard them as they struggled to ascend the slippery slope. Their footwear was not made for the snow and mine was. "That bastard moves faster than a deer!"

"Don't worry, Saelac, he has to come back this way and we can see his tracks."

"What will we say when we return to the village?"

"We say nothing. They will not know we followed him here. They will not miss him until tonight and then it will be too late to hunt for him. The wolves and the foxes will finish off this Dragon Heart."

"Are you sure we can take him? I heard that he killed a wolf with his bare hands."

"Are you afraid? Raldson died because of him and we will avenge his death. Besides, I am sure it was the old man who killed the wolf. I am not afraid of Crow!"

They were both beyond me and I chose my moment well. I leapt out and swung my wooden sword as hard as I could at Saelac's head. He slumped to the ground. Then Tadgh swung his cudgel at me. It was a clumsy blow and I easily evaded it. I suddenly realised that I was now almost the same size as Tadgh who had towered over me when we lived in the land of the Angles. I also felt much stronger.

"Typical Crow! Attacking from behind!"

"Typical Tadgh needing help to attack someone they despise."

He swung his cudgel again and this time I parried with the wooden sword. I saw his arm jar and I punched as hard as I could with my left hand. The blood erupted from his nose. He became enraged and swung wildly at my head. I ducked and swung my sword up between his legs. He went down clutching his groin and let out a wail which sounded like a pig being castrated. I grabbed his cudgel and threw it away. I took a piece the piece of rope I used to hold in my jerkin and tied their wooden collars together. I took my bow and notched an arrow. Tadgh tried to rise and I pushed him to the ground. "You move when I say and not before. Let us wait until Saelac awakens eh?"

After a few minutes Saelac's eyes open and he looked at me. Terror filled them as they widened. "Now you can both rise but do it slowly. I am quite good with this. Now walk before me." They walked awkwardly down the slippery path. I laughed out loud when Tadgh fell bringing Saelac down with him. I made no effort to help them to rise. By the time we reached the house they were tired. I found another piece of rope and I tethered them to a tree. I quickly recovered the sword and then led them by the rope back to the village.

The guard at the gate looked surprised to see a thrall leading two others but he nodded as we entered. I went directly to Olaf the Toothless. He stood looking at us from the steps of Harald One Eye's hall. "What have we here, Dragon Heart?"

"I had been sent on an errand by my master and these two followed me wishing me harm." I smiled, "I have returned them."

He glowered at them. "Why did you leave the village?"

As I had expected they had no excuse and they looked guiltily at each other. "I will have to return to my master. He is expecting his sword."

Olaf nodded and gave me the slightest of winks. "I will see that they are suitably punished."

When I reached Butar's Hall with the sword my mother was standing by the door. "What happened?"

"Tadgh decided I should be quietly killed."

Her mouth dropped open, "But how…"

"I am not the frightened little hare I was." I gestured towards Ragnar who had been listening, "My master has put some iron in my backbone. They will not find me so easy to frighten in the future."

Ragnar chuckled, "Come with me. I think you deserve this."

I placed the sword on his bed and he led me into Butar's sleeping room. He opened a chest at the foot of the bed. I could see that within it were arms and helmets. He took out a long knife or it could have been a short sword. "This is what the Saxons call a seax. It is not as good as a sword but I think that you may have need of it." He gave me the knife and then rummaged around for the sheath. He handed me that too.

"Will Lord Butar not object?"

"These are not his; they belong to me and my other son, Butar's brother, Karl. He was killed in a raid by the men of Stavanger. Take it."

I glanced at my mother, "You might as well, my son. Those boys will not give up just because you have bloodied their nose. Learn how to use it."

Ragnar chuckled, "It is like your wooden sword but you will not need the strength of the wolf this time."

I looked at the blade and felt the bone handle; it seemed made for my hand. The blade was as long as my two hands and the point was sharp as I discovered when I carelessly slipped the blade into the sheath. I held the sheath too high and the razor sharp edge nicked my finger. I sucked the blood and Ragnar nodded. "Now you are one. It has drunk your blood and knows you. Always trust it." He looked at me thoughtfully. "It needs a name but let the blade tell you what that is."

I felt confused. How could a piece of metal talk? But as I discovered, it could. Olaf was as good as his word and the two boys were punished. I heard the lash of the whip on their naked backs. I left the hall to see what the noise was. The two mothers wept and the other four boys glared at me as I stood there. Someone else would try to hurt me. I would have to be even more careful.

I went to Ragnar. "Master, how do I make arrows? We only have six left and if I am to go hunting when the snow melts then I will need more."

"It is good that you wish to learn for this is a skill you will need. Go into the forest and cut thirty of the straightest pieces of wood you can find. They should be as long as your leg. Bring them back here and then collect as many goose and duck feathers as you can."

His task sounded easy but it was not and it took me all day to find the thirty straight pieces of wood. I just had time to find a small bag full of goose feathers before darkness descended. I wanted to begin directly but mother intervened. "The two of you eat first then you can make your arrows but I want no mess in here!"

Even Ragnar quailed before mother and her tongue. She was gentle most of the time but when she wanted her way, she got it. Making arrows was not hard but it was time consuming. I stripped the bark and then made the shaft as smooth as possible. The fixing of the flights was hard and demanded a steady hand and eye. I could see why Ragnar could not make them. After three night's work I had made my un-tipped arrows. "What about the barbs?"

"Metal is best but it is expensive. There is some flint close to our home. Go there and fetch a lump and I will teach you how to nap."

I discovered that you did not need eyes to nap, that is chip pieces, of flint. It was all touch and a firmness of action. After a few disasters I found that I could manage to manufacture many flint arrow heads. "They are plentiful and if they break then no matter. The narrow ones are best for accuracy but the broader ones cause the worst wounds. When I am well and Butar returns we will try them out."

Events occurred which meant that we tried them out sooner rather than later.

Chapter 4

The worst job I had to do for Ragnar was to empty his night pot. His bladder required emptying three times a night. The bowl would be full after the third occasion and he would wake me to get rid of the contents. In his home this was not a problem, I would open the door and hurl the contents into the forest but in the village I had to climb the palisade and empty the pot outside. This particular night I had just found that perfect spot in which to sleep and his voice roused me.

"Yes, master?"

"Time to water the woods," he chuckled.

I wrapped my new cloak about my shoulders and slipped my feet into my boots and took the warm steaming liquid out of the hall. Once outside the blast of cold air hit me like a slap in the face. I headed towards the stairs leading to the palisade. I recognised the young guard, it was Haaken. He was quite friendly towards me and he had asked me many questions about the wolf I had killed. Like many of the young men he envied me.

"The old man's piss?"

"Aye."

"He is so old you know that if you bottled this you could sell it as an elixir of life."

I laughed, "You are more than welcome to this and more believe me."

He sniffed the pungent smelling liquid. "No, I will let you dispose of it. Do me a favour and throw it on the far wall. I am on duty until dawn."

"I will do so." With most of the warriors gone it was down to the young boys and old men to act as guards. I knew that it was yet another reason they wished themselves a-Viking. I walked to the deserted side of the palisade. With just three guards at night one side would remain without a sentry. I headed to the side with the steepest walls. It was the safe section of the wall. There were steep rocks below it and only a determined attacker would risk death to scale it. I held the two handles and hurled the steaming water as far from the walls as I could get. I was about to return to the warmth of the hall when I stopped. After the liquid striking the leaves and bushes I was sure I had heard another noise. I waited. The night seemed as silent as the grave and I was convinced that I had imagined it until I heard the crack of a twig. I peered out into the

Viking Slave

dark but could see nothing and then I glanced to the fiord. I caught the sight of the tip of a mast. There was a dragon ship there.

I moved swiftly to Haaken. "I heard a noise and there is a dragon ship in the fiord."

Haaken was bright and he was decisive. "Go and wake Olaf the Toothless."

I scurried down the steps and went into the almost deserted warrior hall. Almost before I had reached him Olaf was awake and was glaring at me. "What?"

"I heard a noise outside the walls and I saw the mast of a dragon ship."

"If you are making this up I will lay open your back."

I put my hands between my legs and said, "I swear."

He nodded, "Awake and to arms." He looked at me. "Go and get your bow, wolf killer."

I took the bowl back to the hall and Ragnar said, "You were some time..."

"There is a dragon ship in the fiord."

"Take your bow. I will wake your mother. Make sure you have your blade."

I grabbed my bow and other weapons and ran back to the wall. Olaf was there with Haaken. He whispered, "You have good ears. It will be the men from Stavanger. They are cowardly bastards; they wait until our warriors are gone before they attack. You two stay here and kill anything that moves. The gate is where they will attack."

When he left it felt lonely on that wall with just the two of us. Every shadow seemed to move. Suddenly I sensed a movement behind me and I whirled, an arrow already notched. It was Ragnar with his sword. "Master, what are you doing here? You should be in the hall."

"What and be killed in my bed? If I am to die tonight then let it be with my sword in my hand. I will watch your back."

Haaken said quietly, "Watch with what?"

He didn't realise how sharp the old man's ears were and he received a blow to the back of his head. "I can see well enough to hit you, Haaken Haakenson." He stopped and cocked an ear to the outside wall. "They are coming. They will stand close to the wall. Lean over carefully and watch."

I leaned over and saw something glint in the moonlight. It was a helmet. I jerked my head back. "They are below us."

"Think of them as deer, thrall and you will do well."

Haaken and I leaned over. I drew back the bow and the arrow plunged down to strike the warrior in the neck. Haaken's arrow hit another in the arm. Realising they had been seen the raiders raced to the wall and began to climb. They used their shields to hoist each other up. Haaken killed one standing on the shield. I sent an arrow into the leg of one of the men holding the shield and the three of them collapsed into a heap. I could hear the sounds of combat on the other side of the village and knew that the three of us would get no help from that quarter. I loosed arrow after arrow until I reached in and they were all gone. Haaken said, "I emptied mine some time ago. It will be knife work."

I took out my seax and Ragnar placed himself between us. "Protect each other's backs. They will have to kill you before they can move into the village." The raiders had moved further down the walls. They had climbed an empty section and now three of them came towards me.

"Master, there are three of them."

"They can only come at you one at a time. I am behind you." I heard the sword slip from the scabbard. "What weapon does the first one have?"

The warrior who came at me had a helmet, a shield and a spear. "A spear."

"Then his shield is next to the wall. You can grab his spear head and stab with your blade."

The old man sounded confident but then he could not see this huge warrior who raced at me. I suspect he saw only a stripling and thought to knock me from the wall but I was standing before my master and I would let no harm come to him whilst I lived. I was not sure that I would be able to do as Ragnar wished but when the blade came at me it seemed to move in slow motion. I moved to my right and, grabbing the shaft, stabbed upwards with the seax. He caught sight of the seax and tried to bring his shield over to protect himself. He merely succeeded in losing his balance and, as I let go of the spear he fell to his death on the rock strewn slope.

The next warrior had a sword, "A sword, Master!"

"When he strikes use both your hands with your seax."

This time I was sure that I would die. The sword came down and I put the seax up, catching the hilt. I saw the look of triumph on his face. My seax would only slow the blade and not stop it. The look of triumph changed to one of horror as Ragnar's sword ripped into his stomach. The

Viking Slave

sword fell from his lifeless hand and he lay dead at my feet. I pick up the sword and transferred the seax to my left hand.

Ragnar shouted, "Haaken, can you move forwards?"

"If I have to."

"Then do so. Thrall, step back. Make him rush at you."

The third warrior also had a spear and a shield. I was just glad none had mail or all three of us would be dead already. He did indeed run at us and failed to see his dead companion. He tripped at my feet. I hesitated for a moment until Ragnar shouted, "Kill him!" I stabbed down, striking his neck I was concentrating so hard that the sword went through his neck and pinned his body to the walkway.

I heard a cry from behind me and I withdrew my blade. I could see Haaken fighting two men. One, nearer him, had a sword and the other had a spear. Ragnar stabbed forwards, blindly and caught the swordsman on the leg I dived between Haaken's legs and stabbed upwards with my seax. The blade went between his legs and into his body he tore himself from the blade and crashed, screaming, to the ground below. Haaken slumped to the wooden walkway and I stood, using the spear to aid me. I suddenly found myself face to face with a giant of a man. He grabbed and turned me. I felt his left hand come behind me and I knew that he would kill me. I put my left leg on the wall and pushed. We both flew through the air with his arm wrapped around my body. We struck the ground so hard that I was winded. Amazingly I still held the seax and the sword. I tried to stand but my hand was trapped. When I managed to extract my hand and my seax, it came away bloody. The warrior was dead.

I ran back to the wall. Ragnar was slumped close to Haaken. If the old man was dead it would be my fault. I turned him over and he breathed still. "I am just tired Dragon Heart. See to Haaken. He is wounded." I saw that the spear had removed one of Haaken's eyes but the wound which was causing a problem was his arm which was bleeding heavily. I grabbed the hem of the tunic of the dead raider and tied it around the arm. The blood stopped. I suddenly remembered the battle and I stood. There were no longer any sounds of fighting just the wailing of women. The raiders had gone.

My mother rushed to us. "I am well, mother, but see to Haaken." I helped Ragnar to his feet. "Come, master. Now is the time for your bed." I took his sword and sheathed it. "Well master you were wrong you know."

Viking Slave

"What?"

"You said you would never need the sword again and yet you have killed a warrior this night. You are a warrior still."

He chuckled, "As are you Dragon Heart; taking on a warrior armed only with a seax."

"But you told me to!"

"I know but I thought we would both die and it would make a wonderful saga. One armed Ragnar and the Dragon Heart fighting the men of Stavanger."

He was still chuckling when I put him to bed. "Make sure you clean the sword before you put it away. Blood comes away easier when it is wet and make sure you get the scabbard for that sword before someone steals it."

As I passed Olaf he smiled his toothless smile. "If you had not earned the name Dragon Heart before tonight you have now. You did well. Butar will be proud that the village still stands and it is thanks to you and the old man's piss."

I saw Tadgh and the other thralls hauling away the bodies of the raiders, now stripped of weapons and arms. They glared at me with my sword and seax in my hand. I cared not. I had been a warrior, at least for a short time.

Haaken was conscious when I returned. My mother looked at me with pride in her eyes. "You saved his life, my son. He would have bled to death."

"I am in your debt Dragon Heart."

"I am sorry about your eye."

He tried to shrug but I could see that it pained him. "Tonight I saw an old man who was almost blind fighting like a hero so as long as I have one eye I will think myself lucky."

I found the scabbard and sheathed the sword. I took the helmet from the dead warrior to look at his face. I heard Haaken's voice. "Keep the helmet thrall for I believe you will be a warrior one day. Dragon Heart will not be a slave forever." And so I took the helmet.

Mother and I helped Haaken down to the warrior hall where his wounds could be tended to and then Mother took my sword and helmet. "You had better help Olaf. I fear we have lost warriors this night."

As I l looked around I could see that at least five men from the village lay dead. I knew we had killed more of the raiders but that did not help our dead. Olaf wandered over to me. "Go with Grefelle here and show

Viking Slave

him the ones you killed with the arrow." He grabbed Tadgh, "Thrall, go with him and help to pitch the bodies into the fiord."

Tadgh's face was a mask of fury. Grefelle was one of the older warriors. He was closer to Ragnar's age than Butar's. As we walked through the gate he said, "Did I hear that Ragnar killed a warrior?"

"Aye master, with his sword."

He laughed. "At his age that is quite remarkable. And I thought I was doing well. And you Dragon Heart, not content with a wolf you kill three warriors with your own hands."

We found the eight men we had killed. We had hit others but they had left with their wounds. We could see their blood trails in the first light of dawn. We took their weapons and made a pile of them. "You two take the bodies one by one to that rock and pitch them into the water."

It did not take long to carry the bodies and hurl them but I had to endure Tadgh's looks of hate. We had just thrown the last one and I had turned when I felt a terrible pain in the back of my head and I fell into a deep black hole.

When I regained consciousness Grefelle was looking at me with concern on his face. "Thank the Allfather that you live. I could not have faced my old friend Ragnar if his thrall had died."

"What happened?"

"The slave Tadgh struck the back of your head with a rock and then ran towards the fiord. I would have run him down but I was concerned about you."

I stood unsteadily and Grefelle supported me. He looked to the fiord which was now bathed in the sunlight of a new day. "Look! He is there!"

We could both see Tadgh running towards the dragon ship and waving his arms. He was joining the raiders. I wondered if I would ever see him again and then it all went black once more.

When I came to I was in Butar's Hall and I saw mother's anxious face peering down at me. She gave a gasp and put her hands to her mouth, "He lives!"

Ragnar's face appeared next to her and he smiled, "I thought you were gone to the Otherworld, thrall."

I tried to sit up, "Tadgh!"

"You rest. Tadgh has fled with the raiders but that was three days ago. Olaf the Toothless still commands and he has ordered that you be rested until I say you are fit to walk outside again. Head wounds are dangerous." She stroked my hair, "Typical of Tadgh to attack from behind. I will get you some broth."

Ragnar put his face close to mine, "Your mother is a force of nature, thrall. I can see why my son is so enamoured of her." He cackled. "It was she who told Olaf you needed rest and even Olaf quailed before her."

As we waited for my broth Ragnar told me how they had seen the raider's ship sail away. The raid had cost us dearly for six men had died and a slave had run but Ragnar seemed exultant. "The men of Stavanger will not be able to show their faces for many years. A boatload defeated by a handful of warriors, a one armed man and a thrall. When Harald has his saga composed their shame will live forever."

"And Haaken?"

"He has a patch where his eye was and his arm heals. He will still be able to go a-Viking and like all the other warriors he now has another helmet and swords. You have a quiver full of good arrows. Olaf sent the thralls who were friends of Tadgh to collect them from the forest. It may have been an ill wind which blew but it blew for us. The Allfather watched over us and," he reverently touched the wolf charm, "the charm of your ancestors helped. You see we old ones have powers beyond the grave." He cackled again.

My mother came in with my broth. "And you will be in your grave sooner if you do not rest. I will bring your broth soon. A man of your age fighting warriors; who has ever heard such a thing."

Despite her words her face showed me that she was proud of the old man and, by association, of me. She gently sat me up and then fed me the broth. Between mouthfuls I asked her more questions. "The sword and the helmet; they are safe?"

"Aye and a good thing too. The next time you go into danger at least your head will be protected."

"Can a thrall go to war?"

"I do not know. In the land of your father it would not happen and in my land we had no slaves but I do not know these people and their ways yet. We will see what Butar says when he returns."

We heard the snores of Ragnar as he slept and mother smiled. "It is good that he rests. Butar will be glad that he survived."

"Mother you and Butar..."

"Yes, my son, we are as husband and wife." She looked down at me, concern on her face, "Does it bother you? I mean your father..."

"No. I like Lord Butar and I barely knew my father. I cannot remember him speaking to me over much and his face is fading."

"He was a hard man to like but he protected us."

"Lord Butar appears as though he is the leader here and not Harald One Eye. They do not seem to get on. Why is that?"

She lowered her voice, even though there was no-one to hear. "Harald's father and Ragnar were brothers but Ragnar lost his arm defending his brother who abandoned him and Olaf on a raid. They escaped but Ragnar swore he would never speak to his brother again. Olaf was oathsworn and had no choice. It is why Ragnar lives outside the village. When Harald became Jarl he gave all the men the choice of becoming his oathsworn or leaving the village. Butar was going to leave but many of the men would have followed him and Butar had too much honour to destroy his people. He stayed but many of the men look to Butar in battle and not Harald but never speak of this. It is bed talk."

"I will not mother. I have killed in battle. I am a man now and I will take a man's responsibilities."

She took away the empty bowl and kissed me on the forehead. "You are my son and I am so proud of you. Your grandfather was a mighty warrior and he would have been proud of you and your deeds. He slew many Saxons and people feared him. He came from a long line of warriors and you continue that line."

By the time the men returned from the raid I was healed enough to walk about the village. I noticed a change in the attitude of the villagers. They smiled at me more and even Olaf the Toothless seemed disposed to scowl less when I passed. Now that Tadgh had gone there was just Saelac who gave me evil looks. Unlike when I had lived by the river I no longer feared his wrath. I had faced down a pack of wolves and Stavanger raiders; Saelac would not bother me.

The first thing I did when I was allowed up was to clean the sword and helmet. My head wound was too tender for me to try it on but my mother said it would be a little too big. She made a small cap from hare fur to fit inside and I prayed for my wound to heal so that I could try it. I was a conical helmet with a nasal; a piece of metal to protect the nose. Ragnar liked it. "With a leather byrnie you will have much protection. All you need now, Dragon Heart, is a shield." He smiled at me, "But I would keep them hidden from my son until your mother has spoken of them."

Viking Slave

So when the mast of the *'Sif'* was seen I was both excited and fearful. It seemed to take an age for the dragon ship to edge up the fiord. It was low in the water which suggested a successful raid. This time there were few animals and no males. The boat appeared to have many women and girls. I also noticed that at least two warriors were missing. Harald led the way and he was accorded a cheer. I saw Olaf waiting to speak with him. Butar joined them and they huddled together as the slaves and plunder were taken from the ship. Suddenly Olaf pointed in my direction and they all looked at me. Finally they headed up to the warrior hall. I bowed my head as they passed and saw the hint of a smile playing on Butar's lips.

I returned to Butar's hall. The old man was keen to get back to his own home. He had had enough of the company of others. He had promised his son to stay there while he was away but he was desperate for us to return to the cave home he loved. "Thrall, gather my belongings by the door. When we have seen my son and said our farewells, we will depart. Do not forget the bow and the quiver. We still have lessons on hunting."

Butar seemed to take an age to reach us and I could see that my mother was eager to greet him. When he entered she threw propriety to the wind and flung her arms around him to embrace and kiss him. After they had disentangled themselves Butar smiled. "Well Dragon Heart, I hear that you and my father are not content to sit idly by when I am away, you insist on fighting off a band of raiders."

"Pah! It was but the men of Stavanger. The thrall and I could have held them alone." Ragnar was dismissive of the raiders.

I did not believe that for one instant but I think it was Ragnar telling his son that he did not need to be protected. "Well whatever the cause, Harald One Eye is throwing a feast in honour of the defenders of his home. You two, as well as Haaken and Olaf, are to be honoured."

"I wanted to get home."

"Father, is one more night too much to ask? I have not seen you, unless, of course, if you have tired of the company of Myfanwy?"

"No, of course not. One more night but we leave at dawn and Dragon Heart here can take some of our belongings up today."

"Of course."

My heart sank. I had hoped to hear the tale of the raid but I was a slave and I obeyed. I gathered the belongings together and laid them on a sled made of hazel branches. I fixed a rope around my shoulders and

Viking Slave

began to drag it up the hill. I could feel my shoulders burning by the time I reached the house. I unpacked everything and stored them in the correct place. With someone who was half blind like Ragnar, the position of even minor objects was vital. I also cleaned out the material which had blown in and chased away a couple of mice who had tried to set up residence in my bed. I hid my helmet and my sword along with Ragnar's in the shelf in the cave. I chopped more logs for the fire and stacked some close by. I then took my bow and headed up into the higher ground where there was still some snow. I needed to check for any tracks. The memory of the wolf attack was still fresh and I wanted to discover if they had returned. They had not.

By the time I reached the village again it was almost dark and we would soon be getting ready for the feast. Mother insisted that I change from my leather jerkin and put on a tunic. "But I have only my old tunic and that is not fit for a feast."

"No you do not. Butar and the men took a chest of clothes on the raid and we have two fine tunics for you."

They were indeed fine and must have been made for a Saxon who was rich for they were dyed and well dyed at that. My mother stood back and admired me. She took a beautifully carved bone comb Butar had given her and dragged it through my protesting hair. "There. You look a little less like the wild child. You will need to braid your hair or cut it." Men did not cut their hair nor did they shave their faces. I would have to learn the skill. My hair now hung almost to my shoulders. My mother put her arms on my shoulders and looked at me. "You are now the same size as your father was. You have grown over this past year." I realised then that I had been a slave for a year and yet it had been the best year of my life. What horror did the gods and sisters have in store for me? Everyone knew that you had to pay for good fortune one way or another.

This time I was seated between Haaken and Olaf. Haaken looked quite dashing with his leather patch. He grinned as I sat next to him. "Who would have thought that things would turn out like this?" He leaned in to me. "I will confess that I thought the three of us would all die on that wall and I was prepared to go to the Otherworld that night."

I had not thought about it. I had been so scared that I had not thought of death only survival. "I am glad that your wound was not serious."

He shrugged, "A good warrior is measured by his wounds." I thought that the wounds should be on the warrior's enemies.

Harald One Eye stood and all went silent. "This is a double celebration. We have come back richer than we dared dream of and our home was saved by the brave warriors we left behind. Haaken will give us the saga of the defence of Ulfberg."

Haaken stood and began to chant his poem. He must have been preparing it for some time as it flowed like a mountain stream and everyone was enchanted. I heard my name and Ragnar's mentioned more than once and saw Ragnar allow himself a self satisfied smile. As with all sagas we were made to sound braver than we were. The treachery of Tadgh was greeted by scowls and boos as well as sympathetic looks in my direction. The warriors who had been on the raid had no idea what had gone on and I could see the looks of amazement on their faces. When he had finished he took a little bow as the table was banged. He then had to repeat it so that they could all appreciate the music of the poetry and the words. Haaken was much better than Harald had been.

When he had finished for a second time Harald One Eye stood. "I have decided to take a wife on this special night. I will marry the Saxon princess Aethelfrith, daughter to Aethelred." I wondered how that would work for he already had a thin faced wife called Freya. Perhaps a Jarl was allowed more than one wife. It would certainly make life within the hall interesting. I must have been the only one to speculate for everyone cheered and Harald looked well pleased with himself.

I turned to Haaken, "Why are they so happy?"

Olaf answered, "Our Jarl sees himself as a king. If he marries the daughter then he has a claim to the throne."

"But we are but a handful of warriors."

Olaf smiled his toothless smile which was always disconcerting, "We will soon have more warriors. Word will spread of our success and there are always warriors who are eager to follow successful leaders."

Before I could answer Butar stood, "And I too will take a wife. I will marry Myfanwy." My mother was very popular with the men for they admired her stoic bravery and her cooking. The cheers were even louder. Butar held his hands for silence, "And in honour of that and because of his bravery I now free my thrall Dragon Heart and adopt him as my son. Dragon Heart will become a warrior and I think that he will be a great warrior."

Everyone cheered the news and both Olaf and Haaken slapped my back but Harald One Eye threw a baleful glance in my direction. The

Viking Slave

cheers were louder for Butar than they had been for him. He did not like his sun being eclipsed by Butar and I wondered what it presaged.

Chapter 5

I pondered what changes would result as a result of my emancipation. Haaken tried to get me drunk which was the first change but I was wise enough to resist. Eventually Butar rescued me and took me back to his hall. When we reached it my mother was waiting with joy written all over her face. After she had embraced me Butar said, "I did not ask you before but how do you feel about my adoption?"

Both my mother and Butar seemed to hold their breath as they waited for my reply. "I would be honoured to be as a son to you."

"Good!" He seemed genuinely relieved.

"But you still live with me boy!" Ragnar sounded quite concerned that I would leave him.

I grinned. It was the first time he had not called me thrall. I risked some cheek as the mood seemed to merit it. "Of course old man!"

My mother looked shocked for a moment and then Ragnar cackled his ancient laugh. "And I will have time to beat some sense into this new member of the family so that he respects his elders!"

Now I understood the present of the new tunics and the knowing glances my mother and Butar had exchanged. They had wanted me to look like a freeman when the news was announced.

"This means, Dragon Heart that you will need to train as a warrior. When we next go raiding you will be amongst us. Harald One Eye has given orders for a second ship and I am to command it."

The prospect was exciting; I would go a-Viking.

The next day Ragnar and I returned to our home. It felt different somehow when we walked through the door. I had left a thrall and now returned a freeman. I took out my sword and my helmet. They would no longer need to be hidden. I used the cap inside the helmet and tried on the helmet. I found it fitted well.

Old Ragnar could not see it clearly but he ran his fingers around it. "It is a fine helmet. Keep it covered with grease when you are not wearing it and it will not rust. Let me feel your sword."

I handed him my sword and he balanced it. He held the hilt up to his rheumy white eyes. "You will need to take these warrior bands off. It does not do to claim another man's victories. It will bring bad luck." He suddenly peered at me. "Have you named your seax yet?"

Viking Slave

I had not. "No. Not yet."

"Did it not speak with you in the battle?"

I remembered the warrior I had emasculated. "There was a scream when the warrior died."

"Then it did call to you. It is Screaming Death. That is a good name. Your sword has none as yet but it will call to you when it tastes blood."

After I had removed the warrior bands the hilt looked bare and naked. I decided I would put on a new grip which would make it mine. That would have to wait until we visited the village again. When I had finished sharpening it I put in into its fleece lined scabbard. Ragnar was tired but he was still able to give me orders. "Put the pot of food next to the fire to warm and then go and cut some logs."

"But there are plenty for the fire. I did that the other day."

"No, boy. These are for your shield. We must make the new warrior in the family a shield. You will need to cut straight logs which will split easily." My face must have shown my joy for he said, "Next time listen first and moan later."

I knew exactly where to look for my wood. There was one oak tree on the lower slopes of the hill. I rarely used it for firewood, partly because the wood was too good to be burned and partly because it was some distance from Ragnar's home. This time I did not mind the journey. There was a long straight branch which came from the bottom of the main trunk; I decided to use that. I was quite adept with an axe and soon had the branch down. I trimmed off the smaller branches and then dragged them all back up the hill. I was keen to begin making my shield but I did not want to risk making a mistake. The sun was setting and I knew I would have to wait until the following morning. I dragged the branch inside the house and laid it against a wall well away from the fire. It would not do to dry it out too quickly.

Ragnar had awoken and we ate our food. "What do I call you now sir? You are not 'master' and I would not insult you by calling you old man."

He nodded, "Respectful and thoughtful, I like that. Call me Grandfather for you are now the step son of my son and I would have liked a grandson."

I liked that. "Good, then, grandfather, tell me how we will make my shield."

"You need to cut that log into pieces which are as long as your leg. We will strip the bark and then split the wood into planks. It is important that they are the same width. We will need some nails from the smith.

Viking Slave

When the wood is seasoned then we join the planks and cut the shape. We make it from thin planks and we layer them so that the grain goes in two directions. It will give added strength. We use glue made from deer hooves to make sure that the planks are bonded to each other. Then we nail the planks together to give even more strength. We need a metal disk for the middle to protect your hand. Finally we will need a deer hide to cover it with."

My heart sank, "You mean we will not finish it tomorrow?"

He laughed, "This will protect you in battle and when you row aboard the dragon ship. It is not to be made quickly. Your heart needs to go into the construction. You need not fear, One Eye will not raid again until the leaves begin to fall."

"How do you know?"

"He is careful, like his father was. He will want two ships and more warriors. He is ambitious. Marrying the princess was an astute move. Although I think her father cannot think much of her. He has made no attempt to rescue her and he stuck her in the church of the White Christ. Still our Jarl is now a rich man. Watch his oathsworn; soon they will each wear a mail byrnie like One Eye." I could now hear the derision in his voice. He did not like our Jarl. He was his nephew whom he knew well. He knew his son was a better leader.

I enjoyed making the shield. I had to split the log carefully to get the planks cut accurately. Then I had to shave them until they were smooth. It was a soothing experience and I heeded the old man's words. My work now might save my life. I did not mind shaping each plank and making sure it was the right width. Once I had the planks ready I was sent to buy some nails from the smith. The old man took some silver coins from a purse. "Here, boy, take these. Call them a gift from your grandfather. You should be able to buy more nails than you can use."

I almost flew down to the village. I waved a greeting to my mother and Butar but I only had eyes for the smith. Bagsecg treated me differently this time. The last time I had been a thrall having a collar removed. This day I was a hero of the village and he was pleasant and polite. Once back at my home I could not wait to begin to build my shield but Ragnar made me wait until the next day.

"We need to do this over a whole day. This part is the most crucial."

Once the shield's structure was acceptable to the fingers of old Ragnar, we began to shape it. I say we, but it was my hands, guided by the touch of Ragnar. When the familiar rounded shape of the shield appeared, all I wanted to do was to hold it but we waited another day. The next day we cut the hole for the boss. The metal disk had cost far more than the nails had but Ragnar assured me that it was worth it. When we hammered the disk into place then the shield looked like a shield. He had me make a slight point to the boss. He said the shield was a weapon too. We had a fine deer hide which covered the shield beautifully. It had spent weeks drying and maturing. The nails hammered around the boss ensured it had strength and integrity. I thought the final part would be to put the leather strap on and the wooden handle but Ragnar shook his head. "Tomorrow we make this into the shield of a warrior."

I barely slept as I imagined what the last step would be. I also heard him coughing during the night. I had a disturbed sleep. Ragnar was up before I was and he was busy with water and leaves. "Make some food, grandson. I am busy."

After we had eaten he gave me the pots with the coloured liquids in and he handed me the brushes made from the tail of a fox we had killed. "Now you paint on your sign."

I looked at him in panic. "What sign? What is the sign of Butar?"

He shook his head. "You are not Butar, you are Dragon Heart who killed a wolf. Close your eyes and let the shield call to you."

I did as I was bid and I found my hand creeping to my neck. The sound came to me as clearly as the wound of the wolf pack baying. "The wolf."

"Aye, grandson, the wolf with the blue eyes. It will mark you out in a battle and men will want to fight you."

It took some time to achieve the effect we wanted. The shield was painted red and then I painted on the black wolf with the sharp teeth and finally the blue of the eye which matched the jewel perfectly. I could not believe how beautiful the effect was. And yet Ragnar was still not satisfied. "And now you need to place nails around the edge of the shield for there it is the weakest."

I was amazed at the old man. He could barely see and yet he knew the design and the effect by mere touch. I did as I was bid and then added nails strategically placed around the shield. "They will protect you and the shield and they will blunt your enemy's weapons." After I had finished he ran his hands around the shield and nodded. "It is good."

Once the shield was finished I could not wait to use it but Ragnar was not ready for that. He bid me cut another log from the oak tree the same size as the first one I had cut. I then had to hold that as a shield when I hit the tree with my wooden sword. I could not see the value in using a log and a wooden sword but Ragnar would not be moved and I obeyed. I found both my arms became stronger and I started to move more quickly. Eventually he was happy with my progress and ordered me to hold my real sword and my new shield. They felt as though they were feathers. I could now see what a wise old man he was. He had made me hold heavier objects to strengthen my arms and back.

That night I noticed him coughing more. It had worsened as spring had progressed. I would have expected the opposite. Eventually I became firm. "Grandfather, let us visit your son. You are not well and you need the healing hands of my mother."

When he relented then I knew that he really was ill and we journeyed down to the village. He allowed me to use the sled but insisted that I carry my weapons. It was not easy but I obeyed. My mother and Butar were shocked at Ragnar's appearance and they put him in their bed immediately. "Why did you not bring him sooner?"

I felt guilty but I had tried. "It only became worse this last week. He would not come. Remember, my lord, I was his thrall for over a year. I am not used to ordering Ragnar around."

Butar's face softened. "You are right and I am sorry. He is a strong minded man and he has a strong will."

I think that Ragnar was just old. There did not seem to be a particular ailment but he slept much more than he had and when he did wake he was not as hungry as he used to be. He enjoyed talking to me and my mother in the evenings but gradually his waking hours became less and less until one morning he just didn't wake up. His last ten days were in the home of his son and he was tended to by all of us. He died happy I think. We gave him a warrior's funeral that I knew he wanted. Butar bought a boat from a fisherman. We cleaned it up and laid Ragnar's furs on the bottom. Ragnar, his sword and his shield, were laid on board. He was dressed in his finest clothes with his weapons and his treasures. As I placed his shield upon his chest I reflected that he had waited until my shield was finished before he chose to leave this life. In my mind I think he was ready to die and he chose his moment. He was passing over to Valhalla to watch over me.

As we watched the burning boat head towards the sea I cried for I missed the old man already. Even when I had been a slave he had not been cruel to me and had shown me real affection. He had taught me much, from the language of his people to the skills needed to become a warrior.

Butar put his arms around my mother and me. "Your coming, the two of you gave him longer life and a better one. I can never thank you enough. The last year was a good one for him and he had more purpose. He got to become a warrior again and that was in no small measure due to you, Dragon Heart. When you called him grandfather he felt fulfilled. A man needs a family to live beyond him and he had that with you. He is in the Otherworld now but he will watch over you."

After they had left and the burning boat had disappeared beneath the waves I stood there and wept still. I had not cried when my father had been killed but I wept for the half blind one armed man who had changed me from a boy to a man and set me on the course to become a warrior. Whenever I fought I was never alone for in my heart and in my mind I had Ragnar to protect my back and I felt safer. He was always there with me. The dyes he had used to make the paints were part of him and my shield always seemed like part of Ragnar.

Butar decided that I should live in the village. I was reluctant at first and then he pointed out that I needed to train with the other warriors; *'Ran'*, the new ship, was almost ready and we would be going a-Viking as soon as she was launched. That convinced me. Butar and I went up to the house to clear out the few belongings which remained there. I found it sad that there was so little remaining of him. When Butar asked me why I looked so unhappy I told him, and he put an arm around me.

"If you leave objects then you will be forgotten. Ragnar lives here." He pointed to my head, "and here, "he pointed to my heart. When we feast he will be remembered as you will in the sagas of warriors. He died as famous as when he was a young warrior and that is hard to achieve when you are as old as he. Other warriors envy him and you in equal measure for you are younger than they are. You have achieved much already. Remember that and be a great warrior for Ragnar trained you and set you on your course."

That helped and I set to my training with a will. The other young warriors, all of whom were older than me, showed me respect because of my achievements. I had killed warriors in combat. I had killed a wolf. They could only dream of such glory. It also helped that Haaken and Olaf held me in high esteem too.

The *'Ran'* was a smaller boat than the *'Sif'* and had fewer in the crew. There would be but thirty of us aboard her. The majority were young untried warriors like but me we had Olaf and Butar to lead us. I think Harald gave Butar men he thought were not of the highest standard so that his boat would have all the glory while we would take all of the risks. It did not work out that way and Butar's boat, as the '***Ran***' became known, became more successful. Butar and Olaf were better sailors than Harald and when we sailed it showed.

For the first month of late spring we just had to learn to row together. That is not as easy as it sounds but we were all young and willing to learn. My past achievements meant nothing to Olaf who laid about him with his knotted rope whenever he thought we were slacking. We soon stopped making mistakes. We learned to row in time with each other using the long smooth strokes which propelled the boat seemingly effortlessly through the icy waters of the fiord. We learned to obey the shouts of Butar or Olaf instantly so that the '***Ran***' could jink and spin in the water. She was an agile boat and there was much adjustment to the weight of the boat and the position of the rowers before we were to achieve that perfection which Butar sought. Finally we painted the dragon head at the prow. It had been well carved from the piece of oak but it had been left bare until we were ready. As soon as the red eyes and flaring nostrils were added the boat seemed to become a living beast; we would be the embodiment of the dragon. It was when we sailed that first time with the dragon painted that the crew began a ritual which continued so long as the boat floated. My position was in the middle of the boat and I was always the first one seated. The others boarded and went behind or before me. Haaken impulsively patted me on the head and I looked at him in surprise. He smiled, "I am just making sure that the Dragon Heart of this boat is beating." The rest of the young crew did the same. I wondered at that until Butar nodded and smiled. I became the lucky mascot of the boat.

Just before midsummer, Harald decided that we should be ready to raid. He was eager to pay back the men of Stavanger for their treacherous attack and to teach them a lesson. This was the first time we had placed our shields along the side of the boat. Thanks to Ragnar mine looked better than the rest. Or perhaps I just thought so. I knew that Ragnar would look down and be smiling. The time I had taken to paint the image and finish off the shield had been more than justified and I felt proud of my work. The next test would be more severe- it would be in battle.

When we left Ulfberg we were able to leave more men than the last time Harald had gone raiding. As the smaller of the two ships we followed *'Sif'*. Our boat was the faster for it was lighter and we had an easy row down the fiord towards the open water of the sea. As soon as we left the protection of the high sides of the fiord I noticed that it was harder to row but the seas were still relatively benign. It was still summer and autumn storms were some way off.

Stavanger was not one place but a number of small settlements with an alliance to Stavanger. That was the port where a Jarl resided but we would not be tackling that one. It would be too hard and we would not have enough warriors. This would be a revenge raid. Harald had chosen the one closest to our settlement and about the same size. It did not matter if the men had not been the ones who raided us, they were part of the same clan, and that was enough. We would leave them a message.

We halted just along the coast in a deserted inlet which Olaf had used before. I discovered that Olaf was the most experienced of all the men in the village and had been raiding the longest time. We threw our sea anchors out and then ate a frugal meal of bread and cheese. We washed it down with beer and then lay down in the thwarts to sleep until early morning. I was woken in the middle of the night for my watch. I wrapped my fur cloak tightly around me to keep out the damp early morning cold. It might have been summer but this far north it was never warm.

Haaken smiled, "When you see the false dawn then wake Olaf or Butar. As for me, I shall find a warm spot and dream of the slave girls I will capture."

There was just me and Heinrik. He was another young warrior, a little older than me. He only had a leather cap and I could see him looking enviously at my iron one. "Did you get that in the raid? From one of the men you killed?"

"I did."

"I will get one today."

"I would only worry about that once we have survived. I do not think that this will be easy."

"No, but it should be a glorious day. If I die with a sword in my hand then I will go to Valhalla and boast of my deeds."

Perhaps you had to be born in this land to understand that idea. I was happy to be a warrior and fight for my stepfather. I was happy for the chance to avenge the attack on my village but I did not want to die; with or without a sword in my hand. It seemed an age but when I saw the false dawn in the east I went to Butar and shook him gently. His eyes opened

Viking Slave

as I shook him. "I was awake already." He looked at the sky. "Good. Wake the others."

Most of the men were barely asleep. There was a great deal of nervous energy about our ship that morning. This would be the first raid for many of us. We all just wanted to get on with it and we had to force ourselves to eat some bread and wash it down with the beer we had left. Butar spoke to us all before we left to follow *'Sif'*. "It is a village the same size as ours. There is a wooden wall but this one does not have the benefit of a steep climb. It is almost on the beach. Harald One Eye and his men will have the honour of breaching the walls and we will follow them." I heard the sighs of disappointment. Butar laughed quietly, "You are all young men and have much to learn. Regard this as your apprenticeship. Watch me and watch Olaf. Listen for commands and obey them. None of you are good enough to engage in single combat. I would like to return home with a full crew and plunder."

I liked the speech. It was reassuring. We donned our helmets and began to row along the dark coastline to the village sleeping peacefully around the headland. It was so dark that I could barely see *'Sif'* and yet I knew she was just ahead from our motion as we crossed her wake. We smelled the village before we saw it. It was the smell of wood smoke and animals. We had practised the hand signals and we all raised our oars at precisely the same moment. We silently slid them into the bottom of the boat. We each took our shields from the sides of the boat. Cnut was the one who had been assigned the rope. As he stood close to the prow I could see the walls of the village ahead of us. Cnut disappeared and then there was a small splash. Although I could not see him I knew what he would be doing. He would be tying the boat to a secure point. The last thing that we needed was to have our means of escape float away. Butar waved us to our feet and we clambered over the side.

The water was icy cold and it chilled my feet instantly. I slid my sword silently from its fleece lined scabbard and looked to Butar. The helmet my step father wore was like Harald's it was a half mask which gave him a terrifying aspect. He made sure we were all ashore and then pointed left and right. We took our places. I was to Haaken's right about four men from the end of the line. Olaf followed us to make sure we did not go astray.

Ahead of us Harald and his men were racing to the gate. He had archers with him and I heard the arrows as they flew to the single tower. Although they hit the sentry he had given the alarm and his warning was

Viking Slave

cut short by his death. Harald's oathsworn ran to the gate and began to hack at the middle with their axes. Men appeared on the walls and began to loose their arrows.

Olaf's voice rang out. "Shields!"

I crouched as I raised my shield; I heard and felt the arrow as it thudded into the oak of my shield. If I had been tardy then it would have struck me. Harald's men put their shoulders to the gate and it split asunder. There was a roar as they burst through the shattered gate and into the village. There was the clash of metal and screams. "

"Forward!" Even as we moved forwards I sensed movement to my right. A party of warriors had left the village, I presume by another gate and they were hurtling rapidly towards us. "Ware right!" My voice sounded high pitched but at least Olaf had heard.

"Warriors to the right. Shield wall!"

I had been dreading this as we had only practised it once. Even then we had not got it right. I stood between Haaken and Cnut. The warriors who raced at us were all full grown men and we were boys. I wondered if Heinrik still thought that this was glorious. The men coming towards us all looked much bigger than we were. Perhaps it was an illusion but they seemed better armed too. I glanced at Haaken who seemed quite calm and remembered the last time I had been in this position I had had no shield and no helmet. I also remembered Ragnar. It was reassuring for I felt his presence. I tucked my shield tighter to my body and readied my unnamed sword. Would it tell me its name this day?

The warriors came at us piecemeal and we were one line; it was a shaky line but we knew that Olaf was behind us. None would retreat. The axe, wielded by the giant before me, swung in a vicious yet ponderous arc towards my shield. Perhaps the warrior thought that I was too young to have a good shield but Ragnar had advised me well. The axe embedded itself in the deer hide and the oak. As he tried to tug it away I stabbed forwards and the sword slid into his unprotected belly. His shield protected nothing. Ragnar had taught me to twist the blade and I did so as I withdrew it. The metal came out easier but it brought with it guts and entrails. The giant collapsed in a writhing heap. I had no time for congratulation; the next warrior tried to stab Haaken as he too fought an enemy. I punched the shield forwards and the axe, which was still embedded, caught the warrior on the side and he overbalanced. I stepped forwards and stabbed downwards. My sword slit his throat and he gurgled his life away.

"We have broken them! Finish them off."

Olaf's voice was reassuring. None of us had the time to look and see the results of our fight but he could. We stepped forwards to finish off those who were wounded and give them a warrior's death. I took the opportunity of removing the axe from my shield. It had a leather strap looped to it and I slung it across my back.

"Carry the wounded back to the ship!"

This time it was Butar's voice and it shocked me. I had given no thought to my comrades who might be wounded or dead. I saw that Cnut had received a wound to his leg. I tied a leather tie from one of the dead men's leggings around the wound and then half carried him back to the *'Ran'*. As I did so I had to step across the body of Heinrik. A sword had laid open his head. He would be in Valhalla now. I had no time to mourn and I helped Cnut over the side. Dawn was breaking now and Cnut urged me, "Go and help the others, Dragon Heart. I can look after myself."

I ran back to the scene of the carnage. We had lost other warriors but Haaken still stood. We followed Butar through the shattered gate. There were men from the *'Sif'* lying dead or wounded. Our leader had not had it as easy as he had thought.

Butar turned to Olaf, "Take most of the men and get these younger women on the ships. Haaken and Dragon Heart, come with me."

We headed up to the warrior hall. I could see fighting still going on. Harald was fighting against what looked like the leader of the village. Harald's oathsworn were watching. This was single combat and no man would interfere. I had never seen Harald fight before and he was extremely quick. The warrior he was fighting stood no chance. I am convinced that Harald could have ended it at any time but he wanted to show how good he was and he killed the warrior with many blows which struck his legs and his arms. He became weaker and weaker to the point where it was cruel to carry on and Harald then chose to finish it with a blow which took the head from the village leader. Harald's oathsworn roared their approbation.

"Get the plunder on to the ships." He saw Butar, "A great victory cousin!"

"It is indeed. I have started to collect the young women."

"Good." He saw me for the first time. "You have survived your first raid. Well done boy!" He turned away and I reddened. I had killed men; I was no boy!

Viking Slave

Butar saw my reaction. "You have done well; now remain silent and collect the weapons and take them to the ship."

As Haaken and I carried the swords and axes from the dead men I thought it a pity that none of the men I had killed had worn a mail shirt. All that I had gained was the axe from the first man. After I had deposited my weapons I went back to the scene of our fight. None of them had mail but the warrior with the axe did have a throwing axe tucked into his belt. That would go with his axe. I picked them up and put them in *'Ran'*.

I saw the flames licking at the warrior hall as I entered the village. Harald was sending a message to the other villages. He was letting them know the price of raiding Ulfberg. As we pushed off I noticed that the only ones he had left alive were the old and wounded. This village would be like mine in the land of the Angles; it would be a memory only. Soon the birds would feast on the dead and the fire would destroy what remained. I had seen my first raid and it was cruel and unforgiving. We could have been defeated if we had not stopped the attack on our rear and it would be our bodies feeding the crows and the gulls. The difference between success and failure was the width of a blade.

As I rowed back to our village I thought of my sword and what it had done. It had seemed to move without me directing its course. I remembered that Ragnar had said it would tell me its name and it had; my sword was Quicksilver for it moved so quickly and was deadly. When we reached home I would put three warrior bands around the hilt for the men I had killed and I would name him up in the home I had shared with Ragnar.

Chapter 6

The homecoming was a glorious one despite our losses. This was not a raid on a simple Saxon settlement; we had been fighting men such as ourselves. Ten warriors had died; three of them boys on their first raid. I wondered how their mothers would feel. I was still becoming accustomed to the different ways of the people. If I had died then I know my mother would have been distraught but the mothers who took the bodies of their sons away looked to be almost proud of their death. The thralls carried the plunder ashore. Saelac made the mistake of giving me another of his hateful stares. I was a warrior now and I smacked him hard on the side of the head. "Know your place slave!"

I saw my mother frown but she said nothing. I carried my own plunder back to Butar's Hall. He and Olaf the Toothless supervised the unloading of *'Ran'*. When I reached the hall I carefully took off the helmet to examine it. I did not think it had suffered a blow but I did not know for certain. It had escaped unscathed. I heeded Ragnar's words and I coated it with grease and placed it by my other weapons. I was about to examine the axe when my mother entered.

She turned me to face her. "Before Butar comes I must have a word with you." She looked very serious. "I do not like you speaking to others as you did."

I could not think what she meant and then I recalled, Saelac. "But he is a slave!"

"As you were and as I was. It does not excuse you showing them no respect."

"But he gives me insulting looks."

"Then you do right to beat him but do not insult him as well." She pierced me with her sharp eyes. She seemed to be able to see into your heart and your soul. "It is petty to try to get your own back on those who bullied you. You are now a warrior; are you a man? Or are you still a petulant child with a sword and a shield?"

I was stung by her words for they rang true and I reddened. "I am sorry and you are right. I think I was just over excited after the raid."

She softened and smiled, "I know and that is why I spoke to you alone. I would not belittle you in front of your comrades or your step father. I will not always be there to direct you. You need to think for

Viking Slave

yourself and behave like a true warrior. Be like your grandfather and treat all men the same, slave and free, friend and enemy. Men will think better of you."

When Butar came in he ignored me at first and picked my mother up, almost crushing her in his bear like arms. When he put her down he wrapped an arm around her and faced me, "This Dragon Heart is well named, my sweet. The warrior he killed today was Eric the Bear. He had slain five champions in single combat before the battle and your son killed him with one blow. The others can talk of nothing else."

I shrugged, "Then it was luck for had I known he was a champion I would have frozen and it would be me who died."

Mother gave me a shrewd look, I think she was seeing inside me again, "And when you faced him whose voice did you hear?"

I started, this was frightening, "Ragnar's."

It was Butar's turn to look surprised. "Exactly," said my mother triumphantly, "your teacher. Listen to the voices in your head, my son. They will make you a better warrior." She stood back, "And now the two of you go and wash. There is the smell of blood and death about you. You need to get cleaned up for the feast tonight."

I did drink too much at the feast but that was because of Cnut and Haaken who could not stop talking about my combat with a champion. I kept telling them that I had been lucky but they would have none of it. Eventually I conceded that the stout manufacture of the shield had helped and I gave them Ragnar's secrets. I promised them that I would help them to make their own. Just before I passed out I realised that, for the first time in my life, I now had two friends. I fell happily into oblivion.

What no-one had told me about becoming drunk was that your head felt like there were trolls inside banging hammers against the inside and that you could hold no food inside your stomach. Mother smiled ruefully at me. "You have learned another lesson my son; a painful one but a necessary one."

She was right and I did not drink as much ever again. I did take some comfort from the fact that my two friends were as bad as I was and we deferred our shield making until the following day. I did repair my shield for the axe had ripped a hole in the deer hide. I knew that soon I would have to replace the deer hide which meant I needed to hunt again.

I took my two companions up to Ragnar's home. There was still an oak there and we could make the shields out of sight of prying eyes. I placed my axe, sword and seax on the table. I intended to do some work for myself too. I explained how to cut the oak and how to make the planks. "This task will take a number of days so let us not hurry. The more care we take now the better the shields will be."

While they cut the logs and the planks, an easier task for there were two of them, I made the three warrior bands for the hilt. I had the thin strips of metal which I had traded from the blacksmith as well as the liquid which would change their colour. My mother's eyes were green and I wanted three green bands for my first bands. If I managed to be successful again then I would change the colour. It would remind me of the combats and look dramatic. By the time my companions had brought the planks back I had finished and I was proud of my handiwork.

It needed three of us to work on the shields and we only got as far as making the rough shapes. We left them on the table and trudged down to the village. We had an appetite and ate well. It took three days to finish their shields and then they painted their designs on the deer hide. Haaken used an eye, which seemed appropriate and Cnut chose a dragon. "For I fought next to Dragon Heart and I would be the Dragon Warrior."

No one mocked another warrior when he chose names. We all knew how magical that process was. When the shields were finished I had to admit that they looked better than mine. Haaken saw my look and said, "Yours has honourable scars of battle. Ours are still virgins. When they look like yours I will be happy."

Harald One Eye was a little put out that his battle with the village chief had been put in the shade by my defeat of Eric the Bear and so he decided to go on another raid but this time he left Butar and *'Ran'* at Ulfberg. Haaken and Cnut were more disappointed than either Butar or me. We had had good news. My mother was with child and their prayers had been answered. Mother was convinced that Ragnar had had something to do with it but, for the life of me, I could not see how. Still, he was now in the Otherworld and who knew what power was there?

Harald was intent on raiding the lands of the Angles again. The plunder we had secured from our last raid was poor and the slaves also of inferior quality. He wanted thralls from a land where they were better fed and in better condition. It was not just my mother who was with child, all of the other women and girls of child bearing age were expecting children. The people from across the waters were fecund. The only women who were yet to bear children were Aethelfrith, his wife, and her companion. He blamed it on witchcraft but mother thought the two young women might be doing something themselves to stop themselves become pregnant. Now that I was considered a man I sat with Butar and my mother and was included in their conversations.

"Why would a woman not want a child? And how could she stop it?"

"There are ways," my mother said darkly, "and there are potions and draughts you can take. It is evil but then other women are not as lucky as me in their choice of a man."

The two weeks whilst Harald was away helped me to become part of the village. My stay with Ragnar had made me isolated, almost a hermit. My friendship with Haaken and Cnut meant that I had more people to speak with. My lessons with Ragnar had been well learned; I listened more than I spoke. It made me seem quiet and shy when in fact I was learning about my fellows. Haaken and Cnut were similar in outlook to each other. They were both reckless and fearless. Sometimes these were good qualities, as when we had been raided, but sometimes caution was needed. I stored that information for future use. Although we had used the shield wall, which the Saxons used all the time, it had been a rare occurrence dictated by the sudden flank attack. The tactics of Harald and his men appeared to be to close with the enemy and to kill as many as could be killed. This would work against our neighbours but if the Saxons ever organised themselves then we would be in trouble. That would be when Haaken and Cnut would need caution.

The time in the village was well spent. Butar did not allow us to sit idly by drinking and arm wrestling. We had to trim the **'Ran'** for Olaf and Butar knew that we could make her fly faster if the weight was better distributed. We were rowers short, thanks to the deaths and, until we recruited more, we would have to row with fewer men. When Butar was happy with the balance he took us on the fiord where we practised manoeuvres. Although this was tiring it helped to make us stronger. My arms were now knotted with muscles and, despite my smaller frame; I was becoming as strong as the men who were much bigger. Olaf also insisted on training the younger warriors with bows. All of us were well used to the bow but not loosing together. We respected Olaf's words for he had fought longer than any of us and we did as he asked.

One evening, about seven days after Harald had left, I was coming back from Ragnar's house. I went there every couple of days ostensibly to ensure that it was not becoming infested with vermin but really so that I could be alone and think of old Ragnar. I had my bow in case there was any game but I was not hopeful. I had bagged too many animals close to the path and they avoided it. Suddenly I became aware that someone was ahead and waiting in the undergrowth. Mindful of the attack by Saelac and Tadgh I notched an arrow and slipped into the forest. I could move stealthily in this, my domain and I moved without a sound. I saw two shapes crouched close by an elder bush and I pulled back on the bow. I checked left and right to make sure that there were just two of them and then I shouted, "Show yourselves or you will die!"

There were two high pitched screams and Aethelfrith and her companion stood from behind the bush. I lowered the bow. "What are you doing here, my lady? I could have killed you." Even as I said the words I shuddered at the implication. Had I killed the wife of the chief then I would have been exiled from the village.

The princess quickly composed herself. "We were waiting for you, Gareth." This was the first time anyone had spoken to me in Saxon for a long time and I could not remember the last time I had heard my birth name.

"It would have been safer to wait on the path."

Her companion, Morwenna, said, "See, I told you."

She was rewarded by an elbow in the side and a look of hate. "Well we can speak with you now."

I gave a slight bow, "How may I help you, my lady?" I was not sure if she was a lady or a princess now but if I had made an error she said nothing.

"You are now a hero are you not? You are no longer the thin looking waif who cowered at the prow of the ship beneath his mother when we first saw you. Now, you are a warrior." I could not see where she was going with this and I stood there feeling foolish but remaining silent. A slight frown crossed her face and then she put her arm around Morwenna. Her companion was a little older than me with long blonde braided her. When she had first boarded the *'Sif'* I had noticed a sweet perfumed smell about her but now she smelled like the rest of us. "Morwenna here is young and ripe. How would you like her as your woman?" Morwenna tried to move away but she was held tightly by the older girl.

"It is an attractive offer my lady but it would have been better coming from the lady herself."

The hint of a smile appeared on Morwenna's face. Aethelfrith snapped, "She has no say in the matter! She is my handmaiden and will do as I order." Aethelfrith was beautiful but there was a cruelty in her face and her manner which I did not like. Besides which they were both slaves and previous titles meant nothing.

"And what would I have to do to win this worthy prize?" Again Morwenna was pleased by my words but Aethelfrith appeared confused.

"Who says you would have to do anything?"

"The rose is a pretty flower with a beautiful scent but there is a price to pay if you get too close; you can be pricked by thorns."

"Am I the thorn or the rose?"

"I know not yet my lady for you have not said what you wish me to do for you."

"You are a blunt boy!"

I could see Morwenna hiding a smile behind a hand and I gave a slight bow. "I am not practised in the art of fine words, my lady. I apologise."

She took a deep breath as though she had come to a decision. "You are close to Butar and he has a boat. We would have Butar take me back to my father and he will be rewarded."

I laughed. I laughed so hard that tears rolled down my cheeks. I know now that it was a mistake but the idea seemed so preposterous. "How dare you laugh at a princess!"

I regained my composure, "With respect, my lady, here you are not a princess but the wife of a village Jarl and I do not think that he would countenance such an act."

She spat her next words at me. "If you speak of this to anyone I will tell my husband that you tried to take me!"

I smiled, "Believe me, my lady, I will forget your offer before we have reached the village." I looked at the sky. "Now it is getting on towards sunset and the guards will worry. Allow me to escort you down the path."

Aethelfrith stormed off but Morwenna paused and mouthed, "Thank you."

That evening I explained to Butar and my mother what had been said. Butar shook his head, "You have done the right thing but I fear that this will come back to haunt us."

I looked puzzled and my mother put her hand on mine. "Butar is Harald's cousin and is older. He could be the leader of the village which is why he has to be wary of upsetting Harald. Harald is suspicious of Butar."

I remembered Ragnar's words and it all made sense to me. "But you are a loyal warrior."

"I know and I have no ambitions to be Jarl but Harald is ambitious and believes all men are the same."

My mother looked worried. "It will be dangerous for you both to be in the village for a while. Aethelfrith will allow this to fester inside. She will see your rejection of her idea as a rejection of her. She is a princess and was brought up with people just saying yes to her."

"I could take the *'Ran'* and trade. I have thought of this before." Butar stroked his beard thoughtfully.

"Is the boat not Harald's?"

"No, he and I shared the cost. I have a half interest in the boat. If we trade I could buy the boat outright and he would be able to build another. He sees himself not merely as a Jarl but a king with a fleet of ships."

"What would we trade?" I was curious for we never appeared to have a surplus of anything.

He smiled at me. "You missed much when you spent that time with my father. We hunt seals and melt them down for fats. It is good for making boats watertight. Then there are the furs from the animals we hunt and there are the brown stones that we polish. We will have enough to trade."

Mother frowned. "You can only trade if your cousin allows you to go."

"He will sanction it, indeed he may even encourage it, for that way I will be gone and he will lure more warriors who will be loyal to him."

"Does that not worry you?"

"No, I would rather have a man who is loyal because of what I am, rather than because I buy him. We will begin to gather our goods tomorrow. I will see Olaf tonight. I would have him with us on this venture. I think he will be glad to be rid of the settlement for a while."

We soon found that all of the crew of the *'Ran'* wished to be part of this venture. It would soon be autumn and there would be no more raiding. I put my weapons away for a while and became a trader. I returned to Ragnar's house because I remembered that he had had a small chest with different objects within. Perhaps there would be something to trade. I found a treasure trove of the shiny brown stones called glaesum which Butar had said were valuable. I carried the small chest down to my stepfather who beamed with pleasure when he spied them.

Viking Slave

"You will be rich!"

"They are Ragnar's. They belong to you."

"No, you shared the house with him. We will share the profits how is that? Then you will become a man with riches of his own."

By the time Harald returned from his raid on Northumbria with the *'Sif'* laden down with animals, slaves and plunder, we were ready to leave. Butar said nothing until we had had the obligatory feast and the sagas. Everyone praised the heroism and wisdom of Harald One Eye. Women were not allowed at the feast and so I did not have to worry about the evil looks from Aethelfrith. When most men were drunk Butar approached Harald with me at his side.

"Cousin, I would take **'Ran'** and show my step son a little of the world. I have gathered some trade goods and I would trade with the Franks for I hear they have fine goods."

The chief was silent as though considering. "Which of the men would you take?"

"I have spoken with Olaf for he knows the places to trade but I thought I would take the younger warriors for the crew."

Harald looked almost relieved. "Then I give you my blessing." A cunning look came into his eye. "As half owner I would be entitled to some compensation. After all there is the risk that you might not return."

I was shocked at the effrontery but Butar appeared to expect it. "Would you exchange your half for a tenth of the profits?"

I could see Harald weighing up the cost of the **'Ran'** and the possible profits. It had not cost either man much to build the ship. The labour and most of the materials were from the village. The cost had been for the sails and the tackle. "I agree. When will you sail?"

"On the morning tide."

That was the first time I saw Harald surprised and he looked around the long house and realised that Olaf and the younger men were not there. "You always were a good organiser."

Mother looked sad as she stood forlornly on the wooden quay waving us goodbye. She had just started to show her child with a small bump and Butar assured her that we would return well before the child was born. I hoped that she would not be lonely. I knew that most of the other women looked to her for advice and counsel. It was the thralls and the Saxons who did not like her. She had attained real freedom.

We had our weapons with us but they were stored. The shields protected the trade goods and would mark us as a trader rather than a

Viking Slave

pirate. We headed south and I was excited. I watched my new home disappear to the north as we crossed the open water to the land of the Dane. They were a people who had many links to us. Like us they went raiding and they could be belligerent. Olaf had sailed on a Danish boat in his youth and we hoped that we would be able to use his knowledge to avoid any trouble.

He took us to a small inlet on the west coast of Jutland where they had the beginnings of a harbour. We approached slowly so that they could see we were not here for plunder. Even so, it was an armed delegation who met us. We stayed on board to confirm our peaceful intentions and Olaf and Butar went ashore. When I saw Olaf being embraced by the headman then I knew that we would not have to fight.

We went ashore as a crew and we were made most welcome. Like us they had had a successful summer raiding and were in a generous mood. They held a feast for us. Butar counselled us all to watch what we drank. The last thing we needed was a blood feud. I sat with Harald Bjornson who was the son of the village chief. He told me that they had also raided the land of the Angles and it had made them rich. He became a little drunk and also told me that he had heard of Harald One Eye. He heard that he was the mightiest warrior in the north. I kept my counsel. I had seen him fight and thought him quick but as his opponent had been poor I would reserve my judgement. It was at that time when I came to realise about legends and reputations. I suspected the legend came from Harald himself who seemed to have many sagas about his prowess.

We left on good terms and with something more valuable, knowledge. Olaf had been told of a trading centre close to the land of the Franks in the mighty River Rinaz. This was the biggest river in the world and meant that we would be trading within ten days. All of us became excited at the prospect.

The sailing was easy as we hugged the coast. Most of the time the wind was with us and we did not have to row. It was quite pleasant to watch the land slip by and we all said what we would do with the fortunes that we would make. We were young men and we all had plans and ideas. We had an easy time as Olaf and Butar took it in turn to steer the ship. When it was Butar's watch he had me with him so that I could learn how to sail a ship too. At the time I never thought that I would be able to learn but Butar was a good teacher. I suspect that Olaf would have taught me had I asked but it would have been more painful for me. Olaf believed firmly in the power of the knotted rope.

Viking Slave

Seven days after leaving the Danish port we entered the estuary of the Rinaz. It was like a small sea. We now had to return to our oars and we rowed against the current into the heart of the lands of the Franks and the Germans. There were smaller settlements on the river but their gates were closed to us as we rowed up that river. I do not blame the people for a dragon boat normally meant a raid and they were suspicious even of a boat which appeared to be a peaceful trader. When we reached Cologne I could not believe the size of that city. There were many ships there. We had seen huge ships heading down the river and there were still some of these tied up to the quays.

Olaf steered us to a small berth away from the larger ships. They all looked to be tubby little things and not the sleek dragon ship we rowed. I was not envious. He had the name of a merchant who might be able to supply us with what we required. While Olaf and the rest of the crew began to unload the trade goods Butar and I took our swords and headed towards the place where our contact lived. Olaf had his name from the Danes. Sigismund was a little old man who reminded me of Ragnar. He understood our language but he spoke Saxon which we did too and it made life easier. He was more than happy to be our broker and we negotiated a fee. We left his house and went to a large warehouse on the riverside. There were four heavily armed men outside.

"One cannot be too careful. "Cologne is filled with foreigners such as yourself and not all are peacefully inclined. You would do well to keep your swords and wits about you."

While he organised his warehouse Butar and I returned to the boat. We had more than enough men to leave a watch and transport the goods to the warehouse. I carried my precious chest.

Sigismund had a table ready for us. "So my friends would you like me to trade goods or would you prefer coin?"

We had already decided this. As each man had some of the goods as his own to trade as well as the items from the village we would take coins and that way Harald would not feel cheated. I hung at the back as the main items were all traded for coins which Sigismund counted out. Each man watched. Most used a piece of wood into which they carved marks to keep a tally of their own share. When I reached him he looked at the small chest with interest. I called it a chest but it was only a wooden box as long as my seax and about as wide but it was filled to the brim with the polished stones. When I had discovered them I imagined Ragnar smoothing them when he was alone in the house. It was the sort of painstaking activity which the old man would have enjoyed. He would not have needed eyes for that and his touch meant that they were perfectly polished.

I opened the box and not only Sigismund but my companions gasped. "I see you have saved the best until last." He looked up at me. "You are young to have such a treasure." He glanced at my sword, "Although I can see that you are a warrior and have killed three men. How did you come by them?" I must have looked angry for he added, hurriedly, "I mean nothing by that remark. I would just like to know if there is a likelihood of more."

I glanced at Butar. "They were left to me by my grandfather. There may be more but it would take a long time to collect as many."

Sigismund shook his head, "It would take a lifetime." He began to examine them and scribbled on a wax tablet using a stylus. "Do you wish to haggle or shall I speak a price?"

Butar answered for me. "I do not think that you will cheat us for we will be returning here again."

"That is true." He counted out the coins in a separate pile from the others. It rose steadily higher until it dwarfed the rest which were on the table. He looked at me with a smile on his face. "Satisfied?"

"Yes. Thank you." I put the coins back in the box and clutched it to my chest.

"Now you will wish to buy items and I will change my table." He pointed to the front of the warehouse. "There are my goods. If you do not see what you want let me know and I will obtain it by tomorrow."

All of the men from the crew had coins to spend. Olaf and Butar had the village's share. Harald would have his share from my chest. I knew what Butar and I wanted and, while the men haggled and chose we took Sigismund to one side.

"Have you Frankish swords?"

He shook his head and then stopped, "I do not have swords but I have the blanks."

I looked puzzled but Butar nodded, "That is better."

"What are blanks?" I did not mind showing my ignorance to two such men.

"They are the swords without hilts and pommels. They have not been sharpened or polished. They are normally much cheaper."

Sigismund nodded, "That is so. These were ordered by a king of Frisia who was murdered and his heirs did not want them." He shrugged, "That is a risk we take."

"How many do you have?"

"There are ten of them."

"Then we will take them all!" They shook hands and I could see that everyone was happy with the outcome. We could spend the winter finishing off the swords which would make them even more valuable for trade.

As the men were finishing their own trades we spoke with Sigismund. "How is it that you speak our language so well?"

"Many of your fellows came to Frisia and the Frankish lands close to the sea. They liked it and settled there. They are powerful warriors but they like to trade here. There are some Danes and some from your lands further north. It is fine farmland. I have heard it told that you perch on rocky cliffs and inlets. Is that true?"

"Aye it is."

"Then I can see the attraction of the land along the coast. The kings and chiefs around here are all too busy fighting each other to do anything about it."

It was food for thought as we left Cologne. Sigismund would be happy to deal with us in the future. I do not think he robbed us but I suspect he came out of it more in profit than we did. The purpose had not been to make money but to get me and my stepfather out of Aethelfrith's way.

The journey back down the mighty river was much easier as we had the current with us and it had been swollen by the autumn rains. Our offerings to Njoror and Ran had worked for the winds were in our favour as we headed north. Haaken and Cnut spent long hours on the journey back asking me about my fortune and how I had come by it.

Haaken shook his head and idly scratched the socket of his missing eye; it itched a little in the salt air. "You have been singled out by the gods for you were a thrall and now you will be one of the three richest men in the village."

Cnut shook his head, "By my reckoning the richest for he is Butar's heir. We shall be your brethren, Dragon Heart. I see much profit in associating with you."

"I don't know about that but I do feel I am lucky. As we approached Ulfberg we did not know that that luck was going to change or perhaps it

Viking Slave

was the *Wyrd Sisters* who were spinning their threads. Whatever the reason those last peaceful hours on the boat were soon to be forgotten within a few days of reaching our home.

Chapter 7

We were welcomed like returning heroes but that was merely the calm before the storm. Mother threw her arms around the both of us and hugged until I thought her arms would break. Harald One Eye also greeted us warmly. We had seen his new ship being built. I noticed that she was the same size as *'Sif'*. He was ambitious; he must have had more volunteers. We unloaded *'Ran'* and we all went to our own families. That was the way of the raider and the trader. My mother could not believe the coins that her husband and son had collected.

We took Harald his tithe. There were other warriors there, such as Olaf, to witness the payment. When he had his sword blank and coins Harald nodded and clasped Butar's arm. "*'Ran'* is now yours, cousin. You have your own boat."

There was something about Harald's words which I did not like. He had a sly look about him and he had given up his share far too easily. I put it from my mind as we left to celebrate our return. I noticed, at the feast, all the new faces. This was not just the slaves but many new warriors. Harald's success was attracting those who wished to go a-Viking. I did not drink heavily and I rose early to visit Ragnar's home. I did this to be close to the spirit of the old man. He had lived alone in the house and cave for so long that he seemed to ooze out of the very stone of the walls.

I decided to finish searching for the objects he had hoarded for so many years. I knew that his sword, now with him in Valhalla had been stored on the stone shelf above his bed. I stood on the bed and reached up to see what else was there. It seemed empty until my fingers stumbled upon a piece of cloth. I eased it out and unwrapped the linen. I found inside a piece of carved wood. It was about the size of my hand and it was a wolf. I felt a shudder run through my body. What did this mean? Why had I not found it earlier? I decided to thoroughly search the house for any more treasures. They were no longer safe in the house all alone. I found his warrior bracelets, a long knife and, best of all, his war axe, his skeggox. He had had an ordinary axe which I still used to fell trees and he had a throwing axe. The war axe was finer altogether with a blade inlaid with runes. It had been under his bed! I left the house and returned to Butar's hall.

Viking Slave

I showed Butar the treasures. He remembered the axe but knew nothing about the wolf which he too found strange. "I feel the past at work here." My mother was said to have the gift of second sight and when she spoke as she did we both heeded her words.

We sought Olaf who was now the oldest warrior in the village. He was lost in thoughts for a while. "I have not seen one of these for years but remembering your battle with the wolves, all this begins to make sense." He handed it back to me. "This was meant for you. I am in doubt about that."

"What does it mean?"

He took a large swig from his beaker of ale. "You have heard of Berserkers?"

Butar nodded. "Aye the men who get the madness of battle and throw off their cloak and armour to fight bare chested. It is said they are invincible."

"They are not. The last berserker we had was Bjorn the Bear. He killed many Danes but they finally took him down. The Ulfheonar were a similar cult. They wore only a wolf skin as their armour. They were fierce and had more control than the berserkers. I did not know that Ragnar was one such."

Butar looked amazed. "And I had no idea."

"It was a secret cult. In battle their heads were covered by a wolf's head. He must have been one somewhere else for I have never heard of any here."

I turned the carved piece of wood over in my hand. This was a real secret. They all looked at me. Mother said to me. "Your grandfather, my father, was also a wolf warrior. He too wore a cloak made of a wolf's skin but not the head. This is *wyrd*."

She reached under the neck my tunic and took out the wolf with the jewelled eye. Both Olaf and Butar gasped. "You have always had this?"

"No Olaf, only since I boarded the **'*Sif*'**. Mother gave it to me."

"This is the work of the Norns. Your destiny and that of Ragnar are intertwined."

I did not sleep much that night. I was afraid. I had felt special before and both my friends had noted it but this was different. I had a connection from my adopted grandfather and my birth grandfather and it tied me to the wolf. Perhaps I had been meant to meet the wolf pack that day. Maybe part of the wolf's spirit had entered me.

Viking Slave

The next day the storm broke and it was nothing to do with my find. My mother and Butar were summoned to the Great Hall; Harald's long house. Harald's oathsworn were there as well as all not only the senior warriors but every other warrior from Ulfberg. The hall was packed. Most worryingly of all was the presence of Aethelfrith and Morwenna.

Harald stood and began without any preliminaries. "Myfanwy, wife of Butar Ragnarson, you have been summoned here to answer charges of witchcraft." There was an audible gasp from everyone although my mother appeared calm. I think her calm exterior puzzled Harald. "What have you to say to the charges?" I think he hoped that by coming out without a preamble he would take my mother by surprise. He did not know my mother.

"I am no witch."

Aethelfrith pointed a triumphant finger at my mother, "That is what she would say. It proves she is a witch."

Mother shook her head and smiled, "If I say nothing I am a witch, if I say I am not a witch then I am a witch. Should I lie and say that I am a witch?"

The logic of my mother's words confused the Saxon princess who began to weep. "I can feel her power, husband. She is trying the bewitch me. She is a witch."

I could see Butar becoming angry. "Who lays these charges?"

Aethelfrith stopped weeping for a moment. "I do. I should be with child but I am not because of her spell. You and she are too old to have children and yet she is with child. She has stolen my baby."

The argument was so ridiculous that I thought it would have been laughed out of this court but everyone looked deadly serious. Jarl Harald shrugged as though this was not his doing. "Unless you can prove that you are not a witch then I will have to exile you from this place."

Now I began to see the plan and the thought which had gone into this. It was not about my mother. It was about getting rid of a rival. If Butar had a son and Harald did not then Butar's son would become Jarl. No wonder Harald had been so happy to see us going trading. He had hoped we would not return. He now had more men than when I had arrived in the village and they would all be loyal to him.

Silence descended like a rain cloud on the assembly. My mother's voice sounded pure in the quiet. "I am no witch."

The room remained silent. My mother's fate was sealed for they were all men. Had there been women then there might have been voices

Viking Slave

against her but Aethelfrith was as cunning as her husband. The two young girls played the innocents and no-one would gainsay them. "As you continue to deny the charge I have no choice but to exile you from the village. You must leave by dawn."

Butar had gone beyond anger. He stood by my mother and put his arm around her. "You are doing this because you fear me and yet I have never been anything less than loyal. I will take *'Ran'*, Dragon Heart, and my wife and I will leave this place."

I could see the look of triumph on Harald's face. "Then I hope your son and your wife can row for no-one will go with you."

Olaf stepped forwards, "I will go with you Butar for I wish to serve a man who has honour."

"Me too." Haaken stood beside me.

"And I," Cnut was on the other side.

Soon forty men had stood behind us and Harald was almost apoplectic with rage. He could say nothing for he had created this situation. He expected Butar to be isolated but he was popular. The men were mainly young warriors but there were some experienced ones like Bjorn, Bagsecg the blacksmith and Godfrid. Harald One Eye face reddened and he spat out, angrily, "Then go leave Ulfberg. From this day forth you are no kin of mine. If we ever meet again then I will kill you and all of your family." His one eye wandered from Butar to Mother, finally settling on me. "Watch your back, Butar Ragnarson."

"With you as a cousin Harald One-Eye, I always will."

I said to Butar as we left the hall, "I must do something."

I could see the question on his face but I think he heard the determination in my voice. I took a torch and ran up the path to the house of Ragnar. I was out of breath by the time I arrived. No-one else would live in Ragnar's home. It might be petty, even vindictive but I would not share that memory with anyone. I knew there was nothing of value left inside and I piled the bed and the wooden items together in the middle of the room. "Ragnar, I will give your home a funeral fit for a warrior in Valhalla!"

I thrust the torch into the straw and I was almost scorched by the flames as they leapt in the air. I left the house and shut the door one last time. As I did so I could not resist knocking on it and saying, "Ragnar, it is your thrall."

Viking Slave

I made sure that it was well alight and I turned to descend the path. On impulse I turned one last time and shouted, "Wolf brothers this land is yours now. Protect it for my grandfathers and me."

I ran all the way back. I felt guilty having left my mother and Butar to gather our belongings and place them in the ship. They had, surprisingly gathered all that they needed, I could see a chest with clothes, and the weapons Butar would use as well as the pots my mother would need. They had even gathered my meagre possessions. They both turned when I entered. Butar began to say, "Where..." when he saw the flames on the hillside through the open door. He smiled, "Good. It is what he would have wished. We were just discussing where we should take our people."

"I would have thought down to the land of the Franks. Sigismund the trader told us that the land there is good and our people are there too."

A look of triumph came over Butar's face, "There. Even your son agrees with me."

She gave him a superior smile, "That is because he has not heard of my plan and my destination."

"Go on then tell him."

"Instead of going south let us go west. If we go around the land of the blue warriors we will come to the islands off Cymri."

"Why?"

"Harald One-Eye and his whore have it in for you and me. They will not rest until we are dead. Everyone knows you traded in the south and that it is likely you will return there. Besides we would not be the first settlers. We would have to fight for land and we are too few for that."

That was the argument which persuaded my father. "Very well but I will wait until we are at sea before I tell my people. I do not want to let my cousin know our destination. Come, son, let us load the boat. I fear it will be crowded."

When we reached the boat Olaf and the younger men were on board. They did not have much to take with them. Olaf was grinning when we arrived, which was always disconcerting as it was like a dark empty tunnel looming up at you. "What is making you happy you old pirate?"

He tapped his nose, "The boat will be overloaded will it not." Butar nodded. "We will need spares if we have to repair the ship." Again he nodded. "We have tied four larch trees to the hull. We float higher and we can use them for masts or make planks."

"Excellent. Store our gear. We had best put the sword blanks in the bottom as ballast and to keep an even keel."

Haaken came over. "We also have two small boats and two fishing boats. We forgot that two of the warriors are fishermen. We can use their boats to carry chests and pots."

"Aye, tie the small boats to our stern or they will slow us up."

"And remember, Jarl Butar, we have more rowers and so we will be swifter when we travel."

"Thank you, Olaf, but I am not Jarl."

"You are to us my lord and we will be your oathsworn. All the men will swear once they are aboard. The sooner we leave here the better."

Cnut asked, "And, Jarl Butar, where is our destination?"

Butar winked at me, "You will discover that when we sail."

Olaf took charge of the trim. He ordered everyone around. I noticed that there were only five women on board and just six children. We were all young men. Nor were there any thralls. We would take slaves once we had built our home. We could not take all the animals but we had a couple of pigs and some chickens. We took a pair of goats mainly for the milk on the voyage. We struggled with food for we had not yet begun to salt the meat and the short deadline imposed by Harald meant we would have to fish for our food for a while. Luckily our two fishermen, both fathers of young warriors, were confident that they would manage. The salt we would use to preserve whatever we caught was in one of the smaller boats with chests.

No-one came to see us off, which I found sad but, as we pushed away from the shore, I saw the glow of the fire of Ragnar's house winking as we sailed down the fiord. I felt comforted knowing that no-one would live in Ragnar's home. As we rowed, I was next to Haaken, Butar, or Jarl Butar as he now became known, spoke to his people.

"I know that you have given up much to follow me and it is not too late to change your mind. I will pull ashore should anyone wish to stay." No one said a word, "I am not telling you where we are going for I do not know its name. It is west of here. We will sail to the land of the Angles and then around the land of the Picts. When we find somewhere we like we will settle."

I thought that sounded daunting but I forgot that the others were young men and to them this was an adventure. They would be living a saga and they all cheered. We sailed on through the dark and sagas were sung to enliven the journey through the night.

I knew, from our journey across, that we would have a few days at sea. We would be out of sight of land too. The last time I had been a prisoner but this time we were all free men. It made life easier. We reached the open sea just before dawn and Olaf loosed the sails. It was a good wind blowing from the north east. It took us due east and was a fast wind; moving **'Ran'** swiftly away from Ulfberg. We were ordered to retrieve our oars. Olaf and four others took the first watch while the rest of us slept. Before Butar joined my mother and me he checked to see that the two fishing boats, each with six passengers were still on station. They were and, from the way that they were sailing, were moving quicker than we. That was good. Our two boats attached to our stern and filled with cargo were acting as an anchor. I knew that we would not survive wherever we landed without them.

Ran is a thoughtful goddess and she was with us as she helped out little fleet across the waters. Once dawn broke that first day we had used the sun to sail north west. We devised a system at night to have a light from all three boats and by sailing in a line we could navigate when the clouds hid the stars. After three days we spied land. The Picts were known to be a fierce people and Butar did not risk a landing. The fishermen had caught fish and we still had stale bread and some dried meat. We were not starving. The rainwater was collected so that we had water. Olaf made us clean the filth from the bottom of the boat on a more regular basis. All of us, Butar, Olaf and the women excepted, each took a turn. I think it helped us. We were all equal.

The first squall hit us on the first morning after we had struck land. It gave us plenty of water but upset both the women and the animals. Olaf just chuckled. "Do not worry, the goddess Ran wanted to let us know she was changing the wind. " He pointed at the pennant flying from the masthead. "See it now blows from the south east."

The wind from the south was warm and we flew. This time the fishing boats did not outpace us and we made many miles until we saw, at last, the headland of the land to the south. We turned west again. This time the wind pushed us hard to the north west and, when we awoke we found no land at all in sight. Olaf took a sun sight and we headed west again. The next time we sighted land it was not the mainland but a string of islands and this time there was smoke from the houses we saw there. It was inhabited. We now needed food and Butar took the decision to land. We took out the oars and made swift progress to the island with the largest number of houses. Butar kept us apprised of our position. "There look to be ten or twelve houses and they look like longhouses."

That set the rowers to chattering like starlings. The houses we had seen in the land of the Picts had been tiny roundhouses. Did this mean that there were people like us ahead? The others seemed happy about that but I was not sure. Although they might welcome us they might not want to share what they had. Olaf shouted to the two fishing boats to stand off in case there was a problem and we edged towards the beach.

"There are warriors and they are armed. There are just fifteen of them."

That meant that we outnumbered them but did we really want to fight? We had been at sea for almost a week and our legs would not allow us to fight well. We slowed down as the sail was lowered and the oars retrieved. "Dragon Heart and Haaken, come with Olaf and me. Bring your swords."

By landing with just our swords and neither shield nor helmet we were showing that we wanted peace but we could and would fight if forced. "Haaken, Dragon Heart, secure the boat." We took the rope and waded through the water to tie it to a large barnacle encrusted rock.

The men who approached us kept their swords sheathed but their faces showed their concern. They spoke our language as they greeted us. "I am Hrolf, the headman of this land."

"I am Butar Ragnarson of Ulfberg. What is this land called?"

"It is Orkneyjar. The island of the seals. Forgive my bluntness but why are you here?"

"We left our home to seek a new home."

"Then you will need to carry on. This island supports the few families who live here now and your boatload is too many."

Butar nodded. "We have been at sea for ten days. Could we stay one night and then move on?"

Hrolf looked at his men and they shrugged, "One night." He pointed to the headland to the south. "There is a bay there which will suit you."

I saw Butar and Olaf exchange a knowing look. "You are most hospitable."

We returned to the ship and everyone looked at us expectantly. Was this our new home was the unspoken question on their faces. Butar said, "We will camp here tonight and leave in the morning. The Jarl says it is too poor to support more." As we sailed around the headland he added, "He is a wise Jarl. He shows hospitality but prevents us from a sneak attack in the night."

Viking Slave

It was good to be off the boat and the children ran around in the sand dunes as though they had never run before. Of course they had never seen sand before. Our rocky home just had rocks and steep cliffs. The women set to cooking the fish that the men had caught and Haaken took some of the men further south to forage. They came back with two seals. We ate well that night and made some seal oil which was always useful. The next morning we began to load the boat and Hrolf and some of his men joined us.

"You kept your word, Butar, and I thank you. We thought at first that you were raiders but now I see that you are like us settlers looking for a peaceful life." He pointed south, "South of here are islands but they are occupied by the Picts. They are a fierce people who paint their bodies blue. They can be defeated but they never know when to give in. Further south there is land which has opportunities. There is an island called Manau. The Saxons live there but there are few of them. We have raided the Saxons there. It is good land but we like the seals here. The land to the west is the land of the Irish. Some of our people went there but we have not heard of them since."

"Thank you, Hrolf, for your hospitality."

Hrolf turned to one of his men who had a sack. "Here are some fresh vegetables. You may need them." He gave a rueful smile. "We would have killed to get them when we arrived for we were hungry beyond words." He raised a hand in farewell. "We may see you for we visit the islands when we need sheep."

As we left the island Butar explained to my mother and the others what had transpired. "That is the island my people called Mon. It is not far from my home; the land of Cymri."

That decided Butar. "Then we will go there."

As we rowed Cnut asked, "Why did we not fight them? We will have to fight the Saxons."

"The Saxons are our enemies, certainly the enemies of my mother."

"But you are half Saxon."

"That is the half of me I do not like. That is the half which is like Tadgh and Saelac. Besides I do not think that Butar wishes to fight people like us; those who have been dispossessed. This is better. It is a new start in a new land."

The night ashore had done us all good and, even though the winds were not as favourable, the rowing was not hard. The seal meat had also been a delight. We sailed between the huge islands of the Picts and we saw their settlements. We steered clear of them having heeded the warning of Hrolf. We awoke one morning to see a land to the west and another to the east.

"That must be the land of the Irish to the west and the land of Northumbria to the east." Butar pointed due south. "Soon we will see Manau. Warriors arm yourselves we may have to fight."

As we dressed for battle I was not sure of the wisdom of leaping from our boat to begin a war but Butar knew best and he was our leader. We had all become oathsworn the night we had left Ulfberg. None would leave now save with his permission or they would be the lowest of the low, they would be oath breakers. My weapons were all sharp and protected with seal oil but I checked them anyway. Our shields lined the side of the ship and I would be happier when mine was on my arm. I still needed my leather cap inside my helmet but I was still growing and I knew that soon I would just need a woollen one.

It was noon when we saw the island ahead of us. We could see no sign of inhabitants or settlements but that meant nothing. We cast the two boats with the cargo for the fishing boats to tow and we headed in to what looked like a suitable landing site. There was a small river which tumbled from the wooded hills into the sea. It would provide us with both water and materials to build. As we neared the beach we could see the land to the west was flat and rose to the south and the east but there was still no sign of any people. With so many rowers we were able to have six men ready to leap from the ship and defend us as we beached. Haaken and Cnut were two of those chosen. They jumped and landed waist deep in the water. They surged up the sand to take up a defensive semi circle while Sweyn and I took the two mooring ropes. I found a large rock and I tied it around securely. I drew my sword and joined Haaken and Cnut.

We waited until most of the men were landed and Butar joined us. "Olaf, secure the landing site and get the cargo unloaded." He pointed up the hill, "Haaken, take Cnut and Dragon Heart; find a good place to build our homes up there." He pointed to the hill which rose ahead of us. "I will take the rest and sweep around the headland to see if I can spy any settlements."

As Haaken led us up the hill I wished that I had my bow with me but it was still on the *'Ran'*. My sword would only be useful if I was face to face with someone whereas my bow could kill from a distance. The ridge was only eight hundred paces from the beach. We approached it in a line

Viking Slave

with Haaken in the middle. The time on the boat had taken it out of us and, by the time we reached the top we were all out of breath. This was the steeper side of the valley and would make a good defensive position. We could live by the water but here would be our sanctuary in case we were attacked. We spread out to spy out the island. I could see that the island was not large although it was bigger than Hrolf's. "There Haaken." I pointed south to where a tendril of smoke rose in the sky. There were people there. I turned and saw Butar and his men approaching up the slope from the north. They too were out of breath.

"Jarl Butar, there is a settlement south of here but we thought this would make a good place to build." Haaken was aware of the new responsibility. "The ridge to the east is lower and we are only eight hundred paces from the beach. In case of danger we could easily reach here."

"Good. We will build here. Sweyn and Bjorn, guard this place. Let us go down to the river and walk back to the beach that way."

When we reached the river we noticed that the banks were lined with bushes and trees and there was a strong smell of garlic. We all sniffed until Cnut pointed at the ground. There were bunches of wild garlic. That was an excellent sign that we were meant to be here. Garlic was used in our cooking and to protect us from wolves. Butar nodded. "We will call our new home Hrams-a, the wild garlic river."

Mother changed the moment she stepped ashore. Her face filled with a smile which looked like sunshine on a summer's morning. She giggled as she picked the children up and swung them around. Butar said, with a smile on his face, "Have you the spring madness even though it is autumn?"

"No, my love. I am happy for I am home."

"I thought we came from Cymri."

"This was part of our lands until the Saxons took it. We will make this our home." She set to with a passion and organised the women and the men. She wanted shelters up before dark and she had plans for the houses too.

"But we need to build the walls on the hill for defence."

Mother put her hands on her hips. "You can have half the men. We need the rest."

The men all stared at Butar. Would he be willing to take this loss of face? They did not know him as I did. He shrugged. "Come on then. You fifteen, come with me. The rest stay here and help my wife."

Viking Slave

He took much less than half of the men and this showed what he thought of his wife, my mother. We took the mattocks, axes and spades. There were many trees growing on the valley sides and Olaf and four of the men began hewing trees. The rest of us began to dig the ditch and the holes for the posts. Luckily it was autumn and the ground was damp. It made turning the soil easier. Sweyn still watched the distant settlement and the hillside for the sign of any movement but for the rest of us there was no rest. After the walls had been marked out we began to dig. First we dug the four corner post holes and then the two for the gate. Once they were finished we dug more post holes equally spaced along the wall. Soon we had forty holes ready for the logs. While we waited for the wood to arrive we dug the ditch which would surround it. When the logs reached us we used our axes to cut them to the same length. As soon as the forty posts were in the walls began to take shape. I was not skilled enough with an axe and I continued to dig the ditch while those skilled with axes split the next logs as they were brought up. Once they were ready they were hammered into place using long nails the size of a small dagger.

The sun was setting and we were tired. Butar waved the men down to the beach. Two men were chosen to sleep in the half finished walls and to watch for the approach of an enemy. I promised my friends that I would return with food for them.

Mother had worked wonders at the beach site. The men had erected the framework of a hall and there was a sod roof already in place. Trees were stacked to make a half wall running around the sides. There were three cooking pits and the smell of hot food wafted towards us. We almost broke into a run even though we were exhausted. Our first meal in our new home set the seal on our adventure. We had made it across two oceans and round many islands without loss. We made a sacrifice to Ran in thanks.

I carried the food back up the hill to the two guards. They were grateful. I also gave them a jug with some of the last of the beer. We would need to brew again soon. "Have you seen anything?"

"Not yet but there is a glow close to where the smoke was; I think that it is a settlement."

"By tomorrow we should have a hall for us to sleep within, Harald."

"I do not mind sleeping on the earth and it is warmer here than at Ulfberg."

Viking Slave

As I wandered down I noticed that too. After we had left Orkneyjar I had observed that the sea and the air were much warmer. I did not know why but it boded well for our new life. I touched the wolf charm. Perhaps my grandfathers were working together to guide us to a new home.

Chapter 8

All of our attention was given to the construction of the walls and the houses. Three days later and we had finished both of them. We only had five families, the rest were single men and so we had two halls, one on the hillside in the fort and the other by the beach. There were also five huts for the families. While Olaf repaired the boat and stored the spare masts he had brought, Butar took half of us to explore the island and to scout out our neighbours. We left the hall armed for war; I had my bow, as well as my wolf shield and Quicksilver. We were all rested from the voyage and eager to conquer this new land.

We kept to the western side of the ridge so that we would not be silhouetted against the skyline. Bjorn scouted ahead. He was an older warrior who was quick witted as well as being able to hide well. We too observed everything that we saw. We needed to come to know this new land as well as we knew Ulfberg. I noticed some small wild ponies grazing in the distance. "We could use those beasts, Jarl Butar." I had taken to giving Butar the same title as the others and he had come to accept it."

"Aye. They will help us to get around."

I could see the sea to the west and saw just how small the island was. We could see the mainland to the east as well as to the north. I suspected that Hibernia was not far away to the west. We had travelled about five miles from our new home when Bjorn came scurrying back. "Jarl Butar, there is a Saxon settlement ahead."

"Does it have a wall around it?"

"No, there are fifteen huts and it is close to the sea. They have some fishing boats."

We all looked eagerly at Butar. He knew what we were thinking. "No, we will not just walk in and raid them. I need to know of the other settlements first. These are our closest neighbours. I would know of others. Let us climb that mountain there."

It was not a mountain really but it was the highest point that we could see. We dropped down the valley of the river which seemed to teem with salmon and began to ascend the slope. It had looked higher when we had stood on the other side of the valley but as we climbed I could see that it was a shorter climb than to Ragnar's house. When we stood on the top

Viking Slave

we found that we could see all the way to Northumbria and Ireland whilst to the south I could see a white topped mountain. I wondered if this could be the Wyddfa that my mother had mentioned. If so it was a holy mountain which was said to be the home of a sleeping dragon. While we were admiring the view Butar was using his head and he had seen something more important; the other Saxon settlements.

"Look. There is a wall." We peered towards the south eastern coast and could see a wooden wall with a hall and huts. There were also boats in the bay. On the north western side we could see another wall and another port. There were at least two other settlements and, from what my mother had said, they would have to be Saxon.

"Jarl, there is a road connecting them." Cnut had good eyes.

I turned to look back at the first village we had seen. I stared at the hillside. "And there is one there, Jarl Butar."

"So these look to be the Saxon settlements. Now you see why we waited. Had we rushed in we might have been ambushed. Let us return home and begin to plan."

On the way back we also saw sheep and goats grazing on the hillside. Back at Ulfberg they would have been herded into winter shelters but here it still felt like summer. "Dragon Heart, Cnut and Haaken see if you can drive some of those sheep and goats towards Hrams-a. Take care and do not get spotted by any Saxon shepherd boys."

We set off eagerly. This would be easy. As Butar and the others descended the eastern slope we trotted down the western slope. I was half way down when a thought occurred. "Have either of you ever herded sheep before?" From the looks on their faces it was obvious they had not.

"How hard can it be? They are stupid creatures."

As we discovered, they might be stupid but they were incredibly agile and could run quicker over rocks and gorse than we could walk. After leading us in circles for some time I stopped the other two. "This is getting us nowhere. We will have to use our heads. There is no point running they can out run us. Cnut, go thirty paces to my left. Haaken thirty paces to my right. Let us walk towards them with our arms out. We will drive them down the valley. That one," I pointed to a large brown ram, "looks to be the leader. Let the others go but he is our target. We just have one to watch now."

This time they did not scamper away but walked northwards at a leisurely pace. Whenever we closed with them they hurried off but they did not run any more. I noticed a spur running towards the valley of the

Viking Slave

wild garlic river and I shouted to the other two. "Let us take them in that direction." They nodded and we turned slightly. Two of them did not like this and sprinted out of Cnut's reach. "Let them go. Keep after the leader." Suddenly the land began to fall towards the water and they began to flock together. "Close up a little and just keep walking." Now that they were flocking they seemed easier to control. I saw that the sun was slowly setting to the west and I hoped that we could reach our new home before it was dark. There was the thunder of feet behind us and the two lost sheep erupted between Cnut and me to rejoin the flock. We had all eighteen sheep. It was with some relief that I saw the sea ahead and smelled the smoke of our meal being cooked. I just hoped that the sheep would not be spooked by the sight of so many people.

Someone must have seen our approach for the children, led by Bjorn and some other warriors, appeared. Bjorn must have had skill with sheep for he made the children and warriors form a funnel and the sheep walked happily towards the huts. I was not sure where we would put them but Bjorn had an idea. He led them to the warrior hall and they trotted inside happily. Once inside he slammed the door shut.

Haaken moaned, "And where do we sleep now?"

"In there. All we need to do is build a sheep pen. There are plenty of hazels and hawthorn over there. It will not take long. I'll get the children to cut them. You make sure the sheep don't get out. The door has no latch yet." The three of us leaned against the door and sat on the floor. We had done what was asked of us. We had our first flock.

Now that we knew where the Saxons were we could keep watch for them. We built two towers the next day and began the walkway to run along the top of the wall. Butar and Olaf spent the whole day in the fishing boat sailing around the island with Egill the fisherman. Butar hoped that the Saxons would not try to interfere with the single boat and they kept well out to sea. Mother had the warriors finishing the houses. The final task of the day was to drive a huge tree trunk into the ground so that we could securely moor *'Ran'* to the shore. The rock was fraying the rope we had first used. By the time Butar and Olaf returned we had all finished. Two of the boys had been assigned as shepherds. We just put the hurdles on good grass and then built a second pen for the next day. We had a rope ready for the leader and the flock was becoming tamer day by day.

Butar and Olaf spoke to us in the warrior hall. "There are five villages on the island. There are two on the east coast, one on the south and one

Viking Slave

on the west. We saw no dragon ships just tubby traders. The largest settlement is the one we saw from the mountain. We will destroy the villages one by one until they meet us in battle and we can conquer this island. We came here in hope and now we have it. I believe that we can make this a secure home for us and our families."

We all cheered the prospect. An island of our own would make us safe and we had seen that we could do much with this new land. As our reputation grew then warriors could come to join us for the plunder. Olaf told me that there were many warriors who were no longer welcome in their own homes. For some it was a blood feud and for others they were outlawed. It explained why he followed Butar so readily. "It does not do to give an oath too many times. I gave one to Ragnar and now to his son. I will swear no more oaths." Olaf spoke to me more now. I think that was because I had lived with Ragnar for so long and Olaf had been Ragnar's man before he lost his arm; we shared our memories of the old man. They were close. I think that Ragnar had taken the younger Olaf under his wing; much as he had with me.

While our sheep and the village were becoming tame and controlled we were becoming more warlike. We were young men and many had not been blooded. Haaken and I had fought twice but some had never faced a warrior in battle. With this in mind Butar took the unusual step of explaining what we would be doing the next day.

"Olaf and five warriors will stay here to guard the camp. Those warriors will be chosen by lot. Ten of you will watch the road from the big settlement in the south; they will be led by Bjorn. The rest of us will go to the first village by the Salmon River. We will take the '**Ran**' and land from the sea."

Cnut could never keep his mouth shut." When they see '**Ran**' they will flee, Jarl Butar."

I shook my head as Butar smiled. "I know and Bjorn and his men will capture them." Cnut began to speak again but Butar held up his hand, "And I know that some will escape. They will run to the big Saxon settlement and tell them that a dragon boat has come. They will think that it is from Orkneyjar and will not look on their island." He paused as the warriors nodded. "I intend to conquer this island and make it ours."

I looked around we would have only thirty five men to do this. Would it be enough? And then Ragnar's voice came into my head. I knew that I trusted my friends. I would never let them down and they would be there when I needed them. We would prevail.

Viking Slave

I was proud to be chosen to go with Bjorn. Haaken and Cnut went with me and we liked that for we fought well together. Godfrid had gone with Butar. He would need the better sailors. There were bushes and trees close to the road which led south and we spread ourselves out. Bjorn was older than we were but not my many years. The difference was he had experienced many voyages and raids. Like Olaf he had been restless as a youth and had gone a-Viking. We left before dawn so that we could be there well before the boat.

Bjorn checked our weapons and helmets and nodded. "Remember we only kill the men. The women and the children we need as slaves. Use your pommels to stun them if they struggle. Make sure you have your rope ready to tether them and if any one loses them because of a poor knot then they answer to Olaf." That threat was enough. We then had to wait.

The sun rose in the east but it did not bring warmth. The weather was changing and the rain began to drive from our homeland far to the east. It seemed to rip through our clothes and find flesh despite our layers of clothes. We waited. I had my bow string in my leather purse to keep it dry and I still had my fur cloak. If I had to fight then I would drop it.

Suddenly we heard the sounds of sword on sword. It showed how close we were to the village. Butar was attacking. "Ready yourselves. They will not be expecting us." Four boys ran towards us; looking over their shoulders as they came. They were easily taken and trussed up. The four women and three little children who followed were also easy to contain but then there were six men who followed. None had helmets but three had swords. The others had axes. These would take more than a rope to stop them. Bjorn shouted, "Get them!"

Haaken raced forward flanked by me and Cnut. Quicksilver was ready for the farmer with the axe and I stabbed him in the belly. I stuck my shield in the way of a blow aimed at Haaken who then killed his man. Then it was over. They were all dead. "Take their weapons and let us join Jarl Butar."

Just then two young men who had been hiding behind a rock stood and raced away down the road. Cnut tried to run after them but he slipped on the muddy morass beneath our feet and he fell to the ground.

"Let them go. We have to get back to the ship. Haaken and Dragon Heart, get the weapons from the dead."

The weapons were of poor quality but the metal could be re-used. Bagsecg was a fine blacksmith. We still needed to build him a workshop but it was early days; we had been on the isle a short time as yet. Haaken and I were the last of the column to reach the village. Butar had taken everything of value and burned the houses. The other men from the village lay where they had fought and died.

"Quickly, get back aboard the ship!"

With only thirty five men we had more space than when we had left Ulfberg. Four warriors watched the petrified prisoners. They were all tethered together and if they tried to escape by jumping overboard, they would all drown. I wondered if any of them was like I had been. Were they thinking of a new start? I was the only warrior who had been a slave and it gave me a unique insight into their minds. We headed back north and I assume there were other survivors watching who would tell their chief that the raiders had headed north. And so we did, we sailed the few miles to our new home, Hrams-a. We hoped that the Saxons would believe we had returned to Orkneyjar.

Bagsecg quickly fitted the wooden collars to the new thralls. If they escaped it would be disastrous as they could lead the Saxons to our new home. We put them in the warrior hall in the fort and six men guarded them. Butar was well pleased with the outcome. Although we did not have our own home yet, the three of us had a sheltered corner of the warrior hall. The warriors who shared it with us respected our privacy.

Butar and I cleaned our weapons together. I felt closer to him and Ragnar when I did so. "You did well today, step son. Another warrior band for your hilt." He turned to my mother who now seemed to beam with pleasure the whole day long. "And we lost no men."

Mother was always sensible. "You cannot afford to lose any. Where will we get new ones from? Cnut and my son are barely men. The shepherd boys will not be ready for a few years. We have to be careful and husband what we have." I was the only one who saw the influence she had over Butar. In public she was always quiet and supportive of her husband. In the privacy of our home she offered him advice which he always took. If it had not been for my mother's advice we might be fighting warriors such as us in Frankia.

The slaves were allocated the next day. My mother was given a woman and her three children. One of them was one of the boys who had run quickly from the raid. His name was Aed and I knew that he would take some watching. We spent the first day watching the slaves work as they built a hall for Butar and my mother. I would now sleep with the warriors. I made a coloured band for my sword hilt. This time it was red; all the bands I would use on Manau would be red.

Butar had us split into groups to guard the village at night. He was worried that the slaves would flee and tell the Saxons of our home. We were not yet ready to face them. We needed to weaken them first whilst strengthening our own defences. Cnut and I were on the small hillock overlooking the village and the sheep pens. We talked of the battle and Cnut was disappointed that he had only killed one man. "You have many warrior bands and I have but two."

"I have been lucky and in the right place at the right time."

"No, Dragon Heart you have been skilful. I have watched you fight and you show no fear."

Little did he know the maelstrom that was inside of me. I was scared but I was more fearful of letting down my friends and my step father. When you finally find friends they become as valuable and dear as family. My eyes suddenly caught a movement. Someone was sneaking from the village. "Look, a thrall."

We did not need words. Cnut went in one direction and I went in another we would cut him off. We were unencumbered by shields and helmets and were able to move swiftly. The thrall had his wooden collar on which made it difficult for him to move. He suddenly saw Cnut and ran in the opposite direction. He ran directly towards me. I pulled back my arm as I ran and when he turned, in horror to see me before him, I hit him with my fist and the whole weight of my body. He went down as though I had felled him with an axe. It was Aed. "Come let us take him back to Butar's Hall."

They still slept and so we bound his hands behind him and tied his feet to the post in the middle of the hall. He would go nowhere and he would be punished in the morning.

The village were all summoned to bear witness to the punishment of the slave. His nose was swollen and his eyes were black. I thought that was punishment enough. Butar was dressed in his mail shirt with his masked helmet and looked fearsome. I know now that he was doing this deliberately to frighten the slaves. He was, in reality, a kind and thoughtful man.

"This slave tried to run. In my land there are many punishments for such a crime; he could be blinded, lose a foot or lose a hand."

There was a collective moan from the slaves and his mother fell to her knees at Butar's feet. "Please, lord, it was a mistake. I promise that he will not do it again!"

Butar remained impassive although it was hard to tell behind the helmet. "If I thought that other slaves would run I would kill you all here and now." This time the moan was louder and murderous looks were directed at Aed who sensed the hostility of the others. Slavery was a common occurrence. My mother had been enslaved twice. Most of the women had been slaves. I was sure, from their looks, that some of the women had been captured as children and were only Saxon because of that. "If I choose to be benevolent and leave this wretch intact then how do I know it will not happen again?"

The mother saw a glimmer of hope and grasped the hem of the mail shirt. "I promise he will not run."

"Very well but if anyone runs then the remaining members of that family will be killed." All of our slaves belonged to family groups and that meant they were reliant on each other. I was not sure if Butar would carry out his threat but I had never known him break his word. Aed was released and rushed to his mother sobbing. She smacked him hard on the side of the head fully aware of how close she had come to losing him.

Bjorn and the others who had ambushed the Saxons were chosen to do the same for the western settlement. We all took it as an honour even though it meant we had to leave in the dark of night and wait in the cold autumn air. The first time I had been cold as we had waited for the sun to rise and so this time I took the wolf skin. Mother had fastened a leather tie so that I could wear it like a cloak over my shield. We each took our positions on the valley sides. I was halfway up and I sat next to a rock with the cloak wrapped tightly around me. I enjoyed the quiet and thoughts of Ragnar ran through my head. I imagined him as a young man doing much as I did. As I pulled the skin tighter I thought about Olaf's revelation that he had been Ulfheonar. Olaf had spoken of them in hushed terms. They moved silently in the dark and were masters of disguise and hiding.

I heard sounds from behind me and I glanced over my shoulder. It was Bjorn and Haaken. I turned back to watch the track. "He cannot have disappeared. We would have heard if there had been fighting. He has probably wandered off."

"No, Bjorn. I was the next man and when I looked he was gone which is why I came to you. Perhaps the trolls have taken him."

They walked straight by me and looked towards the road. "I cannot see him either, Haaken. He is not the type to shirk his duty. Perhaps you are right."

I stood up. "Who are you looking for?"

The two of them leapt into the air and then spun around with their weapons in their hands. Haaken clutched his magic amulet. "Where did you come from? Did you come from the ground? Are you a wight?"

"I was here all the time and you walked next to me."

"Impossible. We would have seen you."

I shook my head and stood. I took off the wolf skin. "I used the cloak and that made me invisible." A picture of Ragnar came into my head, "I was like an Ulfheonar."

Bjorn looked intrigued, "A what?" I explained what Olaf had said and Bjorn looked at the skin. "I can see that this would work."

Haaken had regained his composure. "We should be Ulfheonar."

"What do you mean?"

"Jarl Butar thinks highly of us and we could be as wolves. We could learn to hide as Dragon Heart did and we could fight as a pack and defend the leader, you or Butar."

Bjorn liked the idea. "But we would have to put it to the other men and swear them to secrecy. The others might resent this. But I like this idea. We will talk more in the warrior hall."

Now that we had slaves Olaf had his own home built close to the **'Ran'** and Bjorn was the senior warrior in the warrior hall. There was more room than in the one at Ulfberg and we would be able to talk quietly.

We went back to our watching. I had just felt the first rays of the sun warming my back when I spied the masts of a ship over the rise leading to the village. This time we were less than half a mile from the village and we heard the noise of battle sooner. We readied ourselves for the refugees we knew would be fleeing. This time the women were led by four armed men. Two of them had helmets and shields. These were warriors.

Bjorn ran to one while Haaken to the other. I spied a man with a long axe. He saw me and, swinging the wicked looking weapon over his head advanced towards me. I would need all of my skill and agility if I was to survive. His axe had a longer reach than my sword. He suddenly lunged forwards whilst swinging the axe. I stepped forwards and ducked. He had been aiming for my head and my manoeuvre took him by surprise. It would not work a second time and he began to swing in a lower arc. I would not be able to duck beneath it this time. He grinned, his yellow teeth showing in the early morning rays of the sun. He swung at my shield and this time I did not duck, I began to move to my right and spin. The axe started to bite into the leather of the shield but I was moving in the same direction as the axe and it did not connect. I continued my spin and I slashed with my blade at his unprotected side. Quicksilver bit deep into his side and I saw his ribs. He looked at the wound in horror and, before he could react, I had hacked at his neck and killed him.

Once again two refugees escaped but the four warriors lay dead and we had six slaves, two women and four small children. Bjorn was wounded, although not seriously, as was Harald the Quiet. We tethered the slaves and headed into the village. This settlement had been bigger than the first and I think our first raid had made them more alert. I also saw that Olef the Tall was dead. We had lost our first warrior. Flames were already licking the buildings.

"Get on board!"

We embarked as quickly as we could and pushed off to sail north. As we rowed I saw two white faces on the hillside. We were being observed. Hopefully they would report that we were raiders from Orkneyjar or Ireland and would not seek us on Manau.

We had no ships to spare and could not give Olef the burial he deserved. Instead we built a pyre and, laying his sword on his chest, we sent him to Valhalla. That night we drank to his memory and, in the warrior hall told tales of his bravery and the battles in which he had fought. He was, like the rest of us, a young man. We did not feel sadness for him. He would be with Ragnar and the other warriors feasting, fighting and drinking forever. It was a good place to go.

His death acted as a spur to finish our defences and our buildings. Our two towers afforded us clear warning of any stranger who approached. The two fishing boats were also our eyes. One fished to the east and one to the west. They would tell us of any enemy. The new thralls must have been told by the first slaves of the threat from Butar for they behaved impeccably. Perhaps they believed that they would be rescued. We discovered, from our new thralls, who ruled the island; it was a Saxon called Aella. When Edwin had conquered the island, four generations ago it was Aella's family who had been given stewardship of the isle. The main settlement was called Duboglassio and had been the centre when the old people on the island lived there. They had long since disappeared but the name remained.

The fact that warriors had fought us was a warning that Aella would not have to rely on just farmers. We were told that he had Housecarls; he had warriors who were oathsworn and would be both well armed and well trained. We would have to defeat them before Butar could claim the island.

A few days after we had returned from the raid and buried Olef, Bjorn and the rest of his hunters sat in a corner of the warrior hall. Haaken told them of the Ulfheonar and his idea to make us a secret cult who would become like the wolves; invisible and fierce. We could not take another oath but we could all join such a cult and each warrior wished it so. We joined each other with blood. We made a cut and held our hands to each other so that we became blood brothers. That was as strong a union as an oath and Bjorn was happy with the arrangement.

"We still serve Jarl Butar and we are still his oathsworn but now we have a rallying cry, 'Ulfheonar'. When we hear that we fight as a pack and protect the leader."

We all agreed and I slept happier that night knowing that Butar now had eight protectors. I had discovered that Butar and his men did not fight together; they fought as individuals. The Saxons fought as a line, protecting each other. A leader's life only lasted so long as he had skill. I did not want Butar to die. That night, as I fastened another warrior band to my sword I sent my thoughts to Ragnar. He would be pleased that we would be protecting his son.

Chapter 9

We saw Aella's scouts the next day. Godfrid was in the tower and he shouted down, "Saxons." We kept ten men in the hillside fort each day and it happened to be us. I grabbed my bow and raced up the ladder. We still had not built steps to the walkway but we were young fit men and it was not a problem to climb a rickety rough made ladder. I quickly strung my bow and notched an arrow. Godfrid pointed to the south. I could not see anything at first and then I detected a movement. It was beyond my bow range. I could hunt well enough but I was not a good enough archer to hit at distance. The Saxons must have gained confidence that we did nothing for they approached a little closer. They had leather helmets, swords and shields. They stopped about four hundred paces from the walls and had a discussion. Had we had horses we could have run them down but we had not managed to capture the wild ponies we had seen. They began to move down the slope towards the river. Bjorn, who was still bandaged shouted, "Cnut, go and tell Butar there are Saxon scouts. Godfrid and Dragon Heart see if you can hit them with an arrow. The rest of you come with me."

Bjorn led the men out of the gate. I loosed an optimistic arrow and it plunged into the earth fifty paces short of them. It encouraged them to come a little closer and that was a mistake for Godfrid was higher than I was, being in the tower, and his bow had a greater range. It helped that Godfrid was an archer. His arrow soared high into the air and struck one of them in the upper arm. I heard his cry of pain. The other two grabbed him and withdrew. Bjorn and the others gave chase but the three scouts had had enough and fled.

Butar and the rest of the warriors joined us. "So the Saxons know we are here and they will come soon."

Cnut inevitably gave voice to his thoughts, "Do we fight them from the walls?"

Olaf cuffed him about the head, "Foolish boy!"

Butar was more kindly. "No, Cnut, for then they would destroy our homes and our ship. If we had more men then we would be able to do as you say. No, we will put the thralls and the women and children on the walls with Bjorn and four warriors. The rest of us will meet them beard to beard down there." He pointed to the river and the valley bottom. "There, with no room to manoeuvre, our small numbers will aid us."

That was our battle plan. It was the way of our people. There was little planning; you relied on the skill of every warrior. What worried me, as I sharpened my sword and daggers, was that we had too many untried warriors who had not fought in battles. I just hoped that the Saxons were as inexperienced as we were. Bjorn came to Butar's Hall to speak with him. "Jarl Butar, have I offended you? Why cannot I fight with you and the others?"

"Because, Bjorn, you are too valuable. You are wounded still and I need a leader to watch over our people. Haaken can lead your little band. It will do him good to be a leader."

Bjorn could see the sense in Butar's words and realised he was not being punished. "You will only have thirty warriors. Will that be enough?"

"Unless you can think of some way to make more warriors overnight it will have to be." There was a wry smile on my step father's face. "It will all depend upon this Aella and how many men he brings. Thanks to Godfrid's arrow they did not see our numbers they only know that there are enemies and they have a sanctuary on a hill. Let us see what the Norns have planned for us."

Mother had two of the older sheep slaughtered and cooked up with the vegetables which were now looking worse for wear. The cauldron would be carried up the hill and would give food for the next days. The valuables from the settlement were placed aboard **'Ran'** and the fishermen took her into the bay and anchored her there. They would stay with our only means of escape should this sanctuary become a trap.

They did not come the next day. But we had prepared; the women, children and slaves were sent to the fort for their protection. We knew that they would come soon, for within a month we would be in the depths of winter and it would be harder to move even on such a small island. Aella had to protect his domain. Already I could see that he was a cautious man and his attack would be both deliberate and thorough.

They came the next morning. They had not travelled during the night for it was late morning when we saw their scouts coming along the valley. Butar turned to Bjorn, "Look after my family." Bjorn nodded, "Warriors, let us win this land from the Saxon thief."

The men roared but, as we descended I reflected that we were thieving from the Saxons. Perhaps it was because my mother claimed some sort of kinship with the people who lived here that Butar felt justified. I was a warrior without a land at the moment. I would just trust in Ragnar and my blade. Would I add to my warrior bands or would I become a trophy for a Saxon?

We marched down the slope to the river. The water would protect our left and the slope our right. The Saxons would be funnelled towards us. Butar stood in the centre and Olaf to the right. "Haaken, take Bjorn's men to the left, to the river." The place of honour was to the right where Olaf and his men stood. Butar and Olaf were the only ones with mail shirts but the rest of us were armed as warriors. When the scouts halted we saw the Saxon army behind. Their leader, I assumed Aella, had a mail shirt and a full mask helmet. There were also five other warriors with mail shirts but the rest of his bodyguards, all twenty of them, were armed as we were. The rest looked like farmers with axes, daggers and whatever other farm implement they could scavenge. They would not pose a problem save for the fact that there were thirty of them. We were outnumbered. The normal way of fighting for us was a mad charge at the enemy. I was not certain that would work this time. Their leader and his bodyguards were advancing in a shield wall.

They approached at a steady pace for the ground was muddy and slippery. They were cautious. Suddenly arrows began to rain down on the advancing Saxons. Bjorn was using his five men to disrupt the attack. Two of the farmers and fishermen fell to arrows. Neither looked to have a mortal wound but they were incapacitated. The bodyguards held their shields above their heads. They were protected but not those without shields and helmets. They began to edge away from the Saxon left towards the river and us. It meant that Olaf and Butar would face the twenty well armed men and they would have roughly equal numbers but we seven would have to face over forty armed men. This would be a test of my prowess. I slipped Ragnar's dagger into my left hand behind the shield and I tightened my grip on the strap.

Butar judged his moment well and he shouted, "Charge!"

The Saxons had their shields above their heads when Butar and Olaf struck and they drew first blood. I had no time to be a spectator for Haaken shouted, "Forward!" We ran at the mob which approached us. They were doughty men but they were not warriors. I took the blow from the hand axe on my shield and stabbed the farmer, twisting as I withdrew the blade. One of the Saxons had an axe head tied to a long pole and he swung it at me. I held up my shield but the blade deflected and it struck my helmet. It was a warning that I could be killed, even by a farm tool, and I screamed, "Ragnar!" and hurled myself at the man. Quicksilver took him in the throat but I did not stop. I punched the next Saxon with the metal boss of my shield, the point struck him in the face; when he fell, screaming, I stabbed him. I sensed rather than saw a sword coming down at me and I twisted my own sword up and round to parry it. I was below the man and he was heavier than I was. He roared in triumph as my sword was forced down. I ripped sideways with my left hand holding the shield and the dagger; it ripped across his stomach. I pushed his body away and looked for another enemy. I was shocked to see that there were none before me. I turned and saw that I had emerged from a sea of carnage and my comrades were fighting behind me. I ran at the unprotected backs of the Saxons. It was not glorious but I slashed and hacked at their defenceless rear. Suddenly they found themselves attacked from two directions and they broke. They were not to know it was but one warrior. I punched and slashed at every Saxon I could see but they fled, in terror, up the valley to their homes and safety.

    Before we could congratulate ourselves Haaken roared, "Ulfheonar!" and pointed; Butar was in trouble. We all turned as one and, locking shields, followed Haaken at speed into the side of the throng who surrounded Butar. These men were not as easy to kill for some wore mail. I killed one warrior by smashing Quicksilver down on to his helmet. The iron cracked and he fell to the ground. I stabbed him and saw, to my dismay that Quicksilver was bent. I slashed the edge across his throat, just in time to face a mailed warrior. My sword would not survive another such blow and so I roared, "Ragnar!" again and threw myself at him like a human spear. The edge of my shield caught him below the jaw. His head jerked back and I followed up by throwing my head at him. His neck snapped back and I stabbed upwards with the dagger held in my left hand. The blood from his throat sprayed out like a mountain spring.

    Butar was winning against Aella but one of the Saxon's bodyguards was advancing towards Butar's unprotected sword side. I ran, almost slipping and tripping on the bodies and the blood. I would not reach him in time. I saw the Saxon blade rise, ready to hack Butar's arm. I hurled myself as I had at the farmer. I held Quicksilver before me. The tip entered the mail shirt; had I just stabbed him it would not have penetrated but the blade had all of my weight behind it and it started to rip and tear the metal links. My momentum took us both to the ground. I lifted myself to my feet and found that my blade had bent and then shattered. Quicksilver was no more. It had done its duty and saved Butar's life. I grasped the dead warrior's sword. I was just in time to see Aella's bodyguards carrying his wounded body from the field. Haaken, Cnut and the others stood around Butar and I could hear cheering from the hill top. Against the odds we had won.

The end of a battle is never pleasant. This was only my second such event but it was hard to look around and see which of your comrades would not fight again. Then there was the task of despatching the wounded enemies and sending them to Valhalla so that their souls would not haunt you. Before I did any of that I went to Butar. He looked drawn but he smiled when he saw me.

"Dragon Heart indeed! I thought you were a dragon when you flew through the air at that warrior."

Haaken slapped me on the back. "And I thought we had a Berserker here the way you charged through those farmers. You drove them from the field single handed."

Butar winced. I could see that he was wounded and hidden wounds were always dangerous. "Take my stepfather to my mother she will heal him."

Haaken shook his head. "You and Cnut can do that. I will deal with the enemy."

Cnut and I looked at the steep hill. "Let us take him down the river to his hall. It will be more comfortable than the fort and they will not be back tonight."

Even though he was in pain Butar said, "You have the second sight now do you? You can see into the future."

I chuckled, "No, Jarl Butar, but Aella had to be carried from the field and you are walking. We kept the field and they fled to their home. They will lick their wounds and recover before they try us again."

My mother had watched us from the walls and she and the house slaves were waiting at the hall when we reached it. She pecked me on the cheek. "You reminded me of my father today when I saw you fight. Leave Butar with me. You and Cnut will be needed on the battlefield still."

As we walked back I asked Cnut what had happened to him on the battlefield. "I killed or wounded a couple of farmers and then wounded a warrior. It does not compare with you. You are fearless."

"No. It is the opposite. I am afraid of failing and I do all that I can to avoid that."

He looked down at my sword. "That is not your sword. What happened?"

"Mine broke. I will retrieve it so that I can remove the warrior bands and then I will have the smith use the metal to make me a mask for my helmet."

He laughed, "I think he needs to do more than that."

I took off the helmet and saw what he meant. The axe had scored a line almost through to my skull. I had been lucky once again.

By the time we reached the field there were only the Saxon dead. Haaken had had our dead taken to the fort where they would be safe from animals. Bjorn was organising the men to collect the weapons and armour. I found my broken sword and picked it up. It had not let me down but it had been a stolen sword. I would need a new one. I would need one which was mine and mine alone. There would be no shared memories to confuse the sword. Perhaps the sword I had taken from the warrior of Stavanger had originally been taken from a Saxon. That might explain the way it died. I saw that someone had removed the mail shirt from the warrior I had killed. I was slightly disappointed; I had hoped to have my own mail shirt. I still did not know which of my friends had perished on that bloody field. I did not believe for one moment that we could have survived unscathed.

As I entered the gate I saw the cost laid out beneath cloaks taken from the dead Saxons. Six had died. It was better than we could have hoped but it was six we could ill afford to lose. I saw others like Sweyn and Harald White Streak nursing wounds. Bjorn greeted me and Cnut with a bear hug. "I am so proud of my Ulfheonar. Butar was surrounded until the seven of you leapt into his guards. You were the very wolves we spoke of and Dragon Heart you must show me how I too can become a spear!" The mocking was gentle and I did not mind.

"Did we lose any?"

"Aye Eric fell but he killed two of the enemy before he fell."

"And how many of the enemy?"

"Aella will be short of ten of his oathsworn and another ten farmers fell. We won the day."

"But not the island."

"No, not the island but we have the winter to grow."

"Do we plant boys and hope that they grow into warriors?"

"No, Dragon Heart, but Butar and Olaf are clever men. They will think of something."

That evening we sent our friends to Valhalla. We drew lots to see who would stand guard in the tower and the rest of us went to the warrior hall to remember our friends. None of us were in a mood to drink to excess and we just drank steadily until we fell asleep.

The next day I went to see Butar. The wound was in his side and would heal. He pointed to a mail shirt which lay untidily in the corner. "Olaf recovered the mail shirt from the warrior you slew. He did not want a lesser warrior to have it."

I did not know what amazed me more the fact that he respected me or the fact that he had thought to bring me the shirt. "That is a great gift."

"No, it is not a gift. You earned it. It will need some work on it. The shirt was not the best I have ever seen but it will afford you more protection than the leather jerkin."

I showed him my sword. I had removed the rings. "It served me well but…"

"But it can never be trusted again. Take one of the Frankish blades and see Bagsecg."

I was laden when I entered the newly built blacksmith's workshop. He had brought his anvil but he and his son were busy building the fire that would be the heart of the shop. I told him what I wanted. He examined the shirt, the broken sword, the new sword and the helmet. "I will trade with you. You help me and my son to build our furnace and I will do the work in return."

I clasped his hand. "When do we start?"

"Now!"

I stripped off my leather jerkin and set to work. His son, Bjorn, and I went to the beach to bring up the rocks that we would need to build the outside of the furnace. Bagsecg brought the sand and collected the mud that we would need.

During the morning as we sat, sweating, drinking some welcome spring water, my mother and her thralls came down to collect some shellfish from the bay. She looked at us and asked, "How will you make this furnace?"

Normally a woman would have been ignored but this was my mother who was the wife of Butar and a woman respected by the men. Bagsecg explained how he would shape the rocks so that they fitted together and then layer them with mud.

Viking Slave

My mother nodded. "Where I come from in Cymri they have priests who can read the Roman writing. They told my people how to mix rock with water and sand to make a kind of cement which is stronger than mud."

She turned to go. Bagsecg looked confused. "Lady, how would we make the rock mix with water?"

She pointed to the chips of rock which he had already trimmed, "Pound up the smaller pieces until it looks like the sand." Enigmatically she left.

Bagsecg took his hammer and smashed it against the small pieces of rock. It turned it to powder. He grinned. "She is a clever woman, your mother."

"Will it work?"

Bagsecg pointed to the pile of earth he had ready. "That is soft. It is the heat which dries it but the rock is hard already. It would be better to make something hard into the furnace. It will not crack as easily. I believe it will work. It is worth a try."

That day building the furnace made me much stronger than I had been before. After I had lifted the rocks and Bagsecg had trimmed them I was given the job of smashing the chippings with the hammer. I soon became quite adept. Even as I was doing it I was working out how I could transfer the skill to wielding a skeggox. They were of a similar size and weight. I found that, if I slid my hand down the shaft as I swung I could get greater power. It worried me that to get the full effect you had to use two hands. I would work on that. When I had finished and we had the powdered stone, we began. We mixed the sand with the stone. We had to estimate quantities but we had a great deal of rock powder so we used more of that. Layer by layer the furnace built up until by evening it was finished. The smith looked satisfied. "That took less time than I expected. I hope I have not cheated you for I believe I have done better from this trade."

"No, Bagsecg, I think it was a good trade for all of us. I have learned much and I look forward to using my new weapons and armour." That night I slept well.

Bjorn the Wolf, as he was now known was chosen to lead his Ulfheonar on a mission to see what the Saxons were up to. Egill and his fishing boat had established that they were in Duboglassio but that was all that they knew. We were to watch them. My new blade was not even started and my helmet was in need of repair; I took my leather cap and my dead enemy's sword. As I wrapped my wolf cloak about my shoulders the others were envious. We called ourselves the Ulfheonar but only one of us had the cloak. We followed the same route we had taken that first day and trudged below the ridge line. We followed the Salmon River down to the burnt out village. It was a desolate sight. We crept along the tree lined river sprinting from cover to cover until we were sure that the village was devoid of life. The foxes and the crows feasting on the corpses was evidence enough for that. The Saxons had not even returned to bury their dead.

Cnut pointed to the river which teemed with salmon. "We can harvest those, Bjorn."

"Aye. We will do that upon our return."

As we headed back up the river I thought about the circle which had started with me in a river emptying salmon traps to me walking along a river with the very people who had captured me. *Wyrd*!

We avoided all the little huts and farms we saw dotted around the lower slopes of the hills. We wished to be unseen and we moved through whatever cover we could find. We halted on the hills a mile from the Saxons and lay, hidden, beneath the sky line. Duboglassio was a large fortified village on a small ridge overlooking the bay. They had many fishing boats but I could not see any dragon boats. It was a good vantage point and we could see directly into the settlement. It looked to be well established and they had a large warrior hall. It differed in shape from ours but it was clearly a warrior hall. There were guards on the gate. There had not been any at either of the other two sites which showed that they were now worried.

"We need to get closer to the walls. Haaken, take Cnut and Dragon Heart and scout the southern end. We will do the same to the north. We will meet you south of the village on those cliffs there." He pointed across the bay to where we could see the land rising to some low cliffs.

We scurried down the slope away from the coast. We kept low as we ran. We moved so that we were out of sight of any watchers. After the recent raids they would be wary. When Haaken deemed that we had travelled far enough we turned east. The land here was flatter and heavily wooded. We moved through the woods which hid us from prying eyes. We saw game tracks; there were deer and it looked like wild boars as well. Suddenly we heard a noise. Haaken signalled for us to hide. I lay down beneath a blackberry bush and tucked my legs beneath my wolf skin. I could see through the bushes. The ground was muddy and I streaked my face with it to darken my white skin. I saw the Saxon hunters. There were eight of them; two boys and six men. They were heading back to Duboglassio with a deer they had killed. It was slung on a pole. It began to slip and they halted at the other side of the bush and retied the leather thongs to make it more secure.

"I still say the king should have attacked those Vikings today. They would not have expected it."

"That would have been foolish. He was too badly wounded and besides, we do not know how many there were."

"There didn't seem to be that many of them. I only counted twenty or so. We had many more than they did."

"The fyrd were useless, they would not stand. They all ran as soon as they were attacked. We need more warriors."

"The Vikings are fierce fighters look what they did to Terrell's burg and Abelard's burg. They wiped them out."

"All the more reason we should have attacked again."

"Until things are sorted out on the mainland we can expect no more warriors. We are on our own until then."

"You are right brother, let us recover and wait for the men of Udi's burg to come."

I could hear no more for they had moved away. I waited until there was total silence again and then I extracted myself from the bush. Haaken rushed over to me. "I had no idea where you were."

"I was under that bush and I heard them talk. Some of their warriors wanted to attack again today but the king was badly wounded by Butar. They are expecting more men."

"From another settlement on the island?"

"I know not but Egill did say there was another port to the south. Perhaps it is the burg of Udi."

"Udi?"

"It is what they call it."

"We will follow them down this trail. It is obviously the main way into the town."

When we reached the edge of the woods the walls were less than a hundred paces away. We hid in the trees. Like us they had one gate and it faced the sea. We could see that they had a stone wall to which they had tied their fishing boats. I counted six guards on the wall. The men we had seen were also warriors. The fyrd they had spoken of would be the farmers who had fled before us. I could see that they had a ditch running around the edge of the wooden walls and they had wooden towers. It would be hard to assault.

When we had seen enough we melted back into the woods and headed for the cliffs. Bjorn was there already. "We were worried." He stopped and looked at my face. "What have you done?"

"I smeared mud to help me hide in the woods. We saw some Saxons." I told him what they had said.

"Good. That helps us. Let us find this other place, this burg of Udi and then head home."

The cliff path was a dangerous one for it could be seen both from the sea and from the ground below us. The attacks on their villages must have made them wary for we saw no-one. They must all have been keeping close to their homes. We saw the last settlement nestling in a wide bay at the southern end of the isle. It was not as big as Duboglassio but there appeared to be a large number of people there. They were building a wooden wall. We watched them for a while to ascertain their numbers and then headed north.

"We have spurred them into protecting themselves. Looking at the numbers of men we are still outnumbered. I hope Jarl Butar has a plan."

"Knowing my stepfather and Olaf as I do I expect they will." We went further west on our return journey to see as much of this small island as we could. We saw more of the little ponies but they shied away when we approached. A herd of goats were grazing on the upper slopes of the high peak we had climbed and they would also make a welcome addition to our resources.

It was dark by the time we entered the village for we had walked eight hours from just south of Duboglassio. We were exhausted. My mother was quite concerned. "I did not know if you had met with Saxons."

"We did but they knew it not."

Butar and Olaf listened to all that we told them. Butar nodded. "So we have not defeated them yet and they will attack again. I think we will send men out each day to watch further away and they can try to gather in the animals."

"We need men, Jarl Butar."

Even Olaf had started using the title the men liked so much. "I know but we have none. Where will we get them from?"

"I could go with Egill back up to Orkneyjar. If we tell Hrolf that we have settled here then he could direct any other ships from home. There are many landless men are there not?"

"True. That would appeal to many warriors. You could also tell Hrolf that next summer we would be ready to trade."

Olaf looked up, "Trade what?"

"I do not know yet but this island looks to be more bountiful than Orkneyjar so let us just see what we find."

Olaf, Egill and two others set sail the following day and headed north. I did not envy them for the autumn storms were upon us. The waters were warmer than at home but the squalls and storms which blew from nowhere were equally violent. The ones who remained made our homes and defences stronger and we all tried to capture the horses and goats whilst watching for the next Saxon assault.

Viking Slave

Chapter 10

When Bjorn led us across the hills the next day Cnut looked enviously at my cloak. "I have seen no wolves on this island."

Bjorn laughed, "I think it is too small to have any wolves. They would have been hunted."

Haaken was quick thinking, as he had shown on the night of the attack at Ulfberg. "We could go to the mainland and hunt for them there. Those hills that we passed on the way south looked to be forested and perfect country for wolves."

"I do not think that Butar would sanction such a trip for we still need men here and not hunting for wolf skins. That will have to be for the future."

Perhaps we were distracted by the conversation but whatever the reason the Saxons loosed the first arrow without us even seeing them. We were lucky that it was poorly aimed for it missed Bjorn by a hand span. It was warning enough and we unsheathed our swords and ran directly at them. We had no shields but we were warriors and could fight without one if we had to. I took out Screaming Death in my left hand and looked for an enemy. There were ten warriors although none had mail. We were but seven. They had the higher ground but they foolishly relinquished it to charge down to try to finish off what they thought was an easy target. We were not, we were Ulfheonar.

The Saxon warrior is a brave warrior but he is not a reckless warrior; we were. Not only that, we were also fearless. Even though I had been born a Saxon, or at least a half Saxon, I had been trained by Ragnar. Even without a shield and a helmet I thought I could best these. I saw that half of them were my age. I ran at two of them. They each had a bow which they were trying to loose at me. I ran, twisting and turning as I did so, they kept adjusting their aim. They would have been better to have loosed one in the hope that they might hit me but they did not and I was swift! I stabbed forwards with my sword as I slashed blindly with Screaming Death. The sword found flesh while the seax knocked the bow to the ground. I withdrew the sword and stabbed at the second boy but he was on his feet and running like a hare in spring time. An older warrior swung his axe at me and I leaned and twisted backwards. As the axe head whistled but a hand span from my face I jerked my seax forward and felt it bite into his side. He tried to run away from me, the blood seeping from his wound but the blood was in my head and I roared at him slashing with the sword. He held the axe up with two hands to protect himself but the sword smashed through the handle and then split his head in two.

I stopped for there were no more warriors before me. Behind me I saw the archer I had wounded with two other dying boys. The rest of the Saxons were fleeing back towards Duboglassio. Ejnar was nursing a wound to his arm and Aker had been struck by an arrow. "You two get back to the hall we will continue with the scouting. Take the weapons with you. They are of poor quality but I dare say Bagsecg will be able to use the metal."

As the five of us trotted off, a little more carefully than we had before the ambush, I wondered at the attack. They looked to be young men keen to avenge what they saw as dishonour. I doubted that Aella and his warriors would be happy about that. They could ill afford for us to whittle down their numbers like this. We went all the way to the coast and the other burnt out village. We did not need to walk the last mile or so for we saw the same scene with carrion feasting on dead flesh. This one was also a graveyard and we headed back; there was nothing for us here. The goats we had seen previously had now wandered over to the northern side of the island. There were ten of them. I was not optimistic but Haaken insisted on trying to capture them.

We spread out in a half circle and began to walk towards them. They ran off but they ran in the direction of our village. We lost sight of them and we carried on walking. When we crossed the first ridge we saw them in the distance; they were munching the grass there. Bjorn had an idea which way they would go. "If they are seeking grass then they will avoid the river bottoms. The land to the west of the village has woods there. I think we can drive them towards the hill with our fort on top. It worked with the sheep. We have to go that way anyway. Let us just hope they choose the same path as we."

We were less than two miles from our fort and even if we could only capture a couple it would help us through a winter when we might be hungry. The ducks, geese and chickens we had captured already would give us eggs but we had no spare livestock to slaughter. The land began to rise and still they scampered away from us. It all depended now on how alert the men in the fort were. If they could herd the animals to the gate in the fort, we could pen them easily. Luckily for us it was Butar himself. He must have been touring the defences for he saw the goats and organised the remaining warriors. A line of them spread out preventing the goats from descending the hill. When they turned the other way then we were there. We walked steadily uphill and the herd became tighter. Had we had a sheepdog then it would have been easier but when the leading goat walked through the gate, we knew we had them. The last one entered and we all followed, closing the gate behind us.

"Well done Bjorn, you Ulfheonar have been successful again. Aker and Ejnar told us of the ambush, you did well. I think next time we have the warriors take shields and helmets. Now that you have the goats then we are better supplied."

"Do not forget, Jarl, that there is game aplenty close to Duboglassio."

"Aye and Saxons too."

Bjorn bit his tongue. He would have taken the risk. I was beginning to know Bjorn and he would find a way to persuade Butar. We spent the rest of the afternoon trying to tie ropes around the goats so that we could take them to the spare sheep pen. It was not easy but, by dusk, we had succeeded and the women were delighted for they could now make cheese which all of us missed. We were still short of flour for we had not captured much from the Saxons.

Another eight men left the next day to patrol the borderlands. We had worked out a line that was three hours away from us. It took at least half a day for a force of warriors to get to us from Duboglassio and so a three hour line would give us ample warning. The rest of us had a half day duty in the fort and another half day to pursue our own trade. I spent my half day with Bagsecg and we began to work on my sword.

It looked ugly as a blank; there was no sword shape as such. It was a long and narrow piece of metal with a handle. Bagsecg plunged the blank into the fire and his son and I blew air into the fire through bellows made from a sheep's stomach. It was hot work but I knew that it would be worthwhile. When the blank was red hot it was taken out and the two edges hammered until they were thinner. This was repeated until I could see that it had two visible edges. There was no point yet, that would come later. Bagsecg looked up at me. "You can have the sword now if you wish or we can make it even better."

"I want the best sword possible."

He nodded. "It is already the best sword in the village for it is a Frankish blade but we can make it both stronger and easier to use."

He kept heating it but he no longer used the larger hammer. He used quite a small, delicate one and he beat a channel in the centre of the blade. "This will allow the blow to run freely from the tip and make it stronger." He worked a while longer and said, "Now is the time for you to put runes on the blade. I can do this while it is hot."

I thought about this as he heated the sword again. "I would like to honour Ragnar in some way."

He nodded, apparently satisfied with my request. "We can put Ragnar's rune and the rune of the wolf on the blade. They will make it even stronger."

I was delighted with that and I watched fascinated as he made the runes in the red hot metal. The process took as long as both edges had done on the sword. I felt it was worth it. When he seemed satisfied he plunged it into the water.

When he was confident that it was cooled we took it to his grindstone. His son and I took it in turns to turn the huge wheel and the point of the sword gradually emerged. When that was finished he put an edge on to it. He fitted the pommel to the top and handed it to me. It still did not look like a warrior's sword. We now began the laborious process of polishing which would turn it from a metal sword into a warrior's weapon. I say we but it was left to me. Bagsecg's son showed me the technique of taking sand and a sheepskin and polishing away the rough exterior to reveal the shiny sword beneath. The blacksmith and his son went back to making the items the rest of the village would need. I did not mind for the effort I put in would be rewarded when I used it. As night fell I finished the polishing. The runes now stood out really clearly and I took the sword to Butar's Hall. I would eat there with my mother and then fit the warrior bands to the hilt after I had made the grip.

My mother had to force me to stop what I was doing and make me eat. I was obsessed. I had convinced myself that the other sword had failed because it still had the spirit of its previous owner. I needed to have something which was new and was mine. As I wolfed down my food she shook her head. "Why the rush? You are still just a boy."

I looked at Butar for help. He was a warrior and he would understand. He just smiled benignly at me. "How old was Ragnar when he lost his arm?"

Butar was surprised by the question but he answered nonetheless, "Thirty summers. I was a little younger than you are now."

Viking Slave

"And that is why I am rushing. I do not know how long I will have as a warrior. When I am no longer a warrior then I will eat."

"There is more to life than being a warrior my son. One day you will find a wife and give me grandchildren."

The thought had not occurred to me. I did not even notice the girls in the village. It was then that I realised why. I had been away from all of them when I had lived with Ragnar and since then I had been a warrior. I had missed out on those years when boys played games with girls and learned about them. I had been isolated in the Saxon village and isolated in Ulfberg. I wondered how I would find out about women.

My mother frightened me when she said, "Do not worry about learning about women, my son. You will know when the time comes." She could have been reading my mind.

When I had finished my food I completed the work on the hilt. Although it might have been better to wait for daylight to fit the warrior bands I felt that this was the perfect place and time to do that and so I took them from my leather pouch and carefully fitted them. There were eight of them for I did not count the farmers. When I touched the finished sword I felt my hand and arm tingle. This was my sword. Butar and mother admired the sword although I saw the envy in Butar's eyes. Mother just saw the clean lines and the shiny surfaces. Butar saw the weapon.

The next few days saw more patrols and more work with Bagsecg until my helmet was finished and I had a new seax made from my old sword. That evening was my turn at duty in the tower and I was excited to be there in my new helmet with my new weapons. Cnut was jealous of me and begged to hold the blade.

"No, my friend, for I want all of its power for me. What I will do is stick it in the tower wall so that you may admire it, but not touch."

I plunged the tip of the blade into the wooden log at the top of the tower and checked that it was secure. Cnut examined it in minute detail admiring the warrior bands, the sheen and the finishing touches we had applied. I could see him wishing it was his. When he became frustrated at not being able to hold it, we stood looking to the south. We stared at the dark wondering if the shapes we saw were Saxons or just bushes moving. I looked up at the sky; the moon had disappeared. "We will have a storm. I am glad that I have my wolf skin for it will stop me getting wet."

"You are lucky you know, Dragon Heart. Is that because of Ragnar?"

"Aye I think it is. The old man loved me, I think. Well so Butar told me and I like to think he is up there in Valhalla now but I wish he was here. He will be with Thor and Odin."

Just then there was the distant rumble of thunder and Cnut laughed, "There they are now!" I frowned. It did not do to make fun of the gods; even gently.

There was a flash of thunder in the distance and I held my skin above our heads. Despite what I had said I would not let my friend get wet. The rain began to hurtle down and then hailstones the size of small rocks. The thunder cracked and crashed louder and louder until suddenly there was a flash as a bolt of lightning struck my sword and threw both of us to the ground. I think I must have blacked out briefly. When I opened my eyes I expected to see my sword shattered but it still stood in the wood, blackened and steaming but there. I slowly got to my feet and went to withdraw it but it was too hot to touch.

Cnut stood near me, "Is it...?"

"I do not know." Then I saw that my precious warrior bands had all been forged together. There was now just one red band in the middle of the hilt. "This is *wyrd*!"

The rain still pelted down and the sword still sizzled. I heard voices from below and saw Bjorn and Butar. Butar shouted to me, "Are you hurt? We saw the lightning strike the tower."

I leaned over, "We are alive but the bolt struck my sword."

"Come down, your mother is worried and the Saxons will not come on a night such as this."

The sword had cooled sufficiently and I held it carefully as we climbed down the ladder. Butar and Bjorn stared at the sword as we told them what had happened. "This is the work of the gods we must ask your mother what she makes of this. It is beyond my world."

My mother held the sword in her hands and closed her eyes. "There is a power in here which is beyond mere metal. Tell me, both of you, what happened in the tower."

"The lightning struck the sword..."

"No, my son, you both need to tell me what you said and the events which led up to this."

The rain was still pounding on the turf roof of Butar's Hall and the thunder still rolled around outside. I was becoming afraid. What had I unleashed? We told her everything and she nodded. "Now I understand. This is the power of the Otherworld. You have summoned Ragnar back from the dead. His spirit is here in this hall." She seemed almost afraid to touch the sword which lay before the fire. Still the rain crashed and the thunder rolled. Cnut and Butar also looked fearful. "Nature has been upset and we must rectify it. You must name your sword my son and name it well. More rests on this than you can know." She put her arm around me, "Be brave and hold the sword in your hands."

"What do I name it?" I was becoming as fearful as the rest. Why had I not continued to use the other sword? What had made me create this monster?

She smiled, "You will know, believe me. Close your eyes and you will see the name."

I closed my eyes and images suddenly flashed into my head, the wolves, the warriors Tadgh, and then I saw the name as clearly as I could see my hand. "Ragnar's Spirit!" I must have shouted the name in my excitement for it seemed unnaturally loud and suddenly, as though someone had waved a hand, the rain and the thunder stopped and there was silence.

When I opened my eyes my mother was smiling at me and Cnut had his mouth and eyes wide open. "You have put nature back into place and all will be well. You now have the most powerful sword this side of the Otherworld and you must protect it." She drew Cnut and me to her. "You are both joined now as brothers. The lightning of the gods, Ragnar's Spirit and this sword have joined you. This is stronger than any oath and any blood. This is your spirit. Never betray it."

I clasped Cnut's arm. "Brother."

He clasped mine, "Brother."

When I put the sword back in its scabbard I felt as though I had grown taller. It was impossible I know but that is what I sensed as Cnut and I returned to the warrior hall. Our lives changed that night. I never added another warrior band to the hilt for that would have been a sacrilege. I did not need to show the world of my victories; the sword would do that.

The next morning the story was all around the settlement and everyone, thralls included, wanted to see this magical sword and hear the story of Ragnar's Spirit. Bjorn and Haaken could not believe that they had not been there to witness the event. "For once I wish that it had been I who was nearly struck by lightning. Do you realise, my friend, that your sword has been touched by the gods? If you were to sell…"

Bjorn shook his head, "No Haaken, the sword will only be magical for one warrior, Dragon Heart. That is what makes this special, for when

Viking Slave

he fights, he will have Ragnar with him and he was the best warrior ever to come from Ulfberg."

If I thought that a special sword would afford me special treatment I was wrong. I still had duties to perform and I still had to patrol the walls. When I saw Bagsecg he looked at the blade. "I have made many swords in my time but never one which was touched by the gods. I know that it is wrong to ask but, as the maker, can I touch it please?"

"Of course."

I handed it to him and he held it briefly and then gave it right back. "It burned!! I who can stand fires hotter than hell could not hold the hilt. It is true then." He shook his head. "I will make all the other swords the same way. Perhaps one of those will be touched by the gods."

As far as I was aware no other sword was ever struck by lightning but those made by Bagsecg and his son Bjorn were highly prized and he became the finest sword smith on the island. Once the word spread then warriors would come to trade for a sword from Manau. That was the future and, as we emerged from our storm we had to repair the damage wrought by the gods. The tower's damage was easily repaired but the rain had flooded the sheep pens and we had to move them to somewhere higher. Two of the huts had been wrecked by the rains.

Butar was a calm leader. He and my mother looked at the site and chose better ground for the new huts. Being the Jarl he was he shared his home with the new families. He would not have any of his people suffering if he could do anything about it. Mother, of course, saw a way to make things better for them both. Now that she had been in the bay for some time she had spied a better site for their hall. It was on the slopes below the fort. There was a rocky base which would provide a more solid foundation and when the two huts were repaired she set Butar and the rest of us making a new hall for her. Bagsecg appeared to have grasped the idea of making Roman rock, as we called it. She would have a stone base for the hall.

We had just laid the lower levels when Olaf returned. He too had suffered during the storm and it had delayed his return but he brought good news. "We will have new warriors within a month. Hrolf told me that there has been a war in our homeland. Harald One Eye has fought the men of Stavanger and captured their port. They, in turn, have ravaged outlying villages in search of new homes. A small boat with warriors passed through and told them. They said they were heading west to find new lands."

Viking Slave

"Beyond the edge of the world?"

"Aye they were reckless. Hrolf said he would tell all of our new land and he will happily trade with us." He then peered around the village and saw the damage and the new work. "It seems I missed much."

We told him all that had happened. Olaf had never shown much emotion in all the time I had known him but when he heard of the sword touched by the gods I saw a different Olaf the Toothless. He looked in genuine awe of me and my blade. "Ragnar's Spirit." His voice almost trembled. "I can see how the old man would not release his hold on life easily. He fought his whole life and he loved you Dragon Heart, I know that." He dropped to one knee. "I will serve Ragnar's Spirit. I will protect Ragnar's family." It was a simple oath but a binding one. He was already Butar's oathsworn but now he swore to guard my mother and me. I was touched. It was not that long ago that I had been a thrall and now the thrall master was offering me protection.

The storm also marked the beginning of winter. We never had snow on our island, at least not snow which lay on the ground. We had sudden snowstorms which melted straight away. We had frosts but they disappeared with the first rays of the sun. Our land at home would be locked in snow and ice for half the year; here it lasted a night at most. Even the high places escaped the ravages of a true winter. Our patrols did not see any more Saxons. We took one close to Duboglassio and we saw that it too had been badly damaged in the storm. They were too busy repairing the damage from the gods to fight us. We had a breathing space for men to heal and for Bagsecg to manufacture more weapons.

He worked on my mail shirt for me. It was tricky and intricate work. Each link had to be joined to all its fellows and beaten by hand. His son soon became an expert in the work for his fingers were small enough to manipulate the rings. When it was finished it was given to me to clean and polish. I took the sand and the sheepskin and I rubbed it each day until, after a week's work, I had a shiny mail shirt. Cnut was now my brother and he did not exhibit the same envy. He showed pride in my good fortune. "Do not worry Cnut. We will get you a mail shirt in the same way I got this. We will fight the Saxons again in the spring and they have such shirts."

I was loath to lose my captured sword. Olaf heard me talking about it and said, "Why not wear a second scabbard across your back. I have seen you fight and your left hand is almost as good as your right. Ragnar's

Spirit is a special sword and should not be used against the lesser men from the fyrd."

Bjorn disagreed, "I believe that Ragnar entered the blade to be a beacon for our people. I know that if I am going into battle I will feel happier knowing that Ragnar is amongst us again and that we have a sword touched by the gods."

They continued to argue but I was happy to have a second scabbard on my back. I just had to make a new one for Ragnar's Spirit. The winter might have been less harsh but the nights were almost as long and I used the nights in the warrior hall to fashion a scabbard fit for my weapon. I chose oak for the outside. I cut it so that, with the sheepskin inside, it was a comfortable fit. Once I had bound the two sides together I covered the whole in some deer hide I still had from the old country. After the leather was fitted I could give it the decoration it deserved. I spent some time on the beach looking for the crystals which washed down the river. I spent a whole month until I had exactly the right colour. I polished and smoothed them until I was satisfied that they were right and then I began to finish the scabbard. I painted, carefully, a dragon on the scabbard. Its tail was at the bottom and its head at the top. I used the stones to represent the scales of the dragon and I used glue made from goat's hooves to stick them. I knew that I would have to replace some of them after combat but I had collected more than I needed. I kept it secret from all but Cnut. He too began to make one similar for his sword.

"We are brothers, let us look like brothers."

I helped him to make his and my experience made it a quicker process. When Bagsecg brought me my repaired helmet I knew that I had changed. The helmet hid half of my face. I let Cnut wear it so that I could see the effect and it was chilling. Bagsecg nodded his approval. "There is one thing you could do to make it look even better."

"Tell me."

"Most men wear a shiny helmet. You are Ulfheonar and use the dark to hide. If we smear this with charcoal from the furnace and then burn it, your helmet will be black as night."

"Will it harm the helmet?"

"No, I believe, it may make it stronger."

And so we made the first black helmet at Hrams-a. The second was Cnut's. We hurried back to the warrior hall with our helmets wrapped in sacks. We both had chests in the warrior hall and our new, precious objects were placed within.

Our first warriors joined us when the days became a little longer. It was a dragon boat but even smaller than *'Ran'*. There were ten warriors. They had brought with them four families. Their leader was Eric Olafson. He knelt before Butar, "We have heard you seek warriors and we are here to offer our swords. Our land was taken by Harald One Eye. We are the only survivors."

Butar would not just accept any warrior and he asked questions. "Who was the Jarl of your village?"

"My father, Olaf Egillson. He and his oathsworn died defending his hall. I was charged with the protection of my mother and sisters." He pointed at the white haired woman with him. "As you can see our ship was small. We were not a wealthy community."

"Then, Eric Olafson, you are welcome. Your warriors can use the warrior hall." He then pointed to the old Butar Hall which was now empty following the completion of the new one. "You and your family can have my old hall."

Eric's face showed his gratitude and his mother and sisters wept. I know from my mother that men can cope with the loss of a home far easier than a woman and Eric's women could now have their own roof over their head. Eric waved his arm and his warriors all knelt. "We will be your oathsworn Jarl Butar and defend this new land with our lives."

They were the first of many. Hrolf was as good as his word and men came in dribs and drabs. Some of them were sent away. They were the ones whose stories suggested they had broken their oaths or become outlaws. We sent them west to Ireland. As Butar said, one night as we ate, "We want men who will fight for this land as a home and not for plunder. They were a-Viking and Ireland and the west will suit them."

It made more work for us as we added buildings. The warrior halls were now both full. The Ulfheonar moved into the one in the fort. We had now renamed it; Storm Citadel. The new warriors fitted in well. As we feasted with them the first night I was forced to tell the tale of the sword and the lightning. We had not yet made it into a saga; I was not a good story teller. Haaken promised me that he would create one which would do it justice.

Our whole world was turned upside when Mother went into labour and my sister, Eurwen was born. We had hardly noticed that my mother was with child. She worked as hard as any of the women and she never complained. The blond baby was born on the day that the first yellow flowers appeared. Her name meant golden one. Butar had never thought he would father a child and now that he had a daughter he was besotted by her. The men had a celebration where they wet the baby's head. It meant that the men all got drunk and told the father what a lucky man he was. Butar, whilst a little inebriated, confided in me that he did not mind having a daughter as the gods had given him a son. I was proud that he viewed me as such.

We had little time to give to my sister, for Saxon scouts appeared again. They were more cautious this time. They came at night and they came without us knowing they had come so close to our walls. The lesson had been learned. They would not risk us whittling their numbers down still further. They sent a couple of fishing boats to spy the harbour but when they saw two dragon ships they turned tail and fled before we could pursue them.

Eric, Butar, Olaf and Bjorn planned our course of action. As was the way with Butar he gathered all the warriors to explain what we would do. "We will not try to land at Duboglassio; they will expect that. Our scouts, the Ulfheonar, have told us that there is another beach further north which we can use. We will take *'Ran'* and land our men there. At the same time Bjorn will lead another column of warriors to attack the landward side of the town."

Egill, who had a wife and three children asked, "What about our families?"

"We will put them in the citadel with Olaf the Toothless and ten warriors to protect them. We will not risk them. We now have more warriors thanks to Eric and Harald." Harald the Fair had arrived with eight warriors a few days before my sister was born. They had two women with them and brought our numbers up to be the same as the Saxons. King Aella still had his fyrd and the unknown warriors from the burg of Udi but we were confident.

The married men seemed satisfied that their families would be safe. The next day we went to war.

Viking Slave

Chapter 11

Eric and his new men went with Butar on the *'Ran'*. Harald and his men, along with the other six new warriors, went with Bjorn. We had a long journey through the night to reach the hills overlooking their fort but we were all proud to be chosen. We had the harder task, we would be the ones who would have no support if anything went wrong. I did not know, until we began our journey, that they were all excited to be fighting alongside the sword of the gods. My youth was outweighed by my sword and my experience. Even though Harald was older he spoke to me as an equal. When I emerged from Butar's hall with my new helmet and mail shirt I could see the envy on the faces of the others. Cnut had blackened his helmet too. Now that we were brothers we wanted to be seen as the same. The shirt felt heavy but not too heavy. I knew that by the end of the night its weight would be more apparent but I was determined not to weaken. I owed it to Ragnar. I kept touching the lightning sword's hilt for reassurance.

We travelled our ridge road, as we had before. It was early spring and still very cold but we were warmed by the thought of battle. Bjorn led but it was Haaken and then me who followed. The Ulfheonar were the leaders. After two hours or so of walking we halted for we knew we would be halfway there. We squatted on our haunches and chewed on the dried meat we had brought.

Suddenly Cnut held up his hand. We all became instantly alert. We craned our heads to hear what he had heard. At first there was nothing and then we heard the sound of metal on metal. Someone was coming our way. Bjorn signalled for us to spread out. We all slid our weapons silently from our scabbards. The sound of whoever was out there had made us even more cautious and careful. Cnut pointed to the valley below us. That was where he had heard the sound. We peered into the dark and then I saw the shapes. There was a column of men below us. I pointed and Bjorn nodded when he saw them. The Saxons were coming to attack us. It meant that when Butar attacked Duboglassio then he would have fewer enemies to fight but our home might be captured by then anyway. I did not envy Bjorn his decision.

We had no idea how many men were below us. It could be Aella and his whole army or it could be a few scouts such as us. We were thirty eight warriors. He signalled Harald and Haaken to join him. They huddled together and he whispered his instructions. Haaken came back. He said nothing but he pointed to the column and drew a finger across his throat. That was enough for us. Haaken drew us to the right and Harald and his men went to the left. Bjorn went to the middle where the new warriors were. He waved his sword forward and we began to march slowly down the slope. Even had we wanted to run, it would have been a mistake. It would have alerted them to our presence. In addition we could have tripped on the treacherous stone covered slope. The dark of the hillside hid us as we approached. The column which looked to be three men deep, stretched down the valley. It was hard to estimate numbers. What was clear to me, as we closed with the Saxons, was that we could not hope to win. There would be too many enemies for us to fight. All that we could hope to do was to weaken them and make them return to their fort and leave our families alone. It would be a death worthy of a saga.

Bjorn must have given instructions to Haaken and Harald for, as he held up his sword, so did they. "Charge!"

We needed no further urging and we plunged into the column of men. I had seen the men I would strike. I knew that Cnut guarded my right and he would protect me as I protected Haaken to my left. I punched the warrior to Haaken's front with my shield as Ragnar's Spirit spitted the warrior behind him. The next two warriors fell over with the force and weight of our attack. As I stabbed one I smashed the edge of my shield at the head of another. I heard one Saxon cry. "They are invisible! They are ghosts!" I glanced at Cnut and realised that I could barely see him.

I knew we had to take advantage of this fear. We were the end of the line and the warriors lower down the valley could hear nothing save the shouts of battle. "Cnut, Haaken. Follow me! Let us charge them!" It speaks well of my comrades that they did not question my words but turned so that I was in the middle and we ran at the approaching column. I suspect the better, braver warriors were at the front of advancing army for the ones we struck appeared petrified.

The three of us made a solid wall of wood and iron. Our swords whipped savagely out and found flesh wherever they struck. We punched with our shields and men fell. We did it silently and they screamed in panic as the three warriors in black hurtled through them. They began to turn and flee. A well armed warrior loomed before me in the dark, his white face showing clearly. We both stabbed forwards with our blades at the same time. He could not see my face and his sword slid harmlessly over my shoulder. Ragnar's Spirit pierced his mouth. Suddenly I caught sight of a warrior in a long mail shirt with a skeggox and shield and he was moving towards me. I made directly for him and I did not slow down. He swung his axe in a huge arc. I raised Ragnar's Spirit. Without slowing I spun around so that the axe head flew harmlessly through the air and missed me completely. I turned my sword and brought it crashing down on to his helmet. Bagsecg had made a wondrous weapon and the gods had perfected it. The sharpened edge went through the iron of the helmet and through his head. Haaken and Cnut killed the other two bodyguards of this Jarl. I stepped over the body and saw that there were no more warriors before me. They were fleeing down the valley. The warrior in the mail must have been their leader. I saw his three oathsworn lying around him.

We turned to see how Bjorn and Harald were doing with the rest of the column. They were surrounded. We were the only men left outside the Saxon lines. Haaken grinned in the dark and shouted, "Ulfheonar!" We threw ourselves at the backs of the warriors before us. My sword sliced into one Saxon. His companion turned and tried to hit me with his sword. The edge caught on my mail shirt. I was too close to him to use my sword and so I head butted him. The front of my helmet had a metal strip running down the middle and it was sharp. He fell in a bloody heap at my feet. I stepped over him as I stabbed forward blindly. The press of men made it hard to swing our weapons and I took to punching. The cross guard of my sword took an eye from one man and the boss of my shield broke another's nose with a satisfying crack. When these two fell I had a space. I took the opportunity to swing my blade shouting, as I did so, "Ragnar's spirit!" Cnut and Haaken told me later that the sword seemed to glow in the dark but I did not see that. I saw the Saxons quail before me as I hacked, slashed and stabbed in a desperate attempt to reach Bjorn.

Suddenly there were no more Saxons before us. I saw Bjorn and Harald. Both were surrounded by the bodies of the Saxons they had slain. Bjorn shouted, "Shield wall!" We turned into a defensive circle in case the Saxons returned. They did not.

No one had the breath to speak. I was sweating and I felt blood trickling down my arm but I was alive and I knew not how. We stood there as dawn slowly broke. All of us expected the Saxons to attack again. They outnumbered us and we would have kept fighting until our enemies were dead but still they did not come.

"Go and find our wounded. Sweyn, return to the citadel and tell Olaf what has happened. We will continue to Duboglassio." We could see that Sweyn was wounded and he would be no good if it came to a fight.

As Sweyn ran back along the valley Harald said, "We still go on? There are so few of us."

Bjorn nodded, "We gave our word and the Jarl will be expecting us."

"But he would not expect us to go after this."

Bjorn's voice hardened. "We gave our word. We march."

There were just twenty of us left. The four wounded were left to guard the weapons of those we had killed. Including Bjorn, just five of the Ulfheonar lived. It was a grisly path we trod. We could see how many had been killed and it marked the trail to Duboglassio. When we passed the mail shirted warrior I had killed Haaken said, "This mail belongs to Dragon Heart, he slew the warrior with one blow."

I did not say it then but I would give the mail to Cnut. Without him, I would not have survived that day. No Saxon came close to my right arm. We found dead and dying men for the next mile. Many had been wounded and had tried to get home. We saw where they had reached before they died.

Haaken said, "I have counted thirty dead so far."

"Out of how many though?"

It was the first time I had fought with Harald and unlike my friends he was a half empty warrior. He thought the worst in every situation. We preferred to think of what we had achieved. It was mid morning before we reached Duboglassio. We had seen the smoke rising as we had approached. I hoped that Jarl Butar would understand why we were late.

The gate of the fort lay open with dead Saxons around it. I saw some of our warriors too. They had died with their swords in their hands. Butar and Eric strode over to us as we entered the compound. Bjorn dropped to his knee. "I am sorry Jarl Butar, we are late."

"Rise, Bjorn. I know what you did. We captured some of the Saxons with whom you fought. The rest ran to their last refuge. It was you and your men who defeated Aella and his army. A handful of you defeated seventy warriors. They were not the fyrd. You have done more than I could have hoped. The island is nearly ours."

This time we would not be leaving the Saxon fort. Eric and Harald would hold it while we returned to Hrams-a, with the booty and the wounded. For the first time we had male slaves. These were not the warriors whom we had fought, but the fishermen from the village. I wondered how they would be used. The Saxons would kill all the males when they went slave raiding.

Jarl Butar was tireless as he instructed Harald and Eric on what they should do. For their part the two leaders had joined our forces and were now being rewarded. "When we have more men Harald then there is another site on the northern end of the island but for now Eric holds Duboglassio for me."

"I am your oathsworn and I am happy to do your bidding." He looked at me. "And this young warrior is a revelation. He looks barely old enough to shave and yet he is like a berserker when he fights."

Jarl Butar looked at me, "Your mother would not be happy to see you being reckless."

"I was not, Jarl Butar. The three of us knew that they feared us for I heard them shout to each other that we were ghosts." I took my black helmet off. "They could not see us in the dark. It is why we won. Had they known there were so few of us they could easily have beaten us but they had no idea of our numbers and they were defeated by their own fear."

Harald shook his head. "I think you do yourself a disservice, Dragon Heart, and you are truly well named. I saw the Jarl you killed. Your sword went through his helmet and his skull. That was a mighty blow."

"The warrior was Jarl Sigfrid. His men fled when he fell and we captured many of them." Butar nodded. "You did well and we shall reward you. Now let us embark."

I looked at Cnut and shook my head. "My brothers and I would return to the field. There is booty we wish to collect."

"You should come back with the rest of us on the *'Ran'*. You must be exhausted."

"With your permission, Jarl, we will take some of these slaves and a hand cart and bring back the mail shirts we found."

Jarl Butar shook his head, "I owe you that at least, but be back before nightfall or you can answer to your mother."

I had not asked my two companions but I knew that they would do as I asked. The four slaves we took were tethered to each other by a halter around the neck. Their hands were free but they were unarmed. They pulled the handcart looking fearfully over their shoulders at us. I have to

Viking Slave

admit that we did look fearsome. As we walked Haaken said, "I will get my helmet blackened too. It is effective."

"It also makes them stronger. I am glad that I wore my wolf skin too."

"We will go hunting this year and get ours too." We were still excited about the battle which had seemed impossible to survive and yet, somehow, we had.

I found myself thinking of the dead. "The Ulfheonar are fewer now."

"Aye but they are stronger because of it." Haaken looked at me. "You are younger than I am and yet you took the decision you did. How did you know what to do?"

"I cannot put it into words but thoughts came into my head. When I grip the sword I feel that no one can defeat me."

Cnut pointed to the blood on my shirt. "You were lucky that blow was not harder. You should wear your deer hide beneath the mail."

"You are right and if I were you I would have a metal strip put on the front of your helmet. Your head can become a weapon too."

Haaken laughed, "Your head already is my friend. It will be interesting to fight alongside you."

We soon reached the first of the dead Saxons and we collected their weapons. When we reached the man with the mail shirt I said to the thralls, "Who is this?" I needed his identity confirming.

"This was Jarl Sigfrid. He ruled Duboglassio for Prince Aella. He was a mighty warrior."

I had spoken in Saxon and one of the others asked, "Who slew him, lord?"

"I did." They looked at me in amazement and I could see the disbelief in their eyes. "Take off his shirt and put it on the cart with the weapons." His helmet was ruined but his axe could be used. I deigned to use an axe but many of the warriors liked them. I found them too dangerous. If you struck an enemy then he would die but it was too easy to avoid the stroke. I preferred the sword. I said to Cnut, "The mail is for you, my brother."

Cnut was speechless. He embraced me and Haaken looked crestfallen. We would have to get a mail byrnie for him too.

When we reached the wounded I had the slaves lift them on to the cart and they pulled them as well. We had to help push the laden cart up the steep parts but it would be worth it. This was our plunder and we would be rich men. I did not need any of it but I wanted my brothers to share in my good fortune.

Viking Slave

It was dusk when we reached the citadel. We saw a tunnel of torches lining the road to the port and we headed that way. All the warriors were there. The slaves held the torches and the warriors banged their shields chanting, "Ulfheonar," over and over. It was one of the proudest moments of my life. Jarl Butar embraced us all. "With warriors like these our line will last a thousand years!"

There was a huge roar. Bjorn said, "You three have done all that you need to do. We will take over now."

I looked at Cnut and nodded. He grabbed the mail shirt. "And I will take this gift from my brother." All the warriors laughed and I left with Butar.

If I thought I would get the same treatment from my mother I was wrong. "Get that mail shirt off and I will tend to your wound. When will you learn that you cannot fight every Saxon alone?"

As my shirt was pulled from me I said, "I was not alone, I had Haaken and Cnut with me."

"Aye and you took on a whole army. Ragnar would not wish you to throw your life away."

"Mother I will not, I promise." She did not understand what it was like to hold a sword in battle and face an enemy. Ragnar had made me believe in myself. I was not afraid of anyone. Since I had had the sword touched by lightning, I had felt invincible.

We spent the next few months consolidating what we had. Our patrols now left from Duboglassio and were able to control and contain the Saxons who were restricted to the southern side of the island. We had two dragon ships now and other small boats. They constantly harassed the Saxon fishing boats so that they could not fish while all the time we improved our weapons. We were becoming stronger as they were becoming weaker. Butar showed how clever he was at this time. He did not push to finally defeat the Saxons. They were weakening day by day. Instead he sent Olaf with a boat load of warriors to trade with the Franks. We now had much plunder and booty. We needed the swords and the grain which Sigismund could provide. It only left us with twenty warriors to guard the citadel but Jarl Butar was confident that no one would attempt to attack us.

Bagsecg was overrun with work. Everyone wanted a blade or a helmet. It reached the point where Butar had to restrict the number of requests. Bagsecg could no longer be used as a warrior for he worked as a smith full time. Men still came but not in dragon boats. Sometimes four or five half starved warriors would arrive desperate to fight in this haven of our people. The name of Jarl Butar was known throughout the Norse world and was respected.

Olaf returned in time for the midsummer solstice. We had not had time for a feast the previous year but we had food aplenty now. We controlled all of the island save for the southern corner and we had gathered every sheep, cow and goat. The Jarl had had the slaves clear much of the woods close to Hrams-a and the pasture suited them. The only food we lacked was pork. We would need to acquire some pigs which meant we would have to raid the mainland.

Olaf had done well in the trade and we had more of the Frankish blades. The grain was sufficient for the next few months but another reason for raiding would be to get the grain the Saxons harvested in the autumn. The Jarl had already begun to use the male slaves to till the land for our own crops. They would take a year to produce food.

Olaf also brought news and I was able to hear it first hand. My reward for my actions had been to include me in the senior council of warriors: the Jarl, Olaf, Eric, Harald and Bjorn. There was also an acceptance that I would be Jarl Butar's heir.

"Harald One Eye is set to become a king. His little Saxon princess finally bore him a son and it must have been the incentive he needed. The whole of our land from Stavanger south is his and he has ten ships now, all fully manned. It is said that the king of the Danes is worried about his neighbour."

Bjorn's face darkened, "So long as he stays there I care not."

"No Bjorn, he will not stay there. We know what a perilous land it is. He will begin to raid the land of the Angles again. Look what we did with one small boat and a handful of men. Do you think that Aethelred will be able to stop him?"

"It is not Aethelred, Jarl Butar, he died. There is a civil war going on. Osbert and Eardwulf are disputing the throne."

"Then it is even more likely that Harald will seize the opportunity. We may have to fight him one day so let us build up our strength. We will let the Saxons in the south wither and die. We now have three boats. We will use two to raid the mainland and the land to the north. We will leave one to watch the Saxons here. The land to the north looks like wild country and we may achieve much booty. Bjorn I would have you lead this raid with men from the three towns."

Harald was quite an aggressive warrior. "I think that we should finish off Aella. He cannot have many men left now."

"The piece of land he holds will not feed his people and we would not gain enough from a battle. We need more warriors and the pickings will be greater on the mainland."

"I beg permission to accompany Bjorn on the raid then Jarl."

"So long as your town is defended and the roads patrolled I am happy." Eric was always quiet. "And what of you, Eric, how is your family settled in Duboglassio?"

"My mother, the Lady Agnetha, is more than grateful. Aella's hall is very comfortable and Ingrid too is happy."

"And what of your sister, Erica?"

"She mopes and moans. She had not been married long when her husband was killed. She is just a little younger than Dragon Heart here and she feels her life is over."

I shook my head. "Speaking as the youngest here she should be grateful for her youth. She has her whole life ahead of her."

"Perhaps you could speak with here then. I think she might take advice from someone who is closer in age to her."

"I will do so."

"And now we must arrange for the celebrations for Midsummer. Olaf can take the Ran and some hunters. They can go to the mainland and hunt some game. I am desirous of pig!" I must have shown my excitement for he added, "And it will just be hunting. We want no raiding yet. When we do raid I want it to be successful. You can scout out suitable landing sites but that is all."

Olaf chuckled. "Besides we only have ten days until the solstice. We will have to leave at dawn."

We made sure that all of the Ulfheonar save Bjorn were aboard. I knew that Haaken and Cnut would want to hunt the wolf. I just hoped that Olaf would allow it. It was a short journey to the mainland. We headed north east. We saw no towns but there were farmsteads. We also saw fishermen's huts on some of the islands. When we landed, Olaf and five men stayed with the boat. There were twenty of us and we split into four parties. I had left Ragnar's Spirit in the hall for this day I would just need my bow.

Cnut led us through the forests looking for a trail. We soon found the signs of wild boars. Haaken and Sweyn both had boar spears for a wild boar was a fierce opponent. I had heard of a boar charging even though it was riddled with arrows. Cnut and I led. My bow was notched and ready. We heard the snuffling of the pigs just ahead of us. When we stopped we could smell them. There were only five of us and we spread out. Sweyn and Haaken stood in the centre. Cnut and Ejnar were on their left and I was on the right. We approached step by step and we always kept step with each other. They were a family. There was a male and a sow with six suckling pigs. Haaken pointed to the male and then at Cnut and Ejnar. Sweyn pointed at the female and me.

I drew back. When I heard Cnut's arrow being loosed I released mine. I notched another for the sow hurled herself in my direction. My first arrow was in her shoulder and it did not even slow her down. My second struck her eye as she leapt at me. Sweyn rammed the spear down her throat. I whipped Screaming Death out and slashed at her throat as Sweyn fought to hold her. Her body sagged as her life blood erupted across the woodland. The boar had taken more arrows and Ejnar was nursing a bloody leg where the boar's tusk had raked him.

"Grab the piglets!"

That was easier said than done. We had a sack with us and we put each one in as we caught it. I bound Ejnar's leg and gave him the writhing sack of pigs. Haaken pointed to the sea, some two miles distant. "You return the pigs to the ship and we will bring these two."

While he and Cnut found the two straight branches we would use to carry the enormous beasts back I headed up the slope. I was looking for more animal tracks. This land seemed to teem with life and I wanted as much information to give Olaf as possible. I found deer tracks as well as game birds and then I stumbled upon some gold; the spoor of wolves. I discovered the tracks after searching around and I followed them for half a mile until they disappeared into a rocky cleft. I marked the spot in my mind and then returned.

"Where in Thor's name have you been?"

"I was looking for animal tracks and I found plenty."

"Deer?"

"Deer, birds and…" I paused, "wolves."

Cnut's face was like a small child's who has just been given a treat. "Where?"

"Up there in the rocks."

"Come let us take these beasts back to Olaf and we can work out how to get ourselves some wolf skins." The stakes were already sharpened and we thrust them in the mouths of the pigs and out through their rear.

Viking Slave

Then we lifted them. They were incredibly heavy. That meant a fine feast so we did not mind. We were the first of the hunters to return and Olaf was delighted with our catch. "There are two males and two females in those pigs. If we can catch another couple we will have our own herd."

"We found more tracks up there. Can we go and hunt some more?"

"The others aren't back yet. Aye we can. We will leave tomorrow." Olaf was in a good mood and did not suspect our motives.

I did feel a little deceitful as we left. We had not told the truth but we had not lied. "You did not tell a lie, Dragon Heart. You said we would hunt and we will. We will bring back deer. We just might have some wolves too." Haaken tried to make me feel better.

Ejnar stayed with the boat as his wound would hinder us. There were just the four of us and we almost ran back into the woods. I found the spoor again and Cnut and I notched arrows. The other two would use the boar spears. I remembered when Ragnar and I had been attacked; the male wolf took as much killing as the boar had. The higher we went the less cover there was. We lost the tracks on some scree which lay below a ledge. We all looked at each other. That would be where the den was. As soon as we stepped on to the rocks they would make a noise and alert the wolves.

Haaken and Cnut went to the right and edged along the last of the solid ground while Sweyn and I waited. Once they were in position they waved at us to move. As we had expected, the rocks skittered beneath our feet. Surprisingly there was no roar or flash of a wolf's teeth and we edged up towards the ledge. I stopped. I smelled wolf. I knew that Sweyn had not. I could still remember the dead wolf bleeding on top of me and it was a smell so powerful that I would never forget. I touched Sweyn's arm to halt him. It was just in time for the male wolf leapt from his place of concealment. Sweyn barely had time to jab the spear forwards. I loosed an arrow which struck him in his side and then Sweyn and the wolf tumbled down the slope. The female was close behind and I had no chance to fit another arrow I jabbed the bow forwards and she yelped as it pierced her eye. I reached down for Screaming Death as I held my left arm forward. Her teeth grabbed my arm which was, fortunately, covered by deer hide. We, too, tumbled down the slope. I stabbed her in the side with my seax as we fell but her teeth sank into the hide and I felt them begin to puncture my skin. As we rolled over my arm came free and I stabbed her as hard as I could through her eye. Suddenly she went limp as the blade entered her brain and ended her life.

I pushed the beast away and looked for Sweyn. He had also been bitten by the wolf but it was dead and he pushed it away from him. I helped him to his feet. He saw the she wolf. "How did you kill it?"

I held up the seax. "With this."

He shook his head. "They are fierce animals and hard to kill. I am glad that I do not have to do that again."

Just then Haaken and Cnut rushed up. Haaken looked shaken. "I thought they would have fled towards us. Only one young male came that way and we killed him." He looked at the two corpses. "You two did far better."

"Where are the others?"

I pointed up the slope where three wolves led their cubs to safety. "They are a very clever animal and more cunning than we give them credit for." I looked at the wolves. "You three have your skins. It is a shame we could not get one for Ejnar."

Cnut shook his head, "It is *wyrd*. This is how it was meant to be."

It was hard for the four of us, especially with our wounds, but we managed to get the three dead wolves down to the boat where the others were waiting. I am not certain what was worse, the attack from the wolves or the tongue lashing we received from Olaf. Fortunately the others had been as successful as we and they killed eight deer and captured some tame pigs from a farm. If they had not then I think we might have been left on the beach.

Chapter 12

While we received rebukes from Olaf, Butar and my mother, from our comrades we found ourselves drowning in a sea of praise. Our wounds were seen as marks of honour and poor Ejnar cursed his own wound which had prevented him from claiming his skin. The pigs were seen as our greatest triumph. We could interbreed the wild boars which had the best meat and the more docile tame pigs. Once our grain was harvested we would be able to withstand hunger far easier. We had made the whole island more likely to survive and added to our legend- the Ulfheonar.

The women who brewed the beer had been busy brewing ready for the midsummer solstice and there was a yeasty smell in the village. Many young warriors were taking brides at this most propitious time of year. This was also good for the community; we would have more warriors when the children grew. Finally, the wheat was being used to bake bread and the animals prepared for the cooking. We would feast as we had never feasted before. That was certainly true for me. I had not really participated in one of these feasts before and I was looking forward to this one. Mother had made me a new tunic. The ones I had had in Ulfberg were now far too small for me. "I have seen enough of you dressed for war. Just for once I would like to see you dressed as my son." I didn't mind.

The preparations for the day started well before dawn. We had lit the fires in their pits during the night and before the sun rose we had lifted the carcasses on to the metal spits. The slaves would spend the day turning them. There would be no celebration for the thralls. Everyone stood to watch the sun rise in the east. This would be the longest day of the year and was something to celebrate. As soon as the sun fully appeared over the horizon the couples were married. There were ten couples and, while the ceremony was brief, each couple had to have the same attention.

Then the feasting began. We had our wedding breakfast. There was no meat involved but we had freshly caught and cooked salmon and shell fish as well as sweet bread and cakes. I did not drink as much as my fellows. Ragnar had taught me well. It enabled me to watch the others and see how they changed when they drank. Eric just smiled more while Harald became more and more morose. Cnut became silly while Haaken began to play cruel tricks on his friends. I had the greatest time watching them all.

After the wedding breakfast we all retired for a sleep ready for the games. We would have archery contests, axe throwing contests, wrestling bouts and, of course, the tug of war. The tug of war would be the last contest of the day and would be over one of the food pits. The Ulfheonar were a team and everyone wanted to defeat us. There was honour to be had from winning and pain if you lost. The ones at the front could be burned!

After my sleep I went to the archery field. It would be the only contest, save for the tug of war, which I would enter. Some of my opponents were already in their cups and the contest was decided between four of us. After a hard fought contest I won and was awarded ten metal tipped arrows; it was a rich prize. I was happy to have won but I did not feel special. The majority of the archers were in no condition to loose an arrow. I spent the afternoon watching the other bouts.

Eric and his wife sought me out. "Dragon Heart, you promised to speak with Erica did you not?"

I had remembered but now that it came to it I was getting cold feet. I sighed, a promise was a promise. If you were a warrior and said you would do something then you had to. I would have preferred facing a she wolf than speaking to a pretty young and unhappy girl. "I will speak with her now. Where is she?"

Eric pointed to the beach where she sat forlornly alone on a rock at the water's edge. I would rather have faced a warband again but I had given my word that I would help the Jarl and I walked over to her. I had seen her from a distance before but never close up. She was about the same age as I was. She was pretty with blonde pigtails. She looked so slender that I thought a strong wind would blow her over. I put on a smile I did not feel. She heard me coming and stood. "No, please don't get up on account of me."

She looked beyond me. Her brother and his wife were anxiously watching us. "Oh I see, my brother has sent you."

I had never lied and I could not bring myself to do so now. "Yes, he is worried about you."

"And what can you do to help me? Will you fight a wolf for me or kill a hundred Saxons?"

I felt confused and did not know what to say, "If it would make you smile then, yes, I would."

She suddenly laughed and when she did her face changed and became a summer's morning. "I believe you would." She gestured for me to sit next to her. "I admire you although I think your name is a little pretentious, Dragon Heart!"

I blushed, "It was given to me by Butar's father and I loved the old man. My birth name was Gareth but no one could say it and the name the other children in my village called was Crow because they hated me." I shrugged, "I answer to almost anything... even pretentious, whatever that means."

She laughed again, "I like you and I am pleased that you do not take yourself so seriously. My brother does. And yet you are a hero and not much older than me. It is remarkable."

"I have been lucky that is all."

"And I heard that you were a slave once."

"Aye, as was my mother. She taught me to make the best of what you are given. Perhaps you should be that way too."

"My husband was killed almost as soon as we married. You cannot understand that."

"True, I have never been married but I have lost and I have mourned. But I believe that you honour the dead by living as well as you can, and doing the best that you are able."

She took my hand and held it between hers. "I apologise, Gareth. I misjudged you. I thought you were like the other young warriors so full of themselves and their glory that they saw nothing else. You are different and I would talk with you and learn about you."

I smiled back and held her hand in mine, "And I am not like the other young warriors. Saxon blood flows in half of me and the other half is from the old ones from across the sea, the Welsh. I have learned to be like your people but that was because of Ragnar."

We then sat and talked. She told me of her husband whom she had barely known. I think that was part of the problem. She felt guilty because she had not loved him. She had not had time to love him. I told her about my time with the Saxons and Ragnar. I never mentioned any of the fighting. There was no need. She had heard that already. We talked so long that we were not aware of the passing of time until I was aware that it was becoming slightly colder and the sun was setting. Something made me turn and the people of the village were all there looking at us. I had no idea why. We both stood, suddenly aware that we were still holding hands. We disengaged. My mother came forwards and she was smiling.

"I am sorry, mother. I did not mean to keep Erica from her family for so long."

She shook her head and I saw tears coursing down her cheeks. "No my son, the gods have touched you again. We came to say goodbye to the summer sun and your heads were surrounded by a golden halo. Those who follow the White Christ would have taken a meaning from it but for us it is symbol of the future." She came and put her arms around us both. "Come let us all celebrate with the gods for this has been the best longest day ever."

She held our hands as she led us away and everyone cheered and shouted. Erica and I were confused but we smiled and, blushing, went to the others. The Ulfheonar were all drunk but they crowded around me and slapped me on the back. Eric shook my hand and said, "Thank you, Dragon Heart. What a change you have wrought in my sister."

Butar slapped me on the back and said, "Gods but my father was right! There are more layers to you than an onion. Just when you think you know all there is to know your surprise us. Come let us eat."

I wondered if they had all eaten of the magic mushroom while I talked with Erica or perhaps this was a dream and I would wake up. I did not know but the rest of the evening passed in a blur of sagas and songs, eating and drinking until, at some point, I passed out and the day ended for me.

I awoke in my own bed with a thumping head. I could hear a wailing which sounded like a creature from the Otherworld until I realised that it was my sister. She was crying for attention. I opened my eyes gingerly and prepared to face the day. The events of the afternoon and evening came flooding back as I dressed. It was not a feast day and I did not wear the fine linen. Instead I wore my warrior clothes. I would return to the warrior hall this day for it was back to the life of an Ulfheonar.

My mother and Butar were at the table eating when I entered. Mother was feeding my sister. Butar shook his head but there was a smile upon his face. "It is the first time I have seen drink defeat you. Have you learned a lesson?"

"Aye, I have. I do not know what possessed me to do so."

They exchanged a knowing look and my mother said, "Midsummer madness perhaps. It strikes just once a year but the effects can last forever."

It sounded enigmatic as though there was another meaning but I was in no mood for riddles. "Well my madness is over now and I shun powerful drink."

"Eat, my son. It is the best cure. You will not feel like it but it will do you good."

I did not want to eat but I heeded my mother's words and forced the honeyed porridge down. When it stayed down I did feel better. "I will return today to the warrior hall and give you your life back again."

"You are always welcome here." Mother looked sad that I should want to leave her again.

"I know but I am a man now and should live with men."

Again they exchanged a look which I did not understand. I took my belongings and trudged back up the hill to the citadel. The bright sunlight brought my thumping head to the fore. I wondered how long it would take to disappear. When I reached the hall, my comrades were asleep. I could see the signs that they, too, had had too much to drink. Had the Saxons had their wits about them then they could have walked in and captured all of us for there was none in a fit state to fight. The exception was Bjorn who was awake and sharpening his sword.

"I see you have risen." He waved a hand at my comrades. "We will get little work done today."

"And for that I am grateful. But is not our work finished?"

"No my young friend. We need food for the winter. The next two months will see us raiding to fill our larders. Olaf was not idle when you went hunting and he has found us a couple of settlements of farmers we can raid."

"And what of Aella? I know that Harald is a little impatient but I agree with him. We should scotch this snake quickly before he tries another sneak attack on us."

"Butar is right but Olaf will be taking the *'Ran'* to see how many men he has left. Jarl Butar is not reckless. If he feels Aella is a threat then he will be quashed."

I was still not convinced. We would be looking over our shoulders the whole time. We would be waiting for them to attack again. I thought it would be better to risk losing men and rid ourselves of the threat. I was one of the rowers selected by Olaf to take out the *'Ran'* the next day. Some of the warriors had still not recovered from the excesses of the feast. As we rowed I was teased incessantly by Haaken and Cnut.

"So, our Dragon Heart has found a flower to pluck."

Viking Slave

"What do you mean?"

"Do not try to fool us. The whole town saw you holding hands and whispering to each other on the beach."

"Oh Erica, I was just talking to her as her brother asked. I believe she will be happier now."

They both burst out laughing as did the rowers around us. "I can guarantee that for she has her heart set on a Dragon Heart. That is clear to everyone."

They were wrong. She was just a friend and I had had precious few of those before. "You are being a fool now, Cnut."

"I will make a wager then brother. I wager my throwing axe against Screaming Death that you will be married before the year is out and it will be to Erica."

I laughed, "I will take that bet for the throwing axe you have is a fine weapon and I will learn how to use it for the contest next year."

"And I will make a new belt for my seax. It will be an excellent second weapon."

Olaf had heard enough. "If you can talk then you are not rowing hard enough. Let us up the beat." The rate increased until *'Ran'* flew across the water. If he thought he was punishing us he was wrong. I finally sweated out the last of the ale from the feast and I felt that satisfying burn from my arm muscles. I felt better than I had in days.

The last Saxon settlement on the island now had a wall around it. There were ten or so fishing boats in the harbour but nothing larger. Olaf took us really close so that we could see as much of the inside as possible. Twenty warriors marched down to the harbour wall. They had bows but it was unlikely that they could hit us. Half of the Saxons had mail. They were oathsworn of Aella. He still had formidable warriors left. We rowed slowly off shore so that Olaf could see how many men there were still.

When we reached Hrams-a, Butar greeted us. "Well Olaf, do they still remain."

"They do, Jarl Butar. They have increased their defences and look set to stay."

"We need to know what is going on inside there. I thought that they would be becoming weaker by now."

"They are still getting fish. We just wait until winter strikes them then they will hurt."

"No, Olaf. I want a peaceful winter for us this year. We were hungry when we first arrived. I would have our people happy."

Jarl Butar was not the same leader he had been. There would have been a time when he would have heeded Olaf's advice. I knew what it was; it was my sister, Eurwen. She had changed Butar and he was now less a warrior and more a family man. I knew that I could help to change his mind. The idea popped into my head. It may have been Ragnar; I was no longer sure when it was my own thoughts or Ragnar's. "Send me into the settlement."

"Send you? Why?"

"I can pass for a Saxon. I can pretend to be an escaped slave and find out what they are doing."

"How would you escape?" Olaf could see the possibilities.

"He is not going!"

"Jarl Butar, I am Ulfheonar and I am happy to do this." Even as I was explaining my idea I was working out how it would work. "The other Ulfheonar could chase me to make it look as though I was an escaping slave. They would not suspect anything."

"But you have fought them."

"I fought them with a face mask. I will not have weapons and not have armour. They will ask me of your settlement and I can tell them untruths."

"You mean lie."

That did not sit well with me. "I will tell them just enough to frighten them without lying."

I could see Butar wavering.

I think Olaf wanted me to do it and he argued in my favour. "The Ulfheonar could wait nearby to give him aid in case he needed it. It would answer your questions once and for all. I believe Dragon Heart can do this."

"If I were not your wife's son would you sanction this?"

The last argument persuaded him. "If anything happens to you then I will destroy every Saxon who remains on the isle."

Bjorn too was concerned. "This is brave and it is risky."

"It is what we do and who we are. Besides if it makes our life on this island safer then so be it."

Haaken and Cnut were determined not to let me down and they both swore that they would not leave without me. We did not tell my mother or anyone else. It was not only the Ulfheonar who accompanied me.

Viking Slave

Butar and twenty warriors also came. They would wait a mile away from the settlement while the Ulfheonar would hide within sight of the walls. To make it look realistic, Cnut and Godfrid would loose arrows close to me. I had told them how I would run and, hopefully, the Saxons would believe the ruse.

Butar put his hands on my shoulders as he said farewell, "Just find out their numbers and their mood. Escape any way that you can. Egill will be fishing off the harbour. You could swim out to him."

"I am not a good swimmer. I will come out the way I go in; running!" I hoped that I would be able to escape. As long as they did not bind me then I would be able to make good my escape. My five comrades clasped my arm.

Bjorn nodded. He made sure my thrall collar fitted. Bagsecg had weakened the pin which held it and I would be able to break it if I needed to. He seemed satisfied. "This will make a good tale. Come back to us." He clasped my forearm as the older warriors did. It gave me the courage I needed. Bjorn thought that I was an equal.

I started to run. I erupted from the trees some four hundred paces from the walls. I did not look back but I jinked from side to side. The arrows flew by perilously close to me and I hoped that the sentries were watching. I began to shout in Saxon, "Help! Help! They are upon me."

The men on the walls began to loose arrows at my comrades. The first part of the plan had succeeded. When I was fifty paces from the walls one of the sentries pointed to my right, "The gate is on the other side; run around and we will protect you."

I ran around the edge of the ditch and found myself amongst their houses. A gaggle of people started at me but I kept running until I eventually reached the gate. Two mailed warriors roughly grabbed me and hauled me towards the warrior hall I had seen from the *'Ran'*. I was dragged up the steps and there, sitting on a chair on a raised dais was Aella. The last time I had seen him he had been fighting with Butar. He looked thin and drawn and, as he spoke I saw him wincing. My step father had wounded him badly.

"Who are you and why did those warriors pursue you?"

There was suspicion in his voice and his men's swords were in their hands. My story would now either save or damn me. "I am Gareth son of Myfanwy and I was taken, just before the midsummer solstice."

"Where was your village?"

Viking Slave

"It is over the water in the land of Northumbria; the village of Loncastre, near to the old Roman fort. It is there no longer for they killed the men and enslaved the rest of us."

"How did you survive? You look strong enough to be a warrior. They kill such as you."

"I do not know. I had no time to fight for I was captured early in the raid."

There was still suspicion in their voices. I just prayed that no one had visited the place I had described. Olaf had given me the name for he had found it while we were hunting. Other raiders had destroyed it sometime in the past.

"And how did you escape? None have made it from their halls yet."

"I was lucky. They had me collecting wild ponies from the hills and they did not watch me closely enough. I manage to outrun them. I had only been there for a week and I was still strong. Many of the other slaves are weaker."

It seemed to me that their suspicion lessened a little. "So they are capturing horses now. How many warriors do they have?"

I would not need to lie now. I could tell them the truth. "They have three dragon ships and I counted over a hundred warriors in their two warrior halls."

One of the bodyguards sheathed his sword. "I told you, lord, that they were getting more men. We should have attacked them sooner."

Aella waved the argument away with his hand. "We tried that twice and both times we lost more than they did. Until Osbald and Eardwulf have decided who will be king we will get no more men."

"By then it will be too late for the food will have all gone."

Aella shouted angrily, "Silence. I was charged by King Aethelred with holding this island which his forebears captured and I will not relinquish to a handful of pirates. The new king will send us aid once we know who the new king is. Take this man and hold him until I have decided what to do with him."

"I came here for protection!" I had to play the part but I was afraid that I would not see my friends again.

"You would have been better off staying where you were and, besides Saxon, there is something about you which I do not like."

I was dragged roughly away and taken to the far end of the warrior hall. They tied a rope through the thrall collar and fixed it to a ring in the wall. "Can I have something to drink then?"

The guard laughed at me. "Until we know what you are we will waste no water or food on you."

I assumed a hurt look and sullenly sat there watching the hall. It suited me because I could both see and hear all that went on. I pretended to be exhausted from my flight to safety. My appearance prompted a flood of visitors to speak with Aella. They all stared at me as they entered and then they would rush towards Aella. There was a great deal of consternation amongst the inhabitants of this last Saxon refuge. I was able to work out that there were fifty people left who were not warriors. I gathered that many had fled to the mainland on the fishing boats. The civil war had put a halt to that but it explained the small numbers I had seen. It was harder to count the warriors but I did discover that Aella still had twelve oathsworn and all of them had armour of some description. As for the others, I would have to wait until they slept to count them.

I found the most valuable information when they ate. It was a frugal meal by Saxon standards. From the smell it appeared to be a thin soup made from poor quality fish. Many of the warriors looked undernourished and they all complained about the poor rations. They moaned about the lack of beer and water. I knew that the supplies were a problem. I briefly opened my eyes to count the warriors. The hall was not full. There appeared to be less than fifty of them. I knew that there would be a few more on the walls. I closed my eyes and lolled my head forward to rest on the thrall collar. I listened once more. They complained about the houses which had been built next to the walls. They had wanted them pulled down to make their walls safer. They were angry that they had been let down by Aella. The ones furthest from him and closest to me and the door argued that he should have kept his ship and then they could have attacked our settlement. There appeared to be little unity. They were all despondent and appeared to want to either attack us or leave the island. Aella was under siege from without and within.

After they had eaten I was dragged to Aella's throne for more questioning. "Where are all these warriors you talk of?"

"I saw them at the place they call Hrams-a during the midsummer solstice but the next day many of them left. I believe they have two more settlements but I never saw them."

I could see nods from the bodyguards. I had merely confirmed what they had thought already. "And why do they not attack?"

That was a trick question. He was trying to catch me out and I chose my words carefully. "I was a slave and I did not speak their language. How would I know what their plans are?"

They seemed satisfied with that as though I had passed some sort of test. Aella turned to his bodyguards. "Are the pursuers still close by?"

"The sentries report that they think there are men in the woods to the north but they could not discern numbers. When the scouts went to look for them they found nothing. There must be few of them and they are hiding. I do not think that they will be a threat to us."

"Why would they wait around? Perhaps this slave knows more than he is saying."

One of the guards shrugged, "Perhaps he does not know what he knows. We should ask different questions."

Aella winced and clutched his leg as though it pained him. "I am too tired tonight but tomorrow we will find out all that he knows. We will see if hot irons and the loss of an eye changes his story. Make sure he is watched and secured."

The thought of torture terrified me but it did not change what I needed to do. I had to look for a chance to escape with my new found knowledge. The warriors soon ignored me. One young warrior was left to watch me. He stared at me for a while and then, after checking that I was securely fastened to the wall, he lay on the floor. Soon the hall was filled with the sound of sleeping men. I feigned sleep. I heard footsteps and I opened my eyes to see a warrior leaving the hall to relieve himself. The youth opposite popped his eyes open when the footsteps sounded. After the warrior came back into the hall, the young warrior settled back into his stare. After a few moments his eye lids drooped and he slept. I waited until the rhythm of snores and heavy breathing resumed and I removed the wooden peg from the collar. I lay the collar down and slowly rose to my feet. I did it agonisingly slowly. It was agony for I had been in the same position throughout the meal. I stepped backwards, never taking my eyes from the young warrior. I felt for the door behind me and I slowly opened it. As soon as I felt the chill air I slipped through and closed it again.

I pressed my back into the wall of the hall. I could see the sentries patrolling the ramparts. There looked to be four of them. I tried to remember where the ditch had been. It was only around the landward side. On the town side there was no ditch. I would not risk the gate; instead, I would drop from the wall. I had to find out how they patrolled.

Viking Slave

It looked as though they were mainly on the land side and there was just one guard who occasionally went to the gate. I waited until he had checked the gate and, as he went to join his comrades I ran to the ladder and ascended the gate. I reached it unseen and I crouched down low to the wall. I chanced a view over the side and I saw that the ground was just five paces below me. It would not be far to drop. I had just begun to climb over when my absence was discovered. The youth ran from the hall shouting. As soon as they heard the shouting the guards looked over and saw me on top of the wall. There was little point in being discreet and I dropped to the ground.

I ran as fast as I could. Had they been more alert the guards would have run to that side of the wall and tried to hit me with arrows but they ran to where I had been and that gave me time. I knew that the warriors would soon pursue me and I needed to put as much distance between us as I could. I ran through the houses and suddenly a face appeared from one of the huts. I swung my hand and punched the man. He fell forwards into the track. I saw the land rising ahead and the trees at the top of the slope. If I could reach those trees then I might stand a chance for I could hide.

I heard a noise behind me and, after checking that the ground ahead had no obstacles I risked a look behind. The warriors were some three hundred paces behind me, their faces white against the dark of the walls. I could not estimate the numbers but there were too many for me to fight. I dug in and ran even harder up the slope. I hoped that they had eaten and drunk too much that night. The eaves of the wood were tantalisingly close and I risked a look behind me. My pursuers were a little further behind and were spreading out. That helped. I gritted my teeth and ran through the pain which coursed through my side. The ground flattened out almost the moment I stepped into the woods and I jerked to my left and ran along the edge of the woods; hopefully, I would be out of sight.

A day without water and food began to take its toll. I changed direction again and began to run deeper into the woods. They were not thick enough for me to hide within but I could run freely. I risked a glance over my shoulder and disaster struck; I tripped over a tree root and crashed to the ground. I knocked the wind from myself and felt a little dizzy. The noise of my crash had alerted my pursuers to my position and I saw them, less than forty paces away as they raced towards me. There were only ten who were close to me but that would be more than enough to ensure that I was captured. This time they would not be so gentle with me.

I struggled to my feet and lurched off into the woods. I could almost smell their foetid breath and I could hear their grunts as they too struggled to get air into their mouths. I would not risk another look behind me. I would run until I was caught and then I would fight.

Suddenly an arrow appeared to come directly for me. I just moved my head slightly and heard the scream as the pursuing warrior was pierced by the missile. A second one and a third followed and two more Saxons hit the ground. Then I heard Bjorn shout, "Ulfheonar!" It was my brothers. I ran five more steps and stopped. Behind me I could see that the Saxons had also stopped and were looking for this unknown attacker. A wolf clad warrior raced from their left and killed one warrior with his sword. Even as they watched his disappearing back a second figure ran from their right and did the same. Two more arrows found their mark and the remaining four warriors edged back to their comrades who were just arriving in numbers.

Cnut appeared next to me. He was almost invisible with his blackened face, black helmet, black armour and wolf skin. He gave me my helmet and wolf skin and then my sword. While I strapped it on, he smeared mud on my face. He grinned in the dark and I saw his teeth. "Move back into the woods. Haaken is to your left."

I did not look for them but I stepped slowly backwards. We moved a step at a time. I saw the Saxons gather. The ones who had reinforced their comrades were fully armed. There were now twenty Saxons and just six of us. Those were better odds than I had just faced. I knew from Cnut's appearance that we would be hard to see and that meant we had an advantage. We knew how many there were of them but they did not know if they faced a few or many. They too advanced cautiously.

I heard Haaken whisper, "Just keep going, Dragon Heart, and all will be well."

I knew from our scouting expeditions that this was not a deep wood and soon we would be out of it. When the trees began to thin I knew that we had reached that point. Haaken's voice came again. "When we are out in the open then turn and run."

That seemed madness but they had concocted this plan and not me. I would obey, I was Ulfheonar. I heard Bjorn's voice this time. "Now!"

I turned and ran. The ground fell before us and I had to work to keep myself upright. I took longer strides. The efforts of the night began to take their toll and I found that I was falling behind Cnut. To my right I saw Haaken and Godfrid and I assumed that Sweyn and Bjorn were to my left. There was a roar from behind as the Saxons saw us clearly. This would be a short battle but it would be glorious.

Then Bjorn shouted, "Turn and stand!" I obeyed. With my sword in my hand I faced the Saxon horde. To my astonishment they were being attacked from both sides. It was Butar and his twenty warriors. We were just spectators. The Saxons stood no chance and they were almost all slaughtered for they were concentrating on us. The one or two who returned would have a tale of terror to tell Aella. I struggled to get my breath and Bjorn clapped on the back.

My stepfather came over to embrace me. "That was well done. They fell into our trap nicely! Haaken and Cnut escort him home. We will bring the weapons. I hope you found some useful information, my young friend."

"So do I!"

Chapter 13

As we walked back over the hills they explained to me how they had been aware that they had been spotted. Had I not come out then they would have assaulted the fort the following night. I was pleased that they had not had to resort to that because we would have lost many men. I told them how they were suspicious both of me and their hidden watchers.

"Besides I know how we can capture this town."

Haaken stopped. "Suddenly you are a leader and you have a plan? How can we do this?"

"I will explain to Butar when I have worked out the right words and the right strategy. I find that I agree with Harald. I think we can rid the island of them before autumn and not wait for them to leave of their own accord."

"You learned much then?"

"Ragnar taught me to listen well and speak little. Last night I spoke not at all and learned much."

We reached Hrams-a by mid morning. My mother stood anxiously with Eurwen in her arms watching for me. I was grateful that she had my sister in her arms for her face was a mixture of relief and anger. "I am glad that you are safe, my son, but furious that you put yourself in such danger. I have spoken with Butar about this and he knows my feelings." I knew she was upset by the fact that she berated me in public and not when we were alone. This must have been boiling inside of her all night.

Now I knew why he had led his warriors to support Bjorn. He wished to be away from my sharp tongued mother. A Saxon shield wall was less frightening. "I am safe, mother, and I do not think I was ever in danger."

"Do not lie to me. I know how close you came to death." My mother's second sight was terrifying. I could keep nothing from her. She pointed with her free arm towards the warrior hall. "And poor Erica has been beside herself with worry. You are thoughtless. She lost a husband and you just go wandering off without regard for anyone."

Now I was confused, "I am sorry. What has Erica got to do with this?"

Exasperated she stormed into Butar's Hall. "Sometimes you are a complete fool. Come in here and I will explain to you!"

Viking Slave

I went in and poured a jug of small beer. "I am sorry, mother. I have obviously done something wrong but I have no idea what."

A smile appeared on her face. "You know I believe you." She laid the sleeping Eurwen down gently in her cot and sat opposite me. "I thought you were playing games with the young girl and her affection. I am sorry; I should have known you better. I forget that you grew up lonely without friends and you did not play with other children. If you had done so then you would have known what I meant." She sighed and looked me directly in the eye. "Erica sees you as her husband." My mouth dropped open and she held up her hand, "The whole village, including your Ulfheonar, see it too. It seems the only one who is blind to this is you."

"But how?"

"When you spoke the other day you made her love you. She thinks you feel the same way."

"I don't understand."

"I know, which will make this difficult. You enjoyed speaking with Erica?"

"Yes it was very easy."

"You like her?"

"Of course she laughs and smiles a lot."

"She neither laughed nor smiled before you spoke with her but let us go on. Were you aware how long you sat holding hands and talking with her?"

I had no idea and I shrugged. "An hour?"

"It was part of the morning and the whole afternoon. You neither ate nor drank. Now what does that tell you?"

Suddenly I knew what she meant. I had not needed any food or drink for I was satisfied with just her company, "Oh! But I am too young surely to think of taking a wife?"

"Erica was a bride when she was younger than you are now. Do you not want to marry her?"

"I am a warrior and I have no time for such things."

"Jarl Butar is a warrior too. Should he have no time for me?"

"Yes but…"

"Erica will not wish to change you. She loves you for who you are. She knows you are a warrior."

"But her brother…"

"Her family are all in favour of the match."

"You have spoken of it?"

"Of course! The whole village has spoken of little else. They all see it as good match and one favoured by the gods. We all saw how they shone the sunset of the longest day upon you. You are both special and have been chosen."

I started to chew my lip and she held my hands in hers. This was a decision. I never had to make decisions. Events happened and I reacted. I had not chosen to fight the wolf it had happened. It was Ragnar wanting me to take out his night water that had alerted me to the raid. I had not chosen to have my sword struck by lightning. Then I saw it all; this was the Norns weaving their webs and it was *wyrd*. I had not chosen this course, it had been chosen for me. My shoulders sagged in resignation and I gave a slight nod.

"We will arrange it all. You shall be married and we will make a room here in the hall for you. I can look after your wife when you go raiding. She will be here when you return."

I could face and fight wolves, Saxons, Champions and wild boars but I could not stand up to my mother and, as it turned out, to Erica. It was not in my nature. I resigned myself to the fact that I would be married. I didn't mind the change in state; I just wished that I had had longer as a free man with neither responsibilities nor ties. I did not doubt that I would be happy. After all Butar became even happier after my mother entered his life. But I knew I would miss my brothers.

Haaken and Cnut were not surprised when I told them. "We knew this would be. Do not worry. She will not expect you to be there always for her. If you want a slave girl then you can have one."

I was shocked. "That does not worry me. I like being Ulfheonar."

"Bjorn is Ulfheonar and he is married. You will still be an Ulfheonar and we will still be brothers. Unless your wife wishes to come raiding with us?"

Both were mocking me and that was the point when I stopped minding. I looked up to Bjorn. If he could cope with marriage then so could I. I would still have my brothers and I would still be Dragon Heart, no matter how pretentious that name was. I resolved that the first thing I would do when I next saw Erica was to ask her what the word meant.

We were married a week later. She did look beautiful and the whole of our people came to watch us be married. We spent our first night together in the new sleeping room built by Butar and we too made those noises I had heard my mother and Butar make. As we cuddled together she giggled, "My first husband left before we could truly join. I was determined to be as one with you before you went to war. I am glad I did for it was worth it."

"You do not mind me going to war?"

"It is what you do and you are a hero. Besides we will be rich and you will be a Jarl. I am happy and I will be here when you return. You took the sadness from my life and gave me my smile back."

I had thought that it would be more complicated than that but it was not. The next day she shooed me out of the house. "Go. Talk to your Ulfheonar and return here tonight! I have woman's work to do and that is far more important than polishing a sword; even one touched by the gods."

My life had only changed a little. I was warmer at night and had someone I could confide in. I found that Erica's day took my mind off whatever worries had entered my complicated head. Marriage was not that bad.

I took the opportunity of explaining to Butar what my plan for taking the last Saxon town was. I had reported to him on the state of the Saxon town but not how we could capture it. He summoned Harald and Eric to join Bjorn and myself when I explained it. "The ditch they have does not go around the town side. The gate is not strong and they have built houses next to the walls. They are both weaknesses which we can exploit. We can land from the three ships and fire the houses. The walls will burn."

"That sounds too easy. Will they not flee?"

"They cannot, Bjorn. They have but one gate and they have no ships. Besides where would they go? We have the rest of the island. Their only way out is by the sea and our ships will shut that door. The morale of the men is at its lowest ebb. Before I fled I counted fifty warriors and fifty villagers. They lost twenty warriors. They are ripe for plucking, Jarl Butar. We can make the island ours and not lose a warrior."

I saw the other three warriors nod one by one and then Butar smiled and said, "We will attack! My stepson has had fire put in his belly by your sister, Eric!"

Eric laughed, "I hope he has put more than that in her belly. A nephew from this union would be a mighty warrior!"

We left ten men to watch our home. Eric and Harald had left five in each of theirs. If any Saxons did escape and flee north we wanted no one in our homes hurt. We took just two boats for our raid and we set sail in the afternoon. When I told Butar that the Saxons ate at dusk he thought that would be the best time for an attack. The fishing boats would be in port and would not be able to give warning. In addition the men's wits would be dulled by the food and drink; poor though the quality was. We took fifty warriors. It was not many more than the Saxons had but we were well armed, well fed and confident. They were not. We had beaten them every time we had fought them; even when we were outnumbered. We were also led by a warrior whom we all admired, Butar. He had defeated Aella in combat before and my view of Aella had shown me a broken man. He felt betrayed and resentful. This was a good time to strike.

As we rowed south, in the late afternoon sun, it felt good to have Ragnar's Spirit around my waist again and to be amongst my comrades. Although I had escaped from their wooden walls I had not enjoyed being alone. With my brothers around me I felt I was a better warrior. Olaf had put the Ulfheonar together on the rowing benches and it was we who gave the beat for the other rowers. That was a great compliment. It showed that Olaf the Toothless held us in high esteem. He did not suffer fools gladly.

As we were sailing along the eastern end of the island on our journey south we were in the shade of the isle and it began to become dark. I could see the rays of the sun reflecting on the water to the east but we were almost invisible. Olaf had the sails taken down as soon as we had passed Duboglassio. The lights from the settlement were a dim beacon for us and we ghosted in to the harbour. There was no one on watch and our boats slid on to the sandy beach. We leapt over the side leaving Olaf and the other captains to watch the boats.

We did not alert the Saxons to our presence by shouting. We moved purposefully through the huts. We would deal with the villagers once the warriors were eliminated. I saw that the gate was still open and the two guards were lounging at the entrance talking. Butar did not issue a command he just ran. His oathsworn and the Ulfheonar ran with him. The two guards saw us and ran inside to close the gates. We ran faster.

Butar yelled, "Ram the gate!"

We all put our shields before us and we hit the gate together. There were fifteen big, heavy and strong warriors; the Saxons had not put the bar in place and the gate shattered. The two sentries lay beneath the broken gates and were trampled as we ran over them. Although we had heard the two Saxons shout a warning there appeared to be no reaction from those within. We continued our run to the warrior hall and Butar burst through the doors. The Saxons within looked up in shock as the mailed figure of Butar roared, "Aella! Today you die!"

The Saxons ran for their weapons. As we had expected, the oathsworn still wore their mail but the others just grabbed their shields and their swords to defend themselves. The Ulfheonar followed Butar closely. Jarl Butar headed directly for Aella who had grabbed his own sword and shield. I ignored them and aimed for the oathsworn who had three legs painted on his shield and had a sword in his hand. He hacked down at my shield and I slashed at his leg. I caught his sword on my shield and he leapt backwards to avoid my cut. He was agile. I feinted with Ragnar's Spirit and as he brought his shield up I punched with mine and he stepped backwards. I smashed down with sword and he was forced to step backwards again. He was running out of places to move and he was distracted, as he stepped backwards for he feared falling. He was no long attacking me but allowing me to make the attack. I shifted my body to the right and he moved to his left. I slashed again at his leg and this time he did not get out of the way. The edge ripped his knee below his mail shirt. Out of the corner of my eye I caught a glimpse of Aella being beaten back by Butar. His oathsworn would become ferocious once their leader fell and I increased the speed of my attack. I was quick in those days and I struck left and right making him twist and turn. I could see each movement caused agony to him as his wound bled out. His guard dropped briefly but it was enough and I plunged my sword into his neck. The brave warrior fell dead at my feet.

I whirled around as another mailed warrior tried to strike at my unprotected back. I struck out blindly with Ragnar's Spirit and he jumped backwards. Aella's bodyguards were good warriors. I hefted my shield into position and moved forwards. He stabbed at my head and I punched up with my shield and stabbed with my sword at the same time. His shield came up but the edge of the Saxon shield was jagged and it ripped through the leather thong on my shield. The movement of my arm threw the shield across the hall leaving me defenceless on my left side. He anticipated victory and advanced towards me. His face fell when I reached over my head and drew my second sword. I met his blow with my second blade and stabbed at his face with Ragnar's Spirit. He reeled backwards and I struck with both swords at the same time. He hesitated, albeit briefly, but it was enough. He parried neither and the two swords struck him so hard that his head fell from his body.

I turned to seek another enemy but they were all dead. Aella was bleeding his life away at Butar's feet and my comrades all stood cheering their own victories. "We shall have to call you two swords now!"

"No, Haaken, I have enough names already. I will just make my leather strap stronger." I sheathed my swords and retrieved my shield.

"And now you have two more mail shirts!"

"I shall give them to Sweyn and Godfrid; they are Ulfheonar and have no mail."

Sweyn heard me and clasped my hand. "Thank you, brother. That is a generous gift."

"He will get more believe me. They were Aella's best two warriors. One of them killed Harald's man, Ulf." Haaken only had one eye but he saw all.

We had lost a man. I had said we would not. I was foresworn. I felt guilty for his death. The edge was taken from my victory which now tasted bitter.

Jarl Butar sheathed his sword. We left the hall. "Let us round up the villagers. Do not harm them unless they resist." The villagers had nowhere to go and they stood in a defensive circle just outside the shattered gate. The handful of men gathered bravely to defend their women with bill hooks and daggers. Butar held up his hand, "I am Jarl Butar and I now rule this island. Aella and his men are dead. You have a choice. You can take your boats and leave this island or stay and enjoy my protection."

One of them, an old greybeard stepped forwards, "You will not enslave us?"

"No we have slaves enough. We need folk who will farm the land and fish the seas. You have until morning to decide. Do not try to leave tonight. My dragon ships are still there."

He nodded and returned to his people. We had drawn lots before the raid and the men who would crew the ships returned there while we took the bodies of the Saxons outside the walls. We would not despoil their dead and we built a bonfire for their bodies. When we had them all they were placed upon the pyre and it was set alight. We stood there until the flames had consumed their flesh and they went to the Otherworld to tell of our courage and skill. We retired to the warrior hall where we ate the last of the Saxon food, poor though it was and then drank their weak ale.

"It is no wonder they were so easy to defeat they had nothing inside of them to make them fight."

Olaf laughed, "Aye but it was also Butar's skill in leaving them alone for so long. It weakened them further."

We all chanted Butar's name. He stood. "Thank you, my warriors. We have travelled far from our homeland and Harald One Eye. We now have a home which is secure and, when we have raided grain in the autumn we will be well supplied with food. I thank you all!" We all banged our beakers. He held up his hands for silence. "I would like to thank my step son, Dragon Heart. Without his courage we would not have known that this was the time to strike."

This time it was my name which was chanted but I did not enjoy it. Men had died because of me. Butar came to join me, "What is the matter? You do not look happy at all."

"I am foresworn. I said no one would die and men did die."

He laughed, "Is that it? We lost two men. Perhaps it was their time to die. Perhaps the Norns had spun a web to entrap them. Who knows? Your plan was a good one and it worked. Two dead men and a handful of wounded warriors is no price at all." He pointed to Ragnar's Spirit. "If you keep going at this pace you will need a longer hilt for your sword. Already you have more warrior bands than some of the older warriors."

I shook my head. "I told you, Jarl Butar, since the lightning strike I will add no more bands. I like it the way it is."

The next morning the old greybeard, who turned out to be the headman, approached Jarl Butar. "I am Morgan, the headman of this town, and we have decided, Jarl Butar, that we would like to stay here."

Jarl Butar nodded and said, "Then swear allegiance to me and my people; the people of Manau."

He nodded, "On what should we swear?"

Jarl Butar looked to me and asked, "I would have them swear on Ragnar's Spirit; how say you?"

I could say nothing. It was an honour. I took it out and handed it to him. "It is an honour, Jarl Butar."

Butar held the sword aloft. "This blade contains the spirit of my dead father and is lightning struck. If you swear on this then it is a most binding oath for the sword has been touched by the gods."

Morgan nodded, "We are of the White Christ and do not believe in the gods but the sword is the sign of the White Christ, it is the sign of the cross and we will so swear."

I could see the awe on their faces as each man approached and kissed the blade; swearing their fealty to my stepfather. There were only ten men but they all proved loyal subjects.

We left Olaf in command of the burg with ten warriors. The rest of us loaded the booty on the ships and headed home. Harald took his own ship and headed north. We dropped Eric and his warriors at Duboglassio. The last mile or so was a joy for the families had come out to wave us back. "We have our own land now, Cnut."

"Aye. We have come far in a short time. And you have a bride. Soon you will have a son."

"How do you know?"

Haaken laughed, "Ragnar watched over you when you were alive and he does so still. Cnut and I are still looking for a girl pretty enough to marry and you find a noble born beauty. You are the special one and the gods watch over you. You will have a son."

"I am not sure of that. You two have had as much luck."

"That is not true but we will pass over that. You were a slave and now you are the step son of Jarl Butar who is now a king in all but name. If that does not mark you as special, then I do not know what does."

As the oars were raised we pulled on to the beach. Our next task, this winter, would be to build a stone quay so that we could tie our boats alongside. For now we were welcomed as heroes. This was my first time returning as a husband and Erica threw her arms around me and smothered me with kisses. Haaken and Cnut roared with laughter. I felt embarrassed but Erica seemed to think this was acceptable. I disengaged myself from her arms. "I am glad to see you, wife."

"And I can see that you were successful! My husband, the hero again!"

Haaken shouted, "We will see to your booty. You see to your wife!"

We scurried from the boat and Erica linked my arm as we went into Jarl Butar's Hall. She wrinkled her nose once we were alone. "You smell of blood."

"We were fighting. And men died."

She took my clothes from me and took a cloth and some water. She washed every drop of dried blood from my body. The water she used was perfumed. She gave me a sheepskin cloak to put around my shoulders. "I will get these cleaned for you! Stay here."

I lay on the bed to wait. I had to admit that it felt better to be clean and the sheepskin, which I had not seen before, felt soft and comforting.

Within a few moments I was asleep. I began to dream and the dream was of Erica. Suddenly I found that it was not a dream and I was lying with Erica. She was as naked as I was and we were making love. When we had finished I saw that night had fallen. I cradled her in my arms, "That was a pleasant surprise."

"You see husband, there are benefits to being married. This is the welcome you will get each time you return from war!" She stood and went to get her dress. "Your mother is waiting for us. She came while you were asleep. There is food on the table."

I was even more embarrassed than I had been on the boat. The idea that my mother knew what I had just done filled me with horror and I would have to face her and Butar across a table. "I am not really hungry."

"I think you are but we are going to join them anyway. It would be rude not to." Erica was a younger version of my mother and equally determined.

As soon as I entered the room I felt that every eye was looking at me, from my mother through to the slaves. Mother and Jarl Butar did not show any shock or embarrassment. They both smiled at me. Mother said, "I am glad you escaped unharmed again, my son. Jarl Butar tells me you slew two of the best of Aella's warriors."

Erica squealed, "Did you? Why did you not tell me?"

"It seems like boasting. They were brave men and they fought and died well."

Jarl Butar nodded, "That is the right way to look at it. I am pleased that you are not a glory hunter."

"No, I just fight for our people."

"And we shall be doing just that soon enough again. We need to capture some grain for our new mouths. We sail in seven days for the mainland. We will be fighting the Saxons again but this time it will be across the river from where your mother lived and your grandfather died."

I was going back to Cymri, the land of my ancestors.

Viking Slave

Chapter 14

Before we left Butar held a meeting with Olaf, Harald and Eric. All of the warriors were summoned to the great hall to hear the words. Jarl Butar stood on a table so that all could see him.

"Brothers, we have achieved our aim. We have conquered our own land and we will fight to keep it." He gestured to the three men who stood before him. "These men will be my new Jarls and will each be responsible for the defence of one quarter of the island. Bjorn will work with me here at Hrams-a. He too will be a Jarl. All of you will be responsible for a dragon boat and supplying men when we need them for the defence of the isle or to gather what we need."

The warriors began banging their beakers against the table and chanting, "King Butar! King Butar!"

He waved his hands for silence. "I am not King Butar and I have no desire to be king. I will rule you as I do now, as Jarl Butar. I will pass judgement as each Jarl will pass judgement in his own burg and I will settle any disputes between Jarls. We will make our laws here," He stamped his foot on the table, "in this building. We will all have a say in those laws." There was more cheering. "But first, we only have three ships and we need a fourth. Tomorrow we will begin to build another dragon ship and then we will raid the mainland for the food we need for the winter."

We left the hall in high spirits. Jarl Eric took me to the side. "We tried to persuade him to be king you know. This was his doing. Your step father is a remarkable man. He genuinely cares for his people; even the new ones like me and Harald. I am lucky that we stopped off in Orkneyjar."

"I know what you mean. I was lucky to be captured by the boat with him aboard. I do not know what my life would have been like otherwise."

With over a hundred men working we soon laid the keel of the new boat. This would be Jarl Butar's boat and would be the same size as *'Sif'* had been. We needed one big dragon ship at least. We all worked longer and harder than we had ever worked before because this was to be our boat. This would the first one we had built as a free people and it was special. Ten days later and it was ready. We caulked the hull and then the beautiful carved dragon prow was fitted along with her mast. Butar named her after the island; he called her *'Man'*. We had shortened the name Manau and it seemed appropriate that the island which had given us a home should be the name of our ship.

It was six days later when the three ships sailed. We left Harald and his boat to give some defence to the island although he came with us. The men who were chosen to stay were philosophical about the whole thing. They would get to raid next time when the target might be something more exciting than winter grain.

We sailed for the river the Saxons called the Dee. It marked the border between the land of Northumbria and the land of Cymri. My mother had given her husband a great deal of information about what to expect. I had been privy to that information. "There are two estuaries, the Dee and the Maeresea. They both lead inland and will allow you to raid deep into Saxon territory. The Saxons use the old Roman forts and it is there that you will find the granaries. The largest one is Legacaestir which in Saxon means the Roman Fortress. We called it something different, Caerlleon, but they both mean the same. It will be a hard place to capture."

As the three ships sailed across the water to the mainland I wondered what Jarl Butar's plan would be. He was never wasteful with his men but I knew that we needed the grain. We had to have bread for the winter and, until our wheat crop grew, we would have to take it where we could. It had been a good summer and we believed that the Saxons had had a good crop. We would reap the benefit of their hard work. My mother had told me how Mona, the island off the coast of Cymri, was also well blessed with grain but she would not allow her husband to raid her kin.

Bjorn and Butar steered the *'Man'* and she was a fine ship. She was as fast and nimble as the Ran but we could carry fifty warriors if we needed to. We had but forty on this voyage leaving us room for a cargo. We hoped to return with a good haul. Bjorn and Butar spent the first three hours of the voyage in deep conference while they steered. The other two, smaller ships followed dutifully in our wake. Jarl Butar was the leader.

When they had decided Bjorn shouted to us, "We head for the Maeresea." It was all that he needed to say for we knew what the alternative was and none of us relished the thought of trying to take a Roman Legionary fortress.

Viking Slave

The wind was in our favour and we soon saw the mainland looming up. To the north it looked like one enormous beach, stretching as far as the eye could see. Behind the sand and the dunes were thick pine forests. We saw no towns. To the south we could also see beaches but there was at least one settlement nestled in the woods. We could see smoke rising. Cnut hazarded a guess that it would be charcoal burners working deep in the forests.

We lowered the sail and headed to the south bank of the estuary. It was another beach with dunes. We leapt from the prow and secured the ropes to some lonely pine trees. The five Ulfheonar were the first ashore and we quickly ran into the woods to see if anyone had spotted us. It appeared empty. There were animals but it was devoid of human life. All of our warriors were well practised in disembarking and soon the seventy of us who would be raiding were assembled. While the majority of the party would capture whatever they could close to the landing site, the Ulfheonar and Jarl Bjorn headed inland to find somewhere that would supply us with grain. We were patient. If we did not find it this trip then we would the next. It was still high summer and we had plenty of time.

We ran along the river using the trees for cover. The four of us with wolf skins went first. With our black armour and helmets we were harder to see. We soon spied a settlement. It was discernible by the smoke rising from the hearth fires. We spread out in a half circle and moved silently through the undergrowth. Suddenly we came upon a village. There was neither wall nor warriors. Sadly there appeared to be no granaries either and few animals. We would not benefit from raiding such a small place. We slipped back into the woods. We headed across land towards the Dee and left the river. The land was fertile and we could see farms and houses dotted around. We had to move carefully to avoid detection. Eventually we came upon the other river, the River Dee. The ground here was marshy with many wading birds but no towns. We could see further up the river the tower of a stone built building. That would be the legionary fortress.

"Let us give our bad news to Butar."

We made our way back across country towards the boats. We had taken a different route and we suddenly came across a more prosperous looking village. This one had no stockade but there were animals. It looked as though it might be worth raiding and it was close to the Maeresea. When we reached there we found that they had had a little success; there were ten slaves and a few animals. We told Butar about our find. We debated what to do.

It was left to Bjorn to come up with a solution. "My lord, if you sail down the river we can surprise them. I will take the Ulfheonar to the village and we can capture it all."

Once more we took the same route we had taken before. This time the journey seemed to take no time at all. We reached the western side just as we spied the masts of the three ships in the river. The villagers were blissfully unaware of their doom as they went about their business. We unsheathed our swords and stepped into the peaceful village. As soon as we were seen there was a scream and then the villagers panicked. Women grabbed their children and ran like headless chickens; men grabbed axes and sticks and prepared to defend themselves. It was too easy, we ran at them and they fled towards the river. We did not run quickly for we knew what awaited them.

By the time we reached the river two men lay dead and the rest were captured along with the women and children. Bjorn shouted to four of our warriors. "Go back to the village there are many animals and there is a grain store." He looked at me. "Find someone to question; one of the men and find out where they get their grain from."

Haaken and Cnut came with me and we approached the prisoners. I did not choose the greybeard nor the young sullen men but a young man a little older than me who kept looking at a woman and baby. He was a family man. He might have more reason to cooperate. We led him away from the other prisoners and I could see the fear on his face. He thought he was going to be executed. I would let him continue to believe that, he might give us more information.

"What is your name?"

He appeared surprised that I spoke Saxon so well. "Scanlan." He dropped to his knees. "Please don't kill me. I have a wife and child."

"Tell me what I need to know, Scanlan, and you will live and be reunited with your family. I promise you that." He looked a little calmer. "Now where do you get your grain from?"

He pointed to the east. "The headman and others take a cart and walk to Legacaestir. They have granaries there."

It was as we feared. We would have to take it from the fort. "How many warriors live at Legacaestir?"

"I have never been, sir, but I have been told it is a warband."

Viking Slave

I knew from my father that that could be anything from twenty warriors to a thousand and didn't help us. "How far is this place?"

He obviously had no concept of distance. "They can be there and back with laden carts in less than a morning."

"Thank you for your honesty."

We took him back and I led him to his wife and child. It was one of Harald's men who guarded them and he said, "I was told to keep them separate."

"And I am telling you to let the woman and the child go to this man."

He had seen me but did not know me. "And who are you?"

"I am the warrior sent by Jarl Bjorn to find out some information and this man supplied it. The price I paid was to reunite them. Now I have spoken far more than I wish to. Release them."

His eyes narrowed, "Or?"

"Or I shall teach you a lesson with my sword."

I honestly thought he was going to take out his sword when Haaken said quietly. "Before you do anything you will regret, this is Dragon Heart the stepson of Jarl Butar and an Ulfheonar. Look at his sword it is Ragnar's Spirit and touched by the gods. Would you fight him?" We had both noticed that this young warrior had but one warrior band on his sword. He was a novice.

His eyes widened and he stuttered, "I am sorry. I was only obeying orders."

I smiled to make it easier. "And I was doing the same. Thank you for your help." I turned to Scanlan, "Keep your family close and I will try to keep you together."

We went to Bjorn who was speaking with Butar and the other Jarls. "The grain is in Legacaestir but we do not know how many warriors are there."

Butar looked at the prisoners and the plunder. We could not fight a battle and guard the prisoners. Bjorn said, "If I might suggest? We send two boats back with the plunder and the Ulfheonar scout out Legacaestir. When the boats return we will know what we have to do."

That decided Butar. "I will return with Eric and Olaf and the prisoners. You keep the *'Ran'* and take it closer to Legacaestir."

Bjorn's smile told us all that he was happy about this. As they turned to leave I said to Jarl Butar. "I promised the man who gave us the information that I would let him be reunited with his wife and child."

"We do not normally do that."

"I know but I gave my word and I would not be foresworn. I will have the three of them as my part of the plunder. They can be the thralls in my home."

He smiled, "You have your mother's heart and I will grant you your wish. Which ones are they?" I pointed them out. "They shall be in your home when you return. Take care, Dragon Heart."

And so when the other two ships sailed west we rowed the *'Ran'* a few miles down the river seeking a quiet and safe anchorage. The wolves would be hunting again soon.

It was dark by the time we found a suitable place. It was sheltered by a low bank and some trees. We put guards out and slept aboard our ship. Jarl Butar would not return for a day at least and we had much to do. Bjorn divided the sixteen scouting warriors into four groups; each would be led by an Ulfheonar. We were there to find and not to fight. We would be best placed to discover what treasures there were.

We left well before dawn. I led my group south east. We would approach the fort from the east and we would be the furthest group out. From what Scanlan had told me I estimated that we would be between five and seven miles from our target. We had plenty of time to get there. The important thing was to stay out of sight. If the Saxons knew that raiders were in the vicinity then the fort would be packed with the civilian population and every warrior who could wield a weapon. It would make it impossible to take.

We found the tiny village soon after leaving the boat. There were six huts. I heard the sound of animals but saw no-one. I ghosted back to the rest of the group and we skirted the village. It was a difficult land to traverse as it was flat and there was a great deal of cultivation. The woods and hedgerows we normally used for cover were absent. It did bode well for the size of the grain we could capture. Just before the sun came up I smelled smoke. I had the other two warriors hide themselves in the woods and I took Egill's son, Alf, with me. He was small and quick witted. I had promised his father that I would teach him my skills. "You two need to keep watch for when we return. If we have pursuers then you will be the trap."

We found a track between two hedges and we ran down between them quickly. It would soon be dawn and we would be forced to hide. We turned a corner and suddenly the walls of the fort loomed up two hundred paces ahead. We dived into the hedgerow. We now had to find somewhere from which to observe the fort. The other side of the hedgerow was scrubby land with bushes and stones. It looked to me as though there had been a house here a long time in the past and it had been abandoned. If it was made of stone then it would have been Roman. They liked to plant gardens. This one had become wild in the last few centuries; a perfect hiding place. A tumble of stones which had been a building afforded us a good vantage point. I took my seax to cut some branches from the hawthorn bush and used those to cover us. I took some mud and smeared both my face and Alf's. We then peered out. We could see but we would not be seen.

As we chewed on some dried deer meat I began to work out how we could find out the numbers. The best way would be to get inside the fort but that was ridiculously risky. The first rays of sunlight touched the upper levels and towers of the fort. We would soon be able to see the defenders. We needed to count. I looked around our den and found a straight piece of hawthorn. I cut two lengths of it and handed one to Alf.

I began to whisper to him. "When you see a guard make a mark on the stick. Only count a guard once. You will need to remember what they wear. If you see anyone giving instructions or wearing mail then put a mark on the line." I did not explain to Alf but that would tell us who the better warriors were and how many of them were within the walls.

Just then I heard a noise close to my right. I slowly swivelled my head. To my horror there was a hut less than a hundred paces away. It had been hidden in the dark. I touched Alf and held my finger to my lips. We would now discover if my hiding place was secure. I could not see the speakers but I knew them to be men by their voices. After what seemed an age, but must have been a short time, the voices receded as they walked away. As I turned I could see the four of them heading along the track, the way we had come. They had bows and were obviously hunting. I hoped that we would be long gone before they returned.

The sun was now illuminating the whole of the wall and I could see the sentries on the walls. I quickly marked my stick. When the time the sun was fully up I saw twenty warriors emerge from the walls to a flat area before the gate. They began to spar with each other. These were the real warriors for they trained. As soon as they went back inside I tapped Alf on the shoulder. We would not see any more and we needed to return to the ship. It would be a longer journey back as we would be moving more slowly now that it was daylight. We backed out from our den and walked hunched over. Now that I knew there was hut nearby I did not

Viking Slave

want us observed; that would have been a disaster. I led us along the field side of the hedgerow. I did not want to stumble upon the four hunters.

I drew my sword and nodded at Alf. He did the same. We had no shields with us but I wanted to be prepared. We moved silently, albeit slowly, through the field which had yet to be harvested. It was a wheat field and came up to my chest. It would be a good crop. Our silence was rewarded when I heard the voices. It was the hunters and they were on the other side of the hedge.

"I am sure that I saw someone in the woods."

"Get away with you. You haven't seen a game bird all morning so how would you see a warrior?"

"A warrior is bigger than a game bird. He was in those woods yonder."

"Well who could it be?"

"I bet it is those Welsh bastards again. They have been quiet for a while."

"You could be right. Sigismund, you go to the fort and tell the captain that we are going to look for some Welsh warriors who might be hiding in the woods."

"I'll show you and you will apologise."

"Yes well the morning has been a waste so far. If we can find some Welshmen then the captain might reward us."

I guessed that Sigismund moved off for the other three spoke. "Well Ardoch, show us these Welsh warriors that no one else could see."

When they moved down the lane I knew that it was my two comrades they had seen. I gave them a few moments to get ahead and then we slipped from the hedgerow into the green track. "We will have to follow them. When I give the word use your sword and do not flinch. We will have the advantage for they will not know we are behind them."

I knew where the three Saxons were headed and that helped. They would only slow down when they neared the hiding place of Wulf and Olaf. Although we walked down the green sward we kept to the hedgerow. The two sides had grown together so that it was like a green tunnel and my black armour, wolf cloak and helmet made it hard to see me. Alf trotted behind, hidden by my mass. I heard them talking and I stopped.

"Through there, near to those beech trees. That was where I thought I saw them."

"Oh so now you think you saw them."

"He is right. Look. I can see the shape of a man."

Their voices lowered as the leader said. "Ready an arrow and we'll have these Welsh boys for breakfast."

I gestured Alf forwards and we ran down the lane. The three Saxons were heading through the woods and were spread out. We were thirty paces behind. I hoped that Wulf and Olaf were keeping a good watch for I would have to wait until they had loosed their arrows before attacking. Their leader was a big man and he pulled back his bow. I thought that I could see our men and they were not moving. They were asleep! There was no alternative; we had to attack.

"Ulfheonar!"

I leapt forwards as the leader turned around. He was quick for one so big and I saw him adjusting his aim. I jinked left and right to put him off. He loosed the arrow and it pinged from my helmet. By then I was close enough to jam my sword into his middle. I took out my second sword as I withdrew Ragnar's Spirit from the man's body. I heard a cry from behind me and saw Alf clutching his arm. The third Saxon was swinging his bow around to face me. I threw myself at him and my second sword struck him in the neck. I rolled to the right as an arrow thudded into the ground beside me. The last Saxon was drawing his seax. I jumped to my feet and swung Ragnar's Spirit at his head. He was no warrior and moved too slowly. The edge of the blade ripped open his throat and he slumped to my feet in a bloody heap.

Wulf and Olaf had emerged from the woods with their swords in their hands. I would have words with them later. I turned and ran to Alf who was lying in a pool of blood. I ripped the hem from the dead Saxon's tunic and tied the arm above the wound with it. The flood of blood became a trickle. Alf was barely conscious and so I broke the flights from the arrow and pushed it through.

"You two grab Alf and head south."

"But the boat is north!"

"Do not argue with me! I am already angry with you for sleeping on watch."

I grabbed the weapons of the dead men. It is what the Welsh would have done. We had to lay a trail south towards Wales and then we could cut back north. We had only gone four hundred paces when we struck the river. This was another disaster. "Head east! Run along the river bank!"

I was looking for somewhere we could leave the river without a trail. Suddenly, a little way ahead I saw that a huge tree had fallen and lay half in the river. "Halt at the tree!" I also needed to loosen the tunic or the poor lad could lose his arm.

"Take your swords and cut down some branches from this dead tree and then lay them to the north." This time there was no argument. There was steel in my voice and fire in my eyes. I loosened the band and blood dripped from his arm. I tightened it again.

His eyes opened, "I am sorry, Dragon Heart."

"It was not your fault and you're a brave boy. The other two will carry you for you are weak." Wulf returned. "Now carry him across those branches and when you get to the other side make sure that Olaf steps in your footsteps. Look for rocks on which to stand. We leave no trail. Go!"

As they left I looked down and saw that Alf's blood had dripped on to the log. I broke a damaged branch off the tree and walked to the river's edge. I stuck the branch in the water and muddied it and then threw the branch in the river. I hoped they would see the muddied water and assume we had gone across. I had to buy us time. When I reached the branches laid by Wulf I walked backwards and collected them as I went. They had done a good job and had covered ten paces with them. I turned and put my feet in the marks left by Wulf. They could find our prints but it would take time. I dumped the branches and followed my companions.

It was now a foot race. Wulf and Olaf took it in turns to carry Alf. I kept stopping to listen for pursuit but I heard none. We found a stream and I halted us again. I check the wound and then led us along the stream. After two hundred paces I left the stream and we headed north. The afternoon was slipping by and I was worried about Alf. His wound needed stitches. Then I smelled the sea and knew that we were close to the estuary. We burst through the hedges and saw the Maeresea ahead. Now all we needed was the *'Ran'*. When I saw her mast I almost wept with relief. This was the first time I had led men and it had nearly ended with our deaths. I had learned a valuable lesson.

We were the last to return and Bjorn was looking anxiously towards the shore when we trudged up the river. Egill's face showed his distress. "It is just an arrow in the arm. He will live. He is a brave boy."

Egill nodded his thanks and took his son. Bjorn said, "What happened?"

I jerked a hand in the direction of Wulf and Olaf who were looking very sheepish. "These two fell asleep and we were nearly found by the

Saxons." I told them what had happened. Bjorn's face was a mask of anger.

"You two will be punished when we return home. Now get out of my sight." After they had gone he asked, "Are we in danger then? Do they know we are here?"

"They think we are the Welsh and I led the trail south. It is why it took us so long to return here. I think they will lose the trail well south of here."

"Good, you have done well. And did you get the information?"

I took out the two tally sticks. "Here!"

"Then we eat first we will get all the information from the others too."

I was ravenous and ate everything that the cook had prepared. Then the Ulfheonar sat with Bjorn. We each told what we had seen. Because Alf and I had both used tally sticks our numbers were slightly more accurate than the others.

"So it would seem they have a captain, twenty Housecarls and thirty or so warriors. We had come with that figure by counting the men on all of the walls, the ones I had seen at practice and then adding ten. "The numbers seem to tally with what Scanlan said."

Bjorn nodded, "I think we can take it."

Haaken grinned, "I think it would be easy. The gate in the northern wall is not the original gate. It looks to be a poor replacement."

"And it appears that it is an attack from the south which they fear. They see the Welsh as the danger and not their brothers." I suddenly had an idea. "We could march in."

"What?"

"We are armed and dressed much as they are. If we marched down the road they might think that we were reinforcements. Jarl Butar speaks Saxon. All we would need is some indecision and we could enter by deception."

"That is dangerous."

Jarl Bjorn stroked his beard. "I am not so sure. What have we to lose? If we attack the wall by our usual tactics then we would have to approach the gate anyway. This way we might get closer before they see who we are. I will sleep on this and when Jarl Butar and the others return we can all make the decision.

Wulf and Olaf kept out of my way. Haaken and Cnut were as angry as I was. We did not expect other warriors to match our standards but we did want them to do their duty. Alf, a young boy, had been wounded because of their dereliction of duty. I went to see Egill to apologise for the wound suffered when his son was in my care. He waved my apology away. "My son has told me what happened and it is the other two who should hang their heads in shame. You killed three warriors! What a feat!"

"They were not warriors. They had bows and they had swords but they were the fyrd. They were brave men but they were not warriors."

Egill nodded, "I understand and yet others would add warrior bands."

"I need no warrior bands to remember the men I kill."

Viking Slave

Chapter 15

The Ulfheonar were sent by Bjorn, the next morning, to scout the vicinity and ensure that we had not been followed. I took them to the stream we had crossed but we saw only our tracks and not the tracks of any Saxons. It looked like they believed our deception. We could see the smoke from the fort when we reached the stream.

Haaken rubbed his eye patch. "The fort is close."

"Aye, when we fled south to deceive them we found the other river, the Dee. The land is not good to land an assault from but I spied a bridge. If we capture the fort then we can sail the ships around and make loading the grain and plunder easier."

"That is a large mouthful to swallow. How do you think we can take such a fort? We hew men not stones. If it was a wall made of wood then I would be more hopeful but not a stone built fort. We would be slaughtered."

"I don't know. They seem to be thinly spread around the walls." I shrugged, "it will be Jarl Butar's decision."

By the time we reached the camp the other two ships had arrived and the four Jarls were in deep conference. Bjorn summoned Haaken and the rest of us over. "Are we safe?"

"Aye, my lord. They did not follow our men."

Jarl Butar shook his head, "We were lucky. Wulf and Olaf nearly ruined what was a good plan." He looked at me. "Now Bjorn seems to think that we can just walk in? Is that your plan?"

I felt embarrassed with everyone looking at me. "It just seemed to me that you see what you expect to see. If you see a horde of men rushing at the walls and shouting you assume it is an enemy. If, on the other hand, you see men strolling along and smiling then you give them the benefit of the doubt and think they are friends." I could see they were not convinced. "We know that their gates are weak and if we can get close to them without losing men then we have a chance."

Haaken stoutly came to my defence, "No-one knows us here on the mainland. Aella and his men never left Manau. They will have no idea that he has lost the island."

Viking Slave

Eric said, "It seems to me that we have nothing to lose. We can still send men along the river to attack on the bridge side and use a small band of warriors to try to gain entry this way."

"We would be drawing their attention away from the bridge in the south to the gate on the north wall. Haaken has told us how few warriors they have. They will struggle to man the perimeter."

Butar sighed, "It seems I am persuaded."

Cnut put his hand up, a little like a naughty boy would, "Jarl Butar, if the raiders on the bridge side came by boat it would make the loading of the grain easier."

Olaf slapped Cnut on the back, it almost knocked the breath from him, "Aye and it will save a long walk too."

We left two ships on the Maeresea with skeleton crews aboard. The *'Ran'* sailed for the Dee and Jarl Butar led Bjorn, the Ulfheonar and twenty chosen warriors. Each warrior had been endorsed by their Jarl for this would be worthy of a saga if we pulled it off. We all wore our shields over our backs and kept our hands free so that we appeared friendly. As soon as we found the main road we marched boldly down it. We did not hurry, we sauntered. Part of the plan was to allow Olaf and the *'Ran'* to reach the Dee and then disembark the rest of the warriors. We did not see many people but, whenever we did, Jarl Butar and I would be the only ones speaking and we would speak Saxon. I am sure that the fort would soon know that we were coming. Their reaction was another matter.

The road we were using was a Roman one and it was straight. We saw the fort and it was a mile away. Our accuracy in the distance was down to the Roman markers. Butar said to me, quietly, "Now we will see if the gods truly smile on you, my son. This will be the longest mile we have ever walked. We could be walking to our deaths."

"I do not mind what the outcome is, Jarl Butar. I am with men I admire and my oath brothers. It will be a good day to die."

"When you are as old as Olaf and I am then it might be a good day to die but even then I doubt it. Since your mother and sister came into my life I find myself clinging on to it even more. I would prefer it if this was a good day to live for all of us. Let the Saxons do the dying."

"We will not die this day Jarl Butar. I believe we will sail home to my wife and mother."

"I hope that you are right." The Jarl turned to the men behind us. "Start laughing and joking. We are happy. We are Saxons who have marched a long way and look forward to a hot meal and a bed for the night."

We saw men on the walls but the gates did not close. When more men appeared, I was delighted. That meant fewer warriors for Olaf to face. The two guards at the gates were joined by four mailed Housecarls. These looked at us more suspiciously. We were two hundred paces away. Jarl Butar shouted, "We are glad to see you, brothers, we have marched many miles today."

I added, "Our feet are sore and our bellies are empty!"

The sound of two Saxon voices seemed to make them less suspicious and the guards smiled at each other. Under his breath Jarl Butar said, "Be ready to run on my command!"

I suspect that our small numbers lulled them. After all what could a handful of men do? In addition we looked and sounded like Saxons. They could not see the emblems on our shields and our helmets were almost identical to their own. The only difference was the black armour of Cnut and me. In the end that was what gave us away. I saw the frowns on the faces of the Housecarls. Suddenly one of them shouted something to the others and I saw them try to close the gate.

"Charge!"

Even as we ran we pulled our shields around and drew our swords. We had been ready for the command and there was no delay. This time they did not even get the bar down on the gate before we struck it. It shattered as though it was glass. My stepfather and I were at the front and it was us who faced the two Housecarls. They had their axes and they swung them at us. It was easy to avoid the blow if you had room to move out of the way and we did. We both ducked and feinted to the side. As my opponent's axe flew over my head I hacked Ragnar's Spirit at his side. It sliced through some of his rings and into the leather shirt he wore beneath. From the grimace on his face I also thought that I had broken a rib or two. I punched him in his injured side with my shield and hacked down with Ragnar's Spirit. He held the axe up to deflect the blow and my blade sliced the bottom half of his handle off. I punched again with my shield and he fell backwards. I stabbed him between his mail shirt and the coif of his helmet.

The rest of the garrison were now racing towards us. I shouted, "Ulfheonar!" and the five of us formed a barrier around Jarl Butar who had just killed his opponent. With our shields forming a wooden wall we held our swords above them. The Saxons rushed at us; they seemed eager

Viking Slave

to die. There were too many of them to swing axes effectively and when the blows did hit our shields they were weak and ineffective. Our swords darted out to stab faces with little protection or smashed down to crush poor quality helmets. After the initial onslaught they reformed their lines. I heard a wail go up from the southern wall and knew what it meant. Olaf and the rest of the men had arrived.

We were now pressed back against the gate for they had brought many men to kill us. I saw some of our warriors lay dead but the Ulfheonar and Jarl Butar were like a rock around which the sea of Saxons broke. I had swung my arm so many times that the muscles in the shoulder ached but we had to hang on. Olaf would not let us down and he would reach us. Suddenly I saw an archer on the walls and he was aiming for us. I watched the arrow as it flew towards us. I knew that it would miss me but it would strike another of my comrades. I lifted the shield and took the arrow on my shield. As I did so one of the Saxons stabbed forwards with his spear and I felt the head slip into my side. I killed the warrior with a mighty blow from Ragnar's Spirit and, as the pressure lessened, took out the spear and threw it to the ground. Cnut saw it and yelled, "Dragon Heart is wounded! Push!"

The survivors of our attack all heaved and pushed so that the Saxons had to recoil. At that moment there was a roar as Olaf and the rest of our comrades fell upon the rear of their lines. There was a frenzied attack and then the Saxon garrison lay slaughtered. We had won. As soon as the last warrior had been despatched Jarl Butar and Haaken laid me on the ground and lifted my mail shirt. My leather jerkin had deflected the spear head from any vital organs but it had pierced my side and I was bleeding freely. Cnut brought a white tunic he had found and he tore it into a strip. Haaken wrapped it around my body. It hurt when he tightened it but I knew that it was necessary for it stopped the bleeding.

"Get my step son aboard the *'Ran'*. He needs do no more today. He saved my life with his shield. The arrow would have killed me and he nearly paid for that bravery with his own life."

I tried to object but the Ulfheonar were in no mood to listen to me and I was carried through the slaughterhouse that was the legionary fortress, down to the river where the dragon ship waited. Haaken said to Olaf, "He is not to leave, Jarl Butar's orders."

"Don't worry my little man. He is going nowhere!"

It was maddening to lie there. I am not lazy by nature and I felt sure that I could be of some help. Olaf put his huge paw on my shoulder. "I can see the blood where you were stabbed. We would rather you rested now so that you can fight another day. Besides I am not going to face your mother and tell her that you died because I couldn't keep you on a boat."

"But I am not going to die."

"I know because you are staying on the boat."

Soon the slaves and booty began to arrive. Cnut looked in on me. "Jarl Butar has sent for the other boats. There is too much grain in these granaries for one boat. We have enough for the winter."

Olaf grunted, "Now you sit still while I get this boat loaded."

I rested by the tiller and watched Olaf shout and curse until the slaves and plunder were placed where he wished. I had been petrified of him when I had been captured but now I saw him in a totally different light. He was now a friend.

It was getting dark when Jarl Butar came aboard. He strode towards me and looked at my wound. He nodded. "We will be heading home soon. Eric and Bjorn can bring the grain back with the other ships. We will take the rest of the slaves and the plunder." He reached into a chest by the stern and brought out a hunk of pork. "Here chew on that until we can get some proper food inside you."

I felt like a baby as I lay, helpless at the stern while all my comrades worked tirelessly. We waited at anchor until the other two ships arrived and then we cast off. The Ulfheonar all sat facing me with their oars in their hands and they all grinned. Haaken, ever the joker shouted, "If I thought a little wound like that would get me out of rowing I would have had Cnut here slice me himself."

Once we had turned her around we hoisted the sail on the '***Ran***'. We were deeply laden and would need all the help we could get to get home in one piece. The wind was sluggish and we seemed to move at a snail's pace. It gave me time to look at the settlements dotted along the river bank. This would make a good place to raid. The fort had not been the deterrent the Saxons thought it would be and their warriors were not the greatest we had faced. Given time we could take everything and there would be no one to stop us.

I saw the exhaustion on the faces of the rowers. "If you will not let me row, Jarl Butar, at least let me take food and drink to my comrades." His face was dark. "I will move slowly."

"Very well but if I see any blood from your wound then I will tie you to the mast!"

In this way I helped my friends and found out how the battle had ended. "The captain was not a brave man and he was caught trying to flee. The Jarl had him executed as a coward. We have some fine mail shirts and weapons as well as some gold, jewels and those books they like; the books of the White Christ. The Jarl thinks we can sell them to Sigismund the next time we trade for Frankish blades."

"How many warriors fell?"

"A few and there were others like yourself who were wounded but your deception worked. Olaf and his men lost not a warrior. It was those around the gate who died."

I settled back down at the tiller and soon fell asleep. I was woken by the sound of seabirds as we round the headland at Hrams-a. Jarl Butar helped me to my feet. "It is good to see home again. I never thought I would tire of the fiords of the north but I have come to love this little haven of peace."

"I think, Jarl Butar, that is because you have someone to come home to. I feel different this time. I know that Erica will fuss over me but tonight I will also be buried in her arms and thank the Allfather that I am not buried in a grave."

"You are changing, Dragon Heart. You now think as a man as well as acting like a man." He smiled at me and shook his head. "Your mother will not know if she should be angry or happy with you for saving my life and risking you own."

We saw the women and children on the beach watching our approach. The fact that we were a single ship was the reason for the concern on their faces. They did not know that our consorts were close behind. As I thought of the consorts I suddenly remembered the grain. "We will now need granaries Jarl Butar. We cannot just store it in our halls."

"Aye you are right. I will divide it into four and then we will all have some grain. I fear the Saxons will suffer hunger this winter because they stored all their grain in one place. At least you will be spared the work."

"But I want to help. I am part of the people. I should do my share."

"You have done more than your share and besides we need you well again so that we can raid others. There are slaves who will do the hard work."

I suddenly remembered Scanlan. "Did you give the slaves to my wife?"

Viking Slave

"Aye she was pleased and they seemed grateful to be kept together. That was a shrewd move. I think you have bought loyalty at a very small cost. Perhaps we should do it with all families."

"This is only the second time that we have taken male slaves. It is a new experience for us. Besides you allowed the Saxons in the south to live as freemen."

"I do not mind Saxons so long as they adhere to our ways. I will not have the White Christ here on Manau. He makes women of warriors. The Saxons were a fierce people like the wolf until they followed the White Christ and now they are like sheep to be fleeced."

I could see Erica standing with my mother who was holding my sister in her arms. They had seen us and I could see the smiles on their faces. They contrasted with the anxious looks of the other women. As the sail was lowered and the oars rose we slowed down and edged next to the wooden walls of the quay. I could see the new stone quay being built further along. Soon this would be a much easier task. The thralls on the quay grabbed the ropes and another waited with the gangplank. We were so loaded that we were lower in the water than we normally were and we had an uphill struggle to disembark. Normally it was just Jarl Butar who left the ship while the rest of us carried the cargo and herded the slaves but my stepfather took my arm.

"Come, you shall go with me. I want your mother to see to your wound." Mother was still the best healer on the whole island and I knew I would be in safe hands.

The Jarl stepped on to the gangplank and the waiting crowd cheered. It was not a false welcome; all loved Jarl Butar because he was fair and genuinely cared for his people. Most remembered the selfish and ambitious Harald One Eye who was the opposite. When I stepped on the plank they all cheered me too and I felt uncomfortable. I glanced down at the Ulfheonar and saw Haaken and Cnut grinning. They knew that I was not happy with attention.

My mother handed Eurwen to a slave. The Jarl greeted me and hugged her as I walked gingerly on to dry land. My wound had stiffened and was aching. Each movement sent a wave of pain coursing through my body. My step father must have told my mother of my wound for she and Erica rushed to my side. My mother's eyes flashed at her husband. "Could he not have been carried from the ship? Was that too much to ask?"

Viking Slave

I saw the helpless look in Jarl Butar's face. He had done all that he could to keep me still and to care for me. "I am a warrior and I can walk mother."

My wife also had an angry look upon her face. "You are a wounded warrior and your mother is right."

They both chuntered and complained all the way to the hall. They tried to get thralls to carry me but I was adamant. Even though it hurt I was determined to walk to the hall. In the end it was too much and I barely made the threshold when my knees gave way and I collapsed.

"Scanlan, carry the master to his bed."

Just before I passed out I saw the face of the Saxon I had captured and I suddenly thought, '*I have a slave.*'

When I awoke I was in my own bed and Erica was holding my hand and looking tearful. She saw my eyes opening and shouted, "He is awake!" She leaned over and kissed me. I felt a pain in my side and I moaned. She leapt back as though scalded. "I am sorry. I leaned on your wound. I am a fool!"

I forced a weak smile, "Do not worry. At least this way I know that I live still."

My mother came in and I saw the relief upon her face, "You had us worried, my son. The wound was worse than Butar and the others knew. They have all been waiting anxiously for news of your recovery."

"I am sorry, Myfanwy, I leaned on his wound."

Mother stroked the hair from Erica's face. "Never mind. I think he will live but I will look at his wound."

She lifted the covers and I saw that I was naked, "Mother!"

She and Erica both laughed. "I think that we have both seen you naked before and, besides, who do you think undressed you and cared for you? Let me see the wound."

I could see that she had stitched my side. They were very neat and precise stitches. When we did that to each other they were ugly and left a scar. She seemed satisfied and she covered me once more. She nodded at Erica and left.

"You are to stay in bed for a week. Those are your mother's orders."

"But…"

"But nothing! Butar agrees. And anyway all they are doing is finishing the granaries. You are missing nothing. If you behave then I may allow Haaken and Cnut to see you this evening. They have been desperate to have words with you."

Viking Slave

I was so bored that I was glad to see my two friends that evening. My mother and Erica, along with my two new slaves, had not stopped fussing over me. Scanlan's wife, Maewe, bowed to me when we were alone. "Thank you, lord, for helping my husband and me. I know that slaves are normally kept apart but I could not bear to be parted. We will work hard for you."

"How old are you, Maewe?"

"I have seen fourteen summers."

"And Scanlan?"

"Fifteen summers."

They were both almost the same age as me and yet she called me lord. *Wyrd.*

When Cnut and Haaken came in they were full of news and questions. It turned out that I had been in and out of consciousness for three days. The spear head had been dirty and my mother had had to clean the wound with a potion she had made before she could stitch it.

"Bagsecg is repairing your armour now and he is putting extra links in. He feels guilty that a spear could pierce his handiwork."

"He need not. It was a powerful thrust. The deer hide saved me."

"Perhaps you ought to face the inside with sheepskin and that will help more."

"Enough of me. Have you two been enjoying building the granaries?"

Haaken sniffed, "We are Ulfheonar and we have been hunting."

Cnut laughed, "Aye and Haaken has caught more than a few deer too."

Haaken looked embarrassed. "What has he caught then?"

"He has been caught himself. One of the daughters of Bagsecg has decided she too would like an Ulfheonar for a husband and has trapped our friend."

"She did not trap me. I went there willingly."

"E'en so they will be married next month."

"Why do they have to wait?"

"Bagsecg insists that his daughter should have her own home and not live in the warrior hall."

I knew what he meant. Women in the warrior hall were considered fair game for any warrior whether they would or no. Butar also preferred married men to live outside the hall. "And when do you raid again?"

They both looked at each other. "Er well."

"Tell him, Cnut. He will find out anyway."

"The day after tomorrow. We go to the land close to where we hunted."

My face must have shown my disappointment. "Do not worry, Dragon Heart. It will be a swift voyage and we will probably not even have to draw our swords."

I became angry. "I do not miss the fighting but you are my brothers and I should be there for you."

"But you nearly died and you are still gravely ill. Would you have us worrying after you when we fight? Would you have us take our eye from our opponent and be killed?"

I was shocked that they would think that. "Of course not but..."

"But nothing. You get well and then we will raid again. Jarl Butar has another raid planned before the autumn storms begin."

I persuaded mother and Erica to allow me to stand in the doorway of the hall and watch the *'Man'* sail east. It was the first time that my brothers had sailed without me and I cursed the Saxon who had stabbed me. It would be a long two or three days before they returned. Jarl Butar had told me that they would spend one day spying out the best target and then make a dawn raid. We were like the squirrels in the forests; we gathered more nuts than we thought we could possibly need for who knew what the winter held.

I used the time to get to know Erica a little better. Apart from the first meeting on Midsummer Solstice I had only spoken to her briefly. Our time together was spent in more physical pursuits. She made me laugh when we talked. It was like having my first friend. We were both young enough to be silly and yet we had both suffered enough to appreciate what we had. I think those three days made me love Erica. I had liked her before but I came to love her. We even managed a couple of walks along the shore, with Scanlan in attendance, to watch the building of the stone quay which would give our ships some protection in the winter storms. It was slow work but it kept our male thralls occupied.

While we were walking we spied a ship approaching. Erica wished to stay to see who it was but I had raided enough to know that this could be a ruse. As I hurried back to the hall I wondered who was in command for Bjorn and Butar were both on the raid. I asked my mother and she looked surprised. "Why it is you, my son."

"But I am not old enough."

"You have enough wisdom and besides, Jarl Butar trusts your judgement."

I strapped on my sword although I was so weak that Erica could have beaten me and I summoned the ten warriors who remained. We would either form a party to greet the visitors or we would die defending the town. Fortunately I recognised Hrolf who stood at the prow. Erica and mother stood by me as the boat tied up. Hrolf strode up to me and embraced me. I winced.

When my mother tutted he stepped back, "I am sorry. Am I stronger than I thought?"

"No Hrolf, I was wounded in a battle. It is nothing. Come, bring your men to the warrior hall and we will talk. Jarl Butar has gone a-Viking."

Hrolf was impressed by our progress. "I had heard that you had defeated the Saxons who were here." He looked a little rueful.

My mother said, "Do you regret not trying it yourself?"

He shook his head, "There were too few of us but if we have another bad winter then I may ask Jarl Butar if we could settle."

"I am sure he would be happy about that."

There was an awkward silence. I think he wanted to ask something but my youth prevented him. I did not mind. I had not expected to be a substitute for Jarl Butar any way. "Do you have news of the lands of the fiords?"

"I have heard that Harald One Eye has begun to send raiders to live in Northumbria. They have taken Bebbanburgh and his men hold that for him."

I frowned. We no longer had an island between us. I worried that Harald would try to take Manau from Jarl Butar. "And you and your people are happy?"

He shook his head, "We were raided by the men from Stavanger who were forced from their homes by Harald One Eye. They killed some of my kin and enslaved others before fleeing to Hibernia where they are setting up new settlements."

"We fought them and they are a savage people."

"Aye and like you they have a Saxon hero. A young warrior called Tadgh who is a ferocious killer. It was he who killed my brother."

I suddenly felt cold. My old enemy and tormentor, Tadgh who had fled Ulfberg was now across the sea in Hibernia. The Norns had been spinning their webs once more. "Why do you not stay here until Jarl Butar returns? He will be back tomorrow and I am sure you would rather talk with an elder rather than a stripling who has barely begun to shave."

Viking Slave

"Do not put yourself down Dragon Heart. The stories about you are growing and they all show you to be a warrior of some renown but I will do as you say for I believe Jarl Butar will wish to make the decision."

Chapter 16

Mother enjoyed playing the hostess and Erica loved the attention she received from Hrolf and his warriors. She was an outstanding beauty and I knew from our brief visit to Orkneyjar that Hrolf's women were plain, bordering on downright ugly. Haaken had said they reminded him of trolls. That was a little unkind but I could see where he was coming from. We learned that his people had suffered from a lack of food the previous winter and I suspected that I knew what his request would be. He was quite interested in our last raid. "We are too far from the riches of Mercia and Northumbria. You are ideally placed here."

Mother had the ability to see things that were hidden from others, "So long as the men from Stavanger do not decide that we are a fruit ripe to be picked."

Hrolf shook his head, "I would have thought that they would have chosen the Saxons as the softer target. Everyone knows that Jarl Butar has the finest warriors on this side of the ocean. I have heard he has Ulfheonar."

Erica smiled proudly, "You are sat with one; my husband is an Ulfheonar. Show him your blade."

I reluctantly took out my sword. Hrolf examined the hilt. "I have never seen so many warrior bands on one so young although you have welded them in an interesting way. Tell me, is this the famous sword they talk of, the one struck by the gods?"

"It is Jarl Hrolf and it is powerful beyond words. It can slice through the helmets of the Saxons. The blade came from the land of the Franks but Bagsecg, our smith, has worked his magic on it."

"I have heard that name. Perhaps he would make me a sword too."

"You will have to ask him but many men want a Bagsecg blade." I then told him how the lightning had struck the sword and he was even more envious.

When the *'Man'* entered the port the next day Hrolf and his people joined us to watch its arrival. I could see from Jarl Butar's face that the raid had not gone as well as he had hoped. It was as black as thunder. He had obviously seen Hrolf's ship when he had entered the anchorage and he put on a smile for our visitor when he leapt ashore.

"Ah, Jarl Hrolf. It is good to see you."

"And you, Jarl Butar. I hope it was a good raid."

"I have had better." He came over to me, "See to the men, stepson and I will speak with our visitor."

"Of course my lord." As they left I went to the boat which was now securely tied. I could see that there were empty benches as well as wounded men. There were no slaves but there looked to be plunder beneath some old sails. Haaken looked up at me and I could see the sadness on his face. "We were ambushed as we headed back to the ship. We lost eight men and all the slaves. It was not good."

"We missed your luck, brother." Cnut looked ruefully at my empty place on the bench.

I knew not what to say. I felt guilty that I had not been there. I resolved that the next time I fought I would take more care both of myself and my comrades and blood sworn. "If it is any consolation then Hrolf and his people have had an even harder time than we have. The men of Stavanger raided them and they now live in Hibernia. Tadgh, the slave from my village, is now a warrior."

Haaken shook his head. "We should have filleted the bastard like a fish when we had the chance and saved the world the trouble."

We emptied the ship and took the wounded to the warrior hall. There would be no feast or celebration, too many men had died but we would hold a feast to celebrate our friendship with the men of Orkneyjar. It was as I suspected, Hrolf needed our grain. Jarl Butar traded some for the seal oil which would make our ships better but the most important thing which came out of it was that Hrolf swore fealty to Jarl Butar. We would fight to protect him and he would come to our aid if we needed it. Many of our people thought that Hrolf came out better but, as Jarl Butar told me, if Hrolf had not directed us to Manau, where would we have ended up? We owed our lives to Jarl Hrolf. He did, however, insist that Jarl Butar take the title, Prince of the Isles. Butar thought it a meaningless title but it pleased everyone and so he took it.

After Hrolf had gone Prince Butar of the Isles made sure that every town and village had enough grain and food for the winter. We improved all our defences and Olaf was sent to trade with Sigismund once more. I recovered and resumed training. Two more warriors, Ulf and Torgil, were recommended to become Ulfheonar. We were seen as the warriors who Butar would turn to in times of need and only the best were recommended. Berserkers just happened and you could not predict them. We were different. Olaf had confided in me that, after he had seen me fight he thought I was a berserker. I could not understand that myself. I always felt in total control of my actions.

My sister grew and Erica became pregnant. I would be a father. My mother, and she was never to be gainsaid, told me that it would be in the spring and I would not argue with her predictions. I did not feel as afraid as I thought I would have been. Scanlan's wife, Maewe, had proved to be a perfect slave. She too was young and had had a child and she was the perfect helper for my wife. I thanked the Allfather for my decision regarding Scanlan. He was devoted to me and I think that if I had freed him he would have served me still. He looked after my armour and weapons. He saw to the land that Prince Butar had given me. He made my life so easy that I wondered how I had managed before he came.

The Yule festival was the best one that I could remember. Eric, Olaf and Harald brought their families to Hrams-a for the seven day festival and we told tales and sagas for the whole time. I was embarrassed that many were about me but, as is the way with sagas, I was allowed to add parts which praised others so that Ragnar became more important and Haaken. That year ended blissfully. And I felt so happy and full of joy that I thought that I would burst.

The late winter brought a flood of volunteers and hopefuls who wished to settle on Manau. Prince Butar applied the same rules and more were rejected than accepted. The Ulfheonar were given the task of training them and I enjoyed that work. Bjorn created the framework and we worked with the warriors. Of course they all wished to touch the sword which had been touched by the gods but after that they were willing and hard workers. When Haaken married, Cnut began to look for a bride. As I looked at us three I realised that we were now men and accepted as the elite of the warriors. It had happened without me realising it. I was no longer Gareth the slave; I was the Dragon Heart and the wielder of Ragnar's Spirit.

I had become much stronger since I had been wounded. I worked hard to keep my body as powerful as I could. I was not the tallest warrior nor was I the strongest but I was the quickest and I began to teach myself to use two swords. After my shield had broken I had sworn that I would not be left defenceless again. Prince Butar told us that we would begin raiding in the spring and so we worked even harder. The Ulfheonar were seen not only as the scouts, the eyes and ears of the warriors but, in battle, the leaders. When we practised, warriors tried to defeat us but no-one could for we kept ourselves at the well trained as any warrior. The warriors in the towns would follow us anywhere. We still had three Ulfheonar without wolf skins and we were already planning our next hunt. That would have to wait until after our first raid.

Of course my son, Arturus, changed that. He came into my life like a whirlwind and put all else from my mind. He was named after my mother's father. I liked the name for it was neither Saxon nor Norse; it was an older name. My mother told me it was from the time of the Romans. If the old fortress we had captured was a measure of their work then they were a powerful people. My son would be too. Erica was born to have children and the birth was so swift that even my mother was surprised and she knew everything. Butar was delighted to be a grandfather and Eric to be an uncle but I was more surprised and happier than anyone. I had a son. I had someone to follow me and to carry on my blood. I had wanted to call him Ragnar but my mother felt that as we had Ragnarson as our family name it might sound wrong. I didn't mind. He would have part of Ragnar in him, I knew that.

Butar had to take me aside to speak with me about the way I doted on Arturus. "It is good that you have a son and that you enjoy being with him but you are a warrior and a leader for our people. You need to prepare to lead your men again."

"But I thought that you told me that having a child changed your life."

"And so it does but it does not change who we are. You are still Dragon Heart, the talisman of the warriors. The men still talk darkly of the one raid you were not present and we lost men. When we sail next week they will look to you and they will both fight better and safer with you there."

I could see what he meant. All winter I had heard of the ill luck which had beset our men without me there. It was nonsense of course but our warriors were very superstitious. "I will put my mind to war again. I swear it."

We had replaced the men we had lost but no more and we still had but three boats with which to go raiding. Olaf stayed at home. He was making his town as strong as it could be. Olaf's town would be as protected as Hrams-a. He would build an impregnable castle and his home would be Castletown. He had neither wife nor children but his legacy would be his town and his castle which was emerging from the Saxon ruins.

Eric and Harald took a boat each and we, of course, were on the *'Man'* for it was bigger than the *'Ran'*. We left one cold spring morning and headed towards the Maeresea and the Dee. We would not need to scout this time; we knew where the people lived and we would be in and out swiftly. The winds were precocious at that time of year and we had to row more than we would normally. Haaken was philosophical about that. "We have had a good winter with plenty of food and warm beds. This will do our muscles and bodies good."

Cnut shook his head. Since Haaken had taken a woman he had changed. Some of it was for the better, he was more thoughtful than he had been but he did enjoy his food and drink more. He was a little heavier than he had been. Cnut was still the one true warrior amongst the three of us. He had no woman and he worked at being the best warrior that he could be. He had told me that he always watched my back in a battle for he had sworn an oath to protect me. He still blamed himself for my wound even though he had been guarding my right side. It had been Haaken who had been on my left side that day.

We were glad when we saw the sandy beaches and dunes appear. There was a small port jutting into the sea and we made straight for it while Harald and Eric took their ships down the Dee. The people would flee and fly into the net of warriors who would wait for them. The Ulfheonar were the first ashore. Bjorn and I leapt into the water followed by the others. I had Ragnar's Spirit in my hand and my shield, repaired and strengthened over the winter, across my back. I doubted there would be many warriors in such a small place. I doubted that I would even blood my blade.

A handful of men stood facing us with axes and short, ancient swords. They were fishermen. I could not bring myself to slaughter them, "Do you really want to die? Drop your weapons or you will!" I suspect I terrified them. I was dressed all in black; they could not see my face and I spoke to them in Saxon. All but one did as I asked. The one hero threw himself at me and Cnut took off his head in a single blow. We left the other warriors to secure the prisoners and we entered the village. It was a port of sorts and I could see, from the hut we entered, that they had had some recent trade. There were pots from Frankia and other foreign items. They were high quality. As we had expected there were few weapons and there was little food for it was spring but we took what they had.

We had our plunder aboard quickly and sailed down the Dee. We saw Eric and Harald herding the women and children on board their boats. We had identified some small villages not far from both rivers and we pulled the *'Man'* on to the shore to join our comrades. We divided into five groups. The Ulfheonar were the smallest group and there were just nine of us. We headed north eastwards towards the settlement which was furthest away. We knew that we just had to head in that direction and we would either find the river or the cluster of huts. We knew that the land around the village had been cultivated and promised both animals and feed. We had enough slaves but we desperately needed more animals and more feed.

Sweyn and Godfrid were scouting ahead and they raced down the green track the Saxons used as a road. "The village is up ahead but there are warriors within."

Bjorn frowned; the village was not big enough to warrant armed men. This was the reason my step father, Prince Butar, had sent so few of us. He had not anticipated any opposition. "How many?"

"We counted five but they were the ones in the village. There were others in the main house we think." Sweyn shrugged. "We are guessing."

Bjorn smiled, "And a Sweyn guess is more accurate than another warrior's observation. We will proceed cautiously and see how many there are."

As we walked along the track I knew that Bjorn would not walk away just because there were armed warriors but neither would he throw our lives away recklessly. We smelled the smoke from their fires and we spread out. Haaken, Cnut and I went to the far side of the village. Bjorn would make the decisions; if he attacked then we would join in and if he decided it was too dangerous then he would send a message.

The villagers had cleared much of the land around the village and we were in the hedgerow two hundred paces from the edge. I could see some animals grazing. They had three pigs and a handful of sheep. They would make a welcome addition to our flocks and herds. Cnut was always the reckless one. "I think that we can get closer. If we cover our backs with our wolf skins then we can creep across the field slowly."

Haaken grinned, "That suits me. Wolves in the sheepfold eh?"

"You two are mad! Come on then." We untied our skins and draped them over our backs and our shields. We moved slowly into the field. We moved very slowly but, even so the sheep edged nervously away. We crept slowly like three shadows, unseen by the villagers in their huts. The closer we came the more I could hear. There were angry voices.

"I do not care what you need the captain needs all your food. If you are hungry then come to the fort and we will share what we have."

"But we only need food because you are taking ours!"

"The raiders took all we had last year. The fort is your only place of refuge. The good of that comes before everything else."

I whispered to the others, "The reason the warriors are here is to steal the villager's food. " We crept closer and stood in the shelter of a hut where we could hear more. Suddenly we heard a roar as Bjorn and the others burst into the village. We had an idea where the warriors were and we went for them. They had no mail nor did they carry a shield. Even though they outnumbered us it gave us the advantage.

Haaken took the left and Cnut the right. The Saxons' attention was on Bjorn and the others. The first two died before they knew we were there. The warrior who faced me was quicker than the other two or perhaps I was still slower due to my old wound. Whatever the case his sword whistled a hand's breadth in front of my helmet. I stabbed at him and be beat my sword away. I swung my shield around and smashed it into his side so that he fell over. I plunged my sword into his chest. There was no order to the fighting; the Saxons were striking out blindly. Two of them came at me and I parried one blow with my shield while I slashed at the second warrior's leg. He fell writhing to the floor and his companion glanced at his comrade. It was only a moment but it was enough. I continued the movement of Ragnar's Spirit and its edge buried itself in his side. Cnut finished off the wounded warrior as Bjorn killed their leader.

The villagers had fled but they had left their animals. "There are sheep and pigs in the field."

"You three get them. The rest of you search the huts for anything of value."

The Saxon warriors had thoughtfully provided some rope for they obviously intended to take back the animals. Cnut roped the ram leaving Haaken and me the task of securing the boar. It twisted and turned and tried to bite us but we managed to tie a halter around its neck. Cnut led the reluctant ram and Haaken and I pulled the pig. The other beasts followed docilely along. Sweyn laughed when he saw us. Haaken waved a fist at him. "Next time you get the pig and we search the huts!"

Bjorn followed quickly. I was pleased that we had not hurt the villagers for they were prey to all. They had their huts and they still had their food. True we had taken their pigs and their sheep but the Saxons would have taken it all. I told Bjorn what I had heard.

"So we hurt them more than Prince Butar knew. That is useful information."

Viking Slave

We reached the boat before many of the others. We put the animals and the Saxon weapons aboard. We had a good haul and, when we left, we were low in the water. We had not far to go. This was a much shorter journey than the one Harald One Eye had had to take to reach my land. Perhaps that was why he was now on the mainland. He could save all the travelling across an ocean which could be savage.

We received a great welcome when we arrived home. We had lost no warriors and the animals and food we had secured would give us a good summer and an even better winter. When we shared out the spoils some of the men asked to have some of the sheep for they wished to farm as well. This was our way. Men fought but they all had an occupation. There were many fecund female slaves who were happy to be the wives of warriors and they could look after the home. Within a few weeks of the raid there were small farmsteads blossoming all over the island. We also found that we had more produce to trade. Harald thought he would try to trade with Hibernia. If there were warriors from home then it might be mutually beneficial.

I was too busy to think of farming for my new home had now been built with quarters for Scanlan and his family. Maewe was with child again and that was good for me. Soon I would have another worker to help Erica. Life was good. I also had some idea about how we could make life easier for ourselves. Butar and I went out hunting in the woods near to the high ground. This was the best time to get deer and we could preserve some of the meat for harder times.

We had killed a buck and a doe and were preparing the poles to carry them back. "I wondered if we could use the thralls."

Butar laughed, "I thought we used them already."

"We do but some of them, like Scanlan, can be trusted. They are loyal and hardworking. There are jobs, especially on the raids which they could do. We use warriors at the moment which is expensive for we need all the warriors we can get."

"Hmm. And what would you have them do?"

"There are animals to look after. Food to prepare. And there are many tasks related to the ship."

"Would not Scanlan run?"

"Not without Maewe and his children and they would be on the island watching over Erica." I could see him wavering and I pushed home my advantage. "Let us try an experiment. Let us take Scanlan the next time and then you can judge. The only loser would be me and I am willing to gamble on his loyalty."

"In that case you may bring him. If he is willing."

The thought that he might refuse me had never occurred to me and I began to doubt myself. I chose an appropriate moment to ask him. We were fishing in the Salmon River; it was a task I had done as a thrall and I didn't mind doing it again. "Scanlan, how would you feel about coming on a raid with us?"

"I couldn't fight my own people, sir. It wouldn't be right."

"No, I understand that. I mean to do work for me such as tending the animals we catch. Watching the boat; that sort of thing."

"You are my master and I will do what you command."

"That is not how I do things Scanlan and you know that. You can refuse and I will think no worse of you. You are a valuable servant but it is just an idea I had."

"I will give it a try sir. You have been kind to me and I am better off than most slaves."

Haaken and Cnut were not convinced. "He will run. Believe me he will have no feelings for that slave he is with. What man would not rather have freedom?"

"I will tell you what Cnut. I will give you my spare axe if he runs."

"What? No wager?"

"No I am so confident that I am telling you he will return with us to Hrams-a."

Haaken listened to my voice and nodded. "He has convinced me, brother."

Prince Butar had planned a raid to the north of where we had been pillaging lately. The land to the north of the Maeresea was fertile and had many small settlements. It was now high summer and there would be crops in the fields and plenty of new animals to take. We could fatten them just as easily on our verdant pastures. It made sense to me for we had not raided there before. When Prince Butar had suffered his ambush it had been further north. This land looked perfect.

As usual one warrior in five was selected to stay behind and guard the homes but, since we had rid the island of Saxons we were not worried. Maewe was concerned that her husband would be in danger but Erica put her mind at rest. "He is with my husband, Dragon Heart. Even my father thinks he will be the most powerful warrior we have ever seen. I think that Scanlan will be safe with Dragon Heart."

I felt humbled by such praise and it convinced Maewe to put her dark thoughts away. We left a month after midsummer when all of the animals were bringing forth new life and we were hopeful that what we were doing was making our home stronger than ever. The Norns had other ideas.

The voyage across was perfect. The winds blew from the west and we barely had to row. We landed at sunset and we were unseen. The seventy warriors split into six groups and spread inland. The three boats were guarded by fifteen warriors and we were on a secluded part of the coast. The Ulfheonar were allocated the middle section and the ten of us pushed inland. We enjoyed our status. We were the smallest group and yet we would, if things went as they normally did, collect the largest plunder and kill the most warriors.

We found a track way just after dawn and, as it headed east we followed it. Cnut and I were the scouts and we saw the farmer trudging towards us. He did not see us and we slipped into the two ditches which ran along the track way and hid beneath our cloaks. We waited until he had passed and then rose. He had been coming from somewhere. We turned and went the way he had come. We smelled the stale aroma of a dead fire and moved more cautiously. This was flat land and it was hard to get a view of places in the distance. We almost stumbled upon the cluster of huts. We secreted ourselves in the elder bush and counted the buildings. They would give us a fair assessment of the population. Then I saw another building, a little way from the huts. It was a White Christ church. I could see the cross on the top. We had found our target.

We hurried back to Bjorn. "There is a village ahead and a White Christ church."

Even in the dark I could see his grin. "We will be rich men after this raid!" All of us knew that the churches of the White Christ had great quantities of gold. It seemed strange to me. All of the followers of the White Christ in the village where I grew up told me that the White Christ was a poor man; I could not understand how his priests could hoard such treasures.

The village was coming to life as we fell upon them. Two men were just emerging from their hut when I chanced upon them. I hit one with my shield and one with the pommel of my sword. They both fell to the ground. I did not kill them. Perhaps it was Scanlan who stayed my hand for I had come to see the plight of the farmers. Those farmers near the Dee were at the mercy of all. I could not bring myself to kill them. My sword was for warriors and not farmers. There were some brave men in the village. I saw two men, little older than me, trying to take on Haaken and Cnut with two old swords. One sword broke as Haaken smashed down upon it and both men lay dead in a pool of their own blood. The women and children fled to the church. One of their priests stood in the doorway holding one of the crosses they set so much store by. He was chanting an incantation of some sort. Godfrid was a superstitious man; he did not believe in the White Christ but the last thing he needed was to be cursed by a priest. The incantation was ended with a sword. From the collective wail from the villagers one would have thought that we had killed the White Christ himself.

Godfrid picked up the cross and stepped over the body. A woman threw herself at him, trying to rake his eyes with her nails. It was foolish for he wore a helmet. He punched her and she fell to the ground.

"Get the villagers outside, Sweyn, and watch them. Dragon Heart, take Cnut and Haaken. Find all that you can in the church."

The people were herded out and I grabbed a torch to illuminate the dark little church. At the far end was a table with a white cloth upon it and some objects. We took the cloth and wrapped the objects within. They were gold and silver. There was a large cross and a couple of candlesticks. Cnut found two metal platters while Haaken found a purse with silver coins hidden in a small room to the rear. We had a rich haul indeed. I could not remember so much treasure in one day. As I stepped over the body of the priest I noticed two rings upon his fingers. They joined the other objects.

Bjorn nodded as we emerged into the light. "Time to head back."

"What about the villagers?"

"We have enough slaves and besides," he pointed to the animals, "we will not have the room."

We led the bull and two cows along with the other animals leaving the women wailing and tearing at their hair. Only three men had died and yet they were carrying on as though we had slaughtered all of their men. I was the last to leave and I wondered why they had neither wall nor ditch. These sheep would be shorn again. That was not my problem and I trudged down the track way after my comrades.

It was a longer journey to the coast than the one when we had arrived. The animals were slow. Sweyn and Godfrid were given the task of making sure that no one ambushed us. When we reached the beach others had returned. I saw that Scanlan was still there and I said to Haaken. "It seems that my slave has not rejoined his people."

"We are not back at Hrams-a yet are we? Do not crow until then."

Prince Butar was delighted with the plunder. "How do we get the animals back?"

"We could build a raft." We all looked at Cnut. He pointed to the pine forest. "We cut down the trees and make a raft. We can use the logs when we get home and we can tow them. All we have to do is to walk them aboard and have a couple of men to watch them. We can tie them to the logs."

No one could think of a better solution and so we began making a large raft for the animals. There was plenty of wood and we had rope. The building of the raft meant that we were not ready to sail until the following day. There was no sign of any pursuit and we felt safe. I dare say the ones we had raided had thought that we would have sailed directly home.

We loaded the reluctant animals at dawn. As it was Cnut's idea he sailed with the animals and Haaken and I felt honour bound to go with him. I brought Scanlan with us so that we had four of us to watch the beasts. It made it easier to manage them. We were barely moving at first until Bjorn hoisted the sail and we moved a little quicker. The motion was somewhat disconcerting and the sea water sloshed around. However there were gaps in the logs and the water emptied itself as quickly as it entered. We knew we would have a slower journey home and, once the cows settled we were able to talk.

"If we have more raids like that one then our island will become the most powerful one in these waters."

"We cannot always be that lucky, Dragon Heart."

"I do not know, Haaken, my brother here seems to accumulate luck like a beach with sand. The more you shift, the more you have."

"And why does it have to be my luck? Could it not be yours, Cnut? Haaken's? Or even Bjorn's."

"That might be true but I think of the times you were not with Cnut or me and you still had the luck. The weird sisters must like you."

When he said that, I felt a shiver run down my spine. It might have been the motion of the raft but I think it was something else. I clutched the hilt of my sword until the sensation passed. I closed my eyes and said a silent prayer to the Allfather to forgive Cnut his words. It did not do to disparage the gods and those who worked with them. The weird sisters had been kind but they could also be both petty and precocious. I resolved to make a sacrifice when I returned home.

"Still, Dragon Heart, you must realise that we have more treasure today than we have ever had. That must be a good thing."

"It probably is, but let us get this voyage over with. I would not risk the wrath of Ran while sailing on a few logs held by rope. It is a dangerous thing to do."

I think that I worried them too for they became silent. Only Scanlan smiled. "And why are you smiling Scanlan? Are you protected from the wrath of the god of the sea?"

"No, sir. But I can swim. We lived by the river and I learned."

"It is a long way to swim home."

"I would not have to swim all the way home for the logs would float and I would just need to hang on to the wood and I would be safe."

Scanlan had hidden depths. He was clever and understood matters which some of my comrades did not. In another lifetime he could have fought alongside me rather than being my slave.

The day drifted on and we dozed. The other ships were now in the distance for they were not towing a raft. Suddenly I saw Bjorn and Prince Butar, raise their hands to point at the island. There was smoke coming from beyond the horizon. It was our home and there was trouble!

Chapter 17

I knew now that Butar would be regretting towing us. I could see that the rowers were rowing even harder than before. The other two ships appeared heading east and turned to join the *'Man'*. I could see that Eric and Harald were speaking with Butar but we were too far away to hear. Two ropes snaked towards us and all three ships towed us. We moved much quicker but the water was rushing over the logs and distressing the cows. Scanlan began to sing to them and, amazingly, it calmed them. Once again the slave had come to our aid.

Butar leaned over the rear of the *'Man'* and cupped his hands, "Duboglassio has been attacked. It is on fire!"

Now I knew that the weird sisters were paying us back for our boasting. We should have kept quiet. I could see, beyond the three ships, that there were buildings afire. It was hard to discern anyone but I could see movement. It looked as though the raiders were still there. I cursed the raft. If we had not made the raft then we would have been home a day earlier and we could have met the raiders at Duboglassio.

When we were two hundred paces from the shore, the three ships stopped rowing. The tide and the motion took the raft to ground itself on the sandy beach. "Scanlan stay with the beasts." We grabbed the ropes and hurriedly tied them to two rocks we then hefted our shields and raced up the beach. I could see that warriors were trying to get inside the wooden walls. We were in time. The smoke from the fires they had started had hidden our approach and Prince Butar led us to attack them from behind.

We were angry. Some of the warriors had families on Duboglassio. We became even angrier when we saw that the raiders were not Saxons; they were our people from beyond the seas in the land of the fiords. I had fought recklessly before but, as we tore into the enemy, I did so without any regard to what might happen to me. They had broken the unwritten rule that we do not attack our own and there could be no mercy.

I slashed down on the back of the first warrior I met and I laid him open to his backbone. Two others whirled to face me. I blocked the sword thrust from one with my shield as I hacked at the second warrior. These were not Saxons. These knew how to use their weapons. The man I had struck with my shield punched at me with the boss of his and I had to use all my power to hold him. As the second warrior tried to slash at my head I leaned backwards and tried a blind stab. I must have struck flesh for he recoiled backwards. I continued the swing with my sword and it bit into the shoulder of the first warrior. I now had breathing space.

The two of them had wounds but they were warriors and would not stop until they were dead. One of them grinned at me. "There is a bounty on your head, thrall, and we will share it!"

They knew me. That should not have been a surprise for my shield was well known but who hated me enough to put a price on my head? It determined me to fight even harder. The warrior with the wounded shoulder was the weaker of the two. I feinted at the other and then launched a furious attack with both sword and shield. I rained so many blows that he could not deflect them all and I hacked at his leg. He crumpled when I struck. I felt the blow coming from my right and I rolled just as the other warrior tried to stab me in the side. The sword caught on my wolf skin and pulled the blade away from my body. I could see that my earlier blow had stuck his arm and he was bleeding. He was also panting and out of breath; he was not a fit man. I regained my balance and we circled each other. I was vaguely aware of my comrades fighting for their lives but I could not aid anyone. I had to kill this warrior first.

I swung Ragnar's Spirit at my enemy and he tried to block it with his shield. I felt it shiver and a crack appeared. He began to look afraid. He tried a blow but when I blocked it with my shield I saw him wince with the pain.

"This is the sword touched by lightning. This is the sword of the gods. Do you really think that you can best me?"

"You are a boy and you were a thrall!"

"And now I am the man who will send you to Valhalla."

I brought my blade over my head; I was aiming for his helmet. He hurriedly blocked it with his shield but the force was so great that the shield struck him on the helmet. I swung again and this time the crack widened. I feinted and he brought up the shield. I changed the direction mid-swing and swung across his middle. The sharp edge tore through his tunic and into his body. He tried to push his entrails back inside as he collapsed to the ground.

I saw that two warriors were assaulting Bjorn. I roared, "Ulfheonar!" One of them turned. He had a skeggox and he swung it at me two handed. If it had connected then there would have been two of me. I deftly spun so that the blade whistled just in front of my shield. I hacked down at him and the sword sliced a hunk from the handle. Bjorn now had the mastery of the other. The warrior I faced was much older than I was and his sword had warrior bands on the hilt. It would not do to underestimate this warrior. He whirled the axe above his head, daring me to attack. I knew that once I did so he would bring the axe down. He dipped one shoulder and as I shifted my position he swung the axe head. It seemed to almost touch my nasal. I took my chance and stabbed at him. He let go of the axe with one hand and grabbed my sword with it. He had leather gauntlets on. He pulled me forwards. I knew what he intended. He was going to head butt me. I lowered my head and I heard his nose shatter as it struck the knurled knob on the top of my own helmet. He fell backwards, still holding my sword. The tip touched his chest and the weight of my body drove it in.

Bjorn stood watching. "Well done! Let us get after the others!" He pointed to the ten warriors who were running west, away from the sea. They were beaten. "Haaken, Cnut, Sweyn! Come!"

It pained me to see our dead warriors lying there as well as dead villagers. These animals would pay for their treachery. As we chased after them I wondered where their ships were. We had not seen them which meant they had been somewhere else first. One of the warriors we were pursuing was wounded and he bravely turned to slow us down. Bjorn did not even miss a step he swung his sword two handed as the wounded warrior weakly hacked at him. The sword almost went through to his backbone.

We were gaining on them. We had purpose in our feet. We wanted to avenge our dead. One of them turned and saw that but five of us followed. He said something to the others and they stopped and turned to face their tormentors. None of us hesitated. Cnut and I were to Bjorn's right; the others to his left. We plunged, like an arrow, into the heart of them. Bjorn knocked aside the warrior's sword with his shield and sank his sword into his stomach. Cnut and I faced three warriors. One had a spear while the other two had swords. As the spear head came towards me I chopped at it with my sword and the head was sliced clean off. I hacked backhanded and Ragnar's Spirit cut his throat. A sword smashed into my shield. The warrior was strong. I hacked at his leg but he jumped away from the blow. We circled each other looking for an opening. I raised my sword and brought it down hard. He blocked it with his sword and sparks flew. As I stepped back I saw that his blade had bent slightly.

Viking Slave

It was not a Frankish sword. I swung again and this time he was forced to block with his shield. I punched with my shield and the boss cracked into the back of his sword hand. I knew that I would have numbed it. I swung my sword again and this time there was little resistance. He fought to hold my sword but it drove inexorably and slowly towards his chest. He knew he was going to die and I gave an extra push. The sword sank into his chest. He was dead in an instant as the blade entered his heart.

One warrior had had enough and he was leaving his beleaguered comrades and running up the hill towards the safety of the woods. I had run this way myself when I had fled the Saxons and it gave me the impetus to drive my legs into the hillside. I ate up the distance between us. I could hear him panting and I knew that I would catch him. I slowed down a little to recover some of my energy for I could see him slowing with the effort. He must have heard me for he suddenly whirled around. He had a short axe and a sword in his hands. He swung the axe at my shield as he stabbed with his sword. When the axe head bit I twisted, knowing that the leather would catch the edge and it was ripped from his hand. At the same time I twisted my sword and his moved to his left. I drove Ragnar's Spirit into his neck and he died with a surprised look upon his face.

I turned to look down the hill and saw that my companions had finished off the others. I took the sword and axe and trudged down the hill. There would be no time to bury the dead. We would do them no honour. They were not worthy.

"Come we must get back to Duboglassio. I fear this day is not yet over."

When we reached the town the raiders were all dead. Butar was organising the removal of their bodies. He saw us as we approached. "They came overland which is how they surprised the guards. Had we not arrived then they would have held the town."

"Where did they come from Prince Butar?"

"I think they came from Hibernia or else we would have seen their ships. Bjorn I want you to stay here with ten of my warriors and see to the defence of the town. I will go to Hrams-a and see to our families. The other two Jarls are anxious to sail home as well. Dragon Heart, have your man Scanlan drive the cows up to Hrams-a. We cannot be delayed by the raft."

Viking Slave

When we went down to the boat I saw that Scanlan had unloaded the animals from the raft. He looked pleased to see me. "I am glad you are well, master. I was worried."

"It will take more than a few pirates to kill me. Drive the cattle back to our fort Scanlan. We will go directly by sea."

"Thank you for the trust, master. I hope that I will not betray it."

I handed him the sword and axe I had taken from the dead warrior. "Here take these in case we did not get all the raiders." Haaken looked amazed and I said, "There is still a wager I believe."

As we boarded the ship he said, "You were right about that one but are you sure about arming him?"

We sat at our oars as we prepared to row. "Remember the night the men from Stavanger came to raid? I was a thrall and I was armed. Had I not been, old friend, then you might not be here now."

We rowed hard, even though we were tired. We all worried about our families. Who knew where the raiders would strike next? The first inkling we had of disaster was the pall of smoke coming from beyond the headland. We had thought the smoke was from Duboglassio but now we could see that it was not. Hrams-a had also been attacked. The fort at Hrams-a was much stronger and in a better position. We could rebuild the town and the port. We could not rebuild families.

"We will sail to Hibernia and teach these pirates a lesson."

Even as Cnut spoke those words I thought of what Hrolf had said. I had a feeling that Tadgh was involved in this somehow. I had not seen his body; had he survived? When we rowed around the headland we saw the devastation which had been wrought. The halls and the huts were afire. The wooden quay had been destroyed and the gates of the fort lay open. Where were our families?

The Ulfheonar leapt from the boat first and ran towards the village. We all held our weapons at the ready. When I found the first body it was stone cold. These had not died today. These had been killed earlier. Where were our families? We found Bagsecg close to his beloved forge. He had been cut to pieces, quite literally. From the blood around him he had killed many of his enemies. We found all the warriors we had left and they were all dead. There appeared to be no one left alive. Butar and the rest found us. "Spread out and see if you can find where they have gone. Haaken, take the Ulfheonar up to the fort."

We trudged up the hill. I was almost afraid to go in. If there was anyone left alive why had they not shouted to us? It was strange; there was no one left within the walls. Not a warrior remained and, as far as we could see, there had been no fighting within the walls. It was as though the gates had opened and the warriors just left. Why?

"This is a mystery, Haaken. Where are the women and children? Where are the slaves?"

"I know I can feel an icy chill. Dragon Heart and Cnut you two have the best eyes. See if you can find any clues as to what occurred here."

We split up and began to search. Suddenly I saw a trail of blood and it was headed towards the lightning tower. "Over here!" I ran towards the ladder and saw that the blood was on the ladder itself. I dropped my shield and raced up. When I peered through the entrance I saw Bjorn Bagsecgson, the son of the smith. He was pale and his leg was bleeding. I put my hand on his neck and I could feel the beat of his heart. He lived still. I tore the hem of his tunic and tied it about the wound. Then I hefted him on my shoulder and carried him down the ladder. The others were waiting.

"He lives. Let us get him to the others. Cnut, go and get some gut. His leg needs stitching and, Haaken, we need something hot for him."

They raced away and I carried the survivor down to the devastation of our home. I saw Butar looking at the shell of his hall and shaking his head. "Why were they not in the fort? Where are the women? Where is Myfanwy?"

"We have a survivor here but he is close to death." The warriors made a circle around us. Cnut brought the gut and the needle. He was not as neat as my mother but he had delicate hands and he stitched the wound. Not all of the huts had burned and Sweyn found some honey which we smeared all over the wound. I loosened the tie and allowed the blood to flow again. None seeped out. Haaken had found some ale and he put it in a pot and placed it on a still burning ember of Prince Butar's Hall. We put in a large amount of honey and swirled it around. We knew how powerful honey could be. I held the youth in my arms. When it was warm enough we spooned some into his mouth and held his nose. He swallowed but his eyes remained closed. We kept doing this until he coughed and spluttered and then opened his eyes. He stared at me, "Dragon Heart, thank the Allfather!" He began to cry.

"Bjorn, there will be time for tears later. Tell me what happened?"

"They came before dawn. My father was awake and he raised the alarm. He sent me to tell Prince Butar's wife. I awoke them and she told me to warn the fort. As I ran I was attacked by a warrior and he stabbed

Viking Slave

me in the leg. When I reached the fort Ulf told me to get to the tower while he and the warriors went to help your ladies. I watched it all from the tower." He sobbed a little and I gave him some more of the honeyed ale. Butar's face was a mask of agony. I could see that he was desperate to know what happened to my mother.

"Go on, Bjorn. You are doing well."

"The warriors fought to reach the hall. The women and the slaves grabbed the children. Your mother tried to organise them but there were too many of them. All of our warriors were slain and they surrounded the women." He hesitated and looked fearfully from Butar to me. I nodded and smiled encouragingly. I knew this would be hard for him. "The leader had a helmet with something on the top; a bird of some description. It was a long way away. I could not hear what they said but your mother appeared to know him. I could see her begging and she dropped to her knees." He took a deep breath. "He killed her and then threw her body in the hall and they set fire to it." I heard the collective intake of breath. "They took them over to the north and then I must have passed out. I am sorry I could not stop it."

Prince Butar knelt down and took Bjorn's hands in his. "You have done well and you obeyed your father and Ulf. You have done nothing wrong. If you had not then we would not have known what happened but now we do." He stood.

"It was Tadgh."

"You cannot be sure."

"I can, Cnut, and we now know where they have taken them. They have fled to Hibernia."

"And we will follow. I want messengers sending to the other Jarls. All of the people will go to Olaf's town. We will meet them all there and we will take every warrior and avenge this..." He almost broke down.

The two of us wandered over to the embers of his hall. There was still heat but neither of us cared and we searched until we found what remained of my mother. The two of us carried her to the centre of the village. I looked at Prince Butar, my stepfather and the only man my mother had ever loved. "I swear to you that I will not rest until Tadgh is dead and we have my sister, my wife and my son safely back here on our island."

"And I promise you that I will not return here until we have rescued all those who were under my protection."

Suddenly the men around us dropped to their knees. Haaken said, "I speak for all of us. We were oathsworn before but now we are blood sworn. None of us will rest until everyone is returned here to their home."

And so we began the blood feud and the war with the Norsemen of Hibernia.

The End

Glossary

Bebbanburgh- Bamburgh Castle, Northumbria
Caerlleon- Welsh for Chester
Duboglassio –Douglas, Isle of Man
Frankia- France and part of Germany
Glaesum –amber
Gut- animal gut
Hrams-a – Ramsey, Isle of Man
Jarl- Norse earl or lord
Joro-goddess of the earth
Legacaestir- Anglo Saxon for Chester
Manau – The Isle of Man
Njoror- God of the sea
Orkneyjar-Orkney
Ran- Goddess of the sea
Rinaz –The Rhine
Seax – short sword
Skeggox – an axe with a shorter beard on one side
Sigismund- Frankish trader living in Cologne
Sif- Goddess of battle and the name of Harald's ship
The Norns- Fate
Thrall- slave
Ullr-Norse God of Hunting
Ulfheonar-an elite warrior with a wolf skin over his armour
Wyrd- Fate

Historical note

The Viking raids began, according to records left by the monks, in the 790s when Lindisfarne was pillaged. However there were many small settlements along the east coast and most were undefended. I have chosen a fictitious village on the Tees. As buildings were all made of wood then any evidence would have long rotted save for a few post holes. My raiders represent the Norse warriors who wanted the plunder of the soft Saxon kingdom. There is a myth that the Vikings raided in large numbers but this is not so. It was only in the tenth and eleventh centuries that the numbers grew. They also did not have allegiances to kings. The Norse settlements were often isolated family groups. The term Viking was not used in what we now term the Viking age. Warriors went a-Viking which meant that they sailed for adventure or pirating. Their lives were hard. Slavery was commonplace. The Norse for slave is thrall and I have used both terms.

The length of the swords in this period was not the same as in the later medieval period. By the year 850 they were only 76cm long and in the eighth century they were shorter still. The first sword Dragon Heart used, Ragnar's, was probably only 60-65cm long. This would only have been slightly longer than a Roman gladius. At this time the sword, not the axe was the main weapon. The best swords came from Frankia, and were probably German in origin. A sword was considered a special weapon and a good one would be handed from father to son. A warrior with a famous blade would be sought out on the battlefield. There was little mail around at the time and warriors learned to be agile to avoid being struck. A skeggox was an axe with a shorter edge on one side. Honey was used as an antiseptic in both ancient and modern times.

I used the Osprey book Saxon, Norman and Viking by Terence Wise as a reference book.

Griff Hosker November 2013

Viking Slave

Other books by Griff Hosker

If you enjoyed reading this book, then why not read another one by the author?

Ancient History

The Sword of Cartimandua Series
(Germania and Britannia 50 A.D. – 128 A.D.)
Ulpius Felix- Roman Warrior (prequel)
The Sword of Cartimandua
The Horse Warriors
Invasion Caledonia
Roman Retreat
Revolt of the Red Witch
Druid's Gold
Trajan's Hunters
The Last Frontier
Hero of Rome
Roman Hawk
Roman Treachery
Roman Wall
Roman Courage

The Wolf Warrior series
(Britain in the late 6th Century)
Saxon Dawn
Saxon Revenge
Saxon England
Saxon Blood
Saxon Slayer

Viking Slave

Saxon Slaughter
Saxon Bane
Saxon Fall: Rise of the Warlord
Saxon Throne
Saxon Sword

Medieval History

The Dragon Heart Series
Viking Slave
Viking Warrior
Viking Jarl
Viking Kingdom
Viking Wolf
Viking War
Viking Sword
Viking Wrath
Viking Raid
Viking Legend
Viking Vengeance
Viking Dragon
Viking Treasure
Viking Enemy
Viking Witch
Viking Blood
Viking Weregeld
Viking Storm
Viking Warband
Viking Shadow
Viking Legacy
Viking Clan
Viking Bravery

The Norman Genesis Series
Hrolf the Viking
Horseman
The Battle for a Home
Revenge of the Franks
The Land of the Northmen

Viking Slave

Ragnvald Hrolfsson
Brothers in Blood
Lord of Rouen
Drekar in the Seine
Duke of Normandy
The Duke and the King

Danelaw
(England and Denmark in the 11th Century)
Dragon Sword
Oathsword (October 2021)

New World Series
Blood on the Blade
Across the Seas
The Savage Wilderness
The Bear and the Wolf
Erik The Navigator

The Vengeance Trail

The Reconquista Chronicles
Castilian Knight
El Campeador
The Lord of Valencia

The Aelfraed Series
(Britain and Byzantium 1050 A.D. - 1085 A.D.)
Housecarl
Outlaw
Varangian

The Anarchy Series England 1120-1180
English Knight
Knight of the Empress
Northern Knight
Baron of the North
Earl

Viking Slave

King Henry's Champion
The King is Dead
Warlord of the North
Enemy at the Gate
The Fallen Crown
Warlord's War
Kingmaker
Henry II
Crusader
The Welsh Marches
Irish War
Poisonous Plots
The Princes' Revolt
Earl Marshal

Border Knight
1182-1300
Sword for Hire
Return of the Knight
Baron's War
Magna Carta
Welsh Wars
Henry III
The Bloody Border
Baron's Crusade
Sentinel of the North
War in the West
Debt of Honour

Sir John Hawkwood Series
France and Italy 1339- 1387
Crécy: The Age of the Archer
Man At Arms
The White Company

Lord Edward's Archer
Lord Edward's Archer
King in Waiting
An Archer's Crusade

Viking Slave

Targets of Treachery

Struggle for a Crown
1360- 1485
Blood on the Crown
To Murder A King
The Throne
King Henry IV
The Road to Agincourt
St Crispin's Day
The Battle For France
The Last Knight

Tales from the Sword I (Short stories from the Medieval period)

Conquistador
England and America in the 16th Century
Conquistador

Modern History

The Napoleonic Horseman Series
Chasseur à Cheval
Napoleon's Guard
British Light Dragoon
Soldier Spy
1808: The Road to Coruña
Talavera
The Lines of Torres Vedras
Bloody Badajoz
The Road to France
Waterloo

The Lucky Jack American Civil War series
Rebel Raiders
Confederate Rangers
The Road to Gettysburg

The British Ace Series

Viking Slave

1914
1915 Fokker Scourge
1916 Angels over the Somme
1917 Eagles Fall
1918 We will remember them
From Arctic Snow to Desert Sand
Wings over Persia

Combined Operations series
1940-1945
Commando
Raider
Behind Enemy Lines
Dieppe
Toehold in Europe
Sword Beach
Breakout
The Battle for Antwerp
King Tiger
Beyond the Rhine
Korea
Korean Winter

Tales from the Sword II (Short stories from the Modern period)

Other Books
Great Granny's Ghost (Aimed at 9-14-year-old young people)

For more information on all of the books then please visit the author's website at www.griffhosker.com where there is a link to contact him or visit his Facebook page: GriffHosker at Sword Books

Printed in Great Britain
by Amazon